THE DEMON SKIN

A NICK DRAKE NOVEL

DWIGHT HOLING

The Demon Skin
A Nick Drake Novel

Print Edition
Copyright 2023 by Dwight Holing

Published by Jackdaw Press
All Rights Reserved

All rights reserved. Except as permitted under the U.S. Copyright Act of 1976, no part of this publication may be reproduced, distributed, or transmitted in any form or by any means, or stored in a database or retrieval system, except for the quotation of brief passages, without prior written permission from the copyright holder.

This book is a work of fiction. Names, characters, places, and incidents are either products of the author's imagination or are used factiously. Any resemblance to actual persons, living or dead, is entirely coincidental. The author acknowledges the trademarked status and trademark owners of various products referenced in this work of fiction, which have been used without permission. The publication/use of these trademarks is not authorized, associated with, or sponsored by the trademark owners.

Cover photograph courtesy of the Bureau of Land Management.

ISBN: 979-8-9866978-2-6

For More Information, please visit dwightholing.com.

See how you can **Get a Free Book** at the end of this novel.

For Annie Notthoff, Arleen Hiuga, Sara Donart Gorham

Friendships born on rivers run deep

1

The frost of early spring cobwebbed the bedroom windowpanes. Sunbeams streaming through them sent diamonds dancing atop the bed quilt. They spun and leapt like a pair of big city ballerinas. I turned my head to see if Gemma was watching too. Her eyes were open, but she was staring across the pillow at me.

"You were tossing and turning all night," she said.

"Trying to get comfortable, is all. You know, after taking that spill off Wovoka and landing on my shoulder. It's still sore."

"It wasn't from being thrown from your horse."

"Then it must be from clearing out that ditch at the Malheur refuge. It normally channels fresh water into the duck pond, but it was still so clogged even the mud hens were complaining."

Gemma didn't laugh. "You've been restless ever since we brought Johnny home. Me too. Let's face it, he's wearing us down."

"We knew what we were getting into and I don't second guess our decision one bit."

"Nor do I, but you have to admit it's harder than we expected. Johnny's harder. His anger and frustration are putting a strain on everyone. You. Me. Us. He requires so much of our attention that it takes away from Hattie. It's not fair to her."

"She seems to be dealing with it."

"It's not her job to deal with it. She's only five years old. I don't know how I'm going to balance caring for Johnny and doing my job. Spring is my busiest season of the year. Ten thousand calves will drop in Harney County over the next few weeks. Don't get me started thinking about all the foals and lambs."

"I'll pick up the slack," I said.

Gemma's sigh was more of a scoff. "You're as busy as I am this time of year. What are we going to do when you're back out on the road patrolling refuges for days at a time?"

"Remember what we said in the beginning. What we've said all along. Give it time. Give Johnny time."

"Time," she said, her exhale floating across the pillow. "All our time is spent raising the kids, doing our jobs, and keeping the ranch going. There's no time for you and me to work on us."

"We're a job now, like fixing a broken rail on the corral?"

"You know what I mean."

"Then we'll make time."

She sighed again. "That's the trouble. There's never enough of it in life."

And too much of it in death, but I didn't say it out loud.

∼

SEVEN MONTHS earlier Gemma and I had driven to Medford from our ranch in No Mountain. We'd pulled up to a cluster of buildings that looked like an elementary school except for the adjoining two-story dormitory and a chain link fence topped by three strands of barbed wire.

A woman with gray hair greeted us in the lobby with a practiced smile. "Hello, I'm the director, Mrs. Wilsey."

Gemma blew right past the pleasantries as she put her fists on her hips. "Why the barbed wire and locked gate? I thought the children here were orphans and foster kids, not inmates."

Mrs. Wilsey's smile didn't crinkle. "Our wards range from three to twelve years of age and have life experiences you'll never see on *The Waltons*. We have a growing enrollment and a shrinking budget. If forced to choose between nutritious meals or hiring additional staff to patrol the grounds at night, I'll take fresh fruits and vegetables every time."

Gemma's shoulders started to relax. "I'm sorry. I—"

"Don't apologize, dear. I'm glad you spoke up. When a prospective parent doesn't comment on the fence and peeling paint, I find they usually lack the protective instincts required for childrearing. Let's go to my office and make sure your application is in order before meeting any children."

We followed her down a hallway that smelled of Pine-Sol. Her office was tiny and the open window was doing little to cool the summer air. Gemma and I sat on a pair of folding metal chairs that reminded me of school assemblies in an overheated auditorium. The director took a seat behind a desk stacked with leaning towers of manila file folders. A single daisy poked from a cut-glass vase. She noticed me looking at it.

"I grow flowers during the winter under a heat lamp and, weather permitting, in a garden outside. Children are like flowers. They're adaptable. They can bloom anywhere as long as they're provided a solid foundation of love, care, and guidance. Without those, they'll wither."

Mrs. Wilsey opened a folder and scanned the letter and application we'd submitted weeks earlier. "It says here you have a daughter and she's your only child. Is she yours by birth or adoption?"

"Birth," Gemma said. "Her name is Hattie, short for Henrietta, after my mother."

"May I ask why you didn't have other children?"

"I was injured in a crash that left me unable to conceive."

"Oh, I'm sorry. I see your daughter will be five in the spring. Is there a reason you waited until now to consider adoption?"

"I suppose it took that long to accept what'd happened to me."

"That's understandable. You do realize we don't house infants here. We're not equipped for neonatal care."

"My husband and I have given this a great deal of thought and decided a child closer in age to Hattie would be easier on her. Us too."

"Do you have a preference for a boy or girl?"

"No, but when I picture our family, I always see one of each."

"And you, Mr. Drake?"

"Call me Nick. I'm in the either-or camp."

The director studied our application. She took a pen from the top drawer and made some notes.

"According to this, you both work. Do your jobs require travel?"

Gemma nodded. "I have a large-animal veterinarian practice and my patients are on ranches scattered far and wide, but I have a plane and that cuts down on travel time. I'm able to be home most nights."

The papers fluttered from the wafts of hot air coming through the open window. "Mr. Drake, er, Nick, the application states you're with the US Fish and Wildlife Service. In what capacity?"

"A ranger. I operate out of a field office in the town of No Mountain, but my jurisdiction is pretty big."

"Meaning?"

"From the Snake River along the Idaho-Oregon border to the Klamath Basin just east of where we're sitting right now. I'm occasionally called to work on refuges in the northernmost parts of Nevada and California."

"In other words, you must travel great distances too. Do you also fly a plane?"

"No, Gemma's the pilot in the family. I go to work in a pickup or on horseback or sometimes in a skiff."

"My word, that sounds adventurous."

"It has more to do with the remoteness of wildlife refuges and their size. They have few roads by design. Animals don't drive."

"What are your duties?"

"They run the gamut from checking on fences to conducting wildlife population studies to enforcing regulations. There's also paperwork that needs doing. Too much of it, in my opinion."

"The regulations, what sort are they?"

"They're mainly aimed at preventing unlawful activities, such as poaching or grazing in areas where it's prohibited. A major focus now is protecting special plants and animals that came when the Endangered Species Act was passed a couple years ago."

"Do you have to make arrests?"

"Writing a citation is usually enough, but I arrest violators if circumstances warrant. Goes with the job."

"Do you carry a gun?"

"As well as wear a badge. I'm a sworn law-enforcement officer."

"Then your occupation is risky, even dangerous. That's a questionable environment in which to raise a child, especially one who might bear emotional scars from being orphaned or abandoned."

I wanted to remind her that all things in life came with risk, from pulling on your boots and stepping outside every morning to falling in love, but I bit my tongue. "I've been at it several years and I'm careful."

"Have you ever had to fire your weapon in the line of duty?"

"Ma'am, I served three years of combat duty in Vietnam, and as a ranger, I've—"

Gemma cut me off with a throat clearer. "Nick was a sergeant in the war and was awarded medals for bravery, but I think what you're really asking is, do we have firearms in the house. The answer is yes. They're secured in a locked gun safe along with my father's service weapons. He's the county sheriff."

"Yes, I see that on your application. Sheriff Pudge Warbler. Another very dangerous occupation. He lives with you?"

"The other way around. The ranch has been in our family for generations. I was born and grew up there and then came back following veterinarian school. Nick moved in after we were married. If we're fortunate enough to have a child come live with us, they'll not only have their own bedroom, but a doting grandfather as well."

Mrs. Wilsey pressed on. "Your application also mentions an elderly woman who lives with you. What's the nature of her relationship?"

"My mother died when I was Hattie's age and November moved in to help raise me. She's lived on the ranch ever since."

"November, like the month. That's an unusual name. I notice you didn't write down her last name."

"She's Paiute and was sent to a government-run boarding school. The teachers forbid the children to speak their native tongue and named her that because her birth name translates to Girl Born in Snow. They tried to beat the Indian out of her." Gemma folded her arms across her chest. "November succeeded. They failed."

"Please, I didn't intend any offense. You'll find we have children of different races here, including American Indian. I'm asking because I need to know what her relationship will be to a new child in the household."

"If our daughter is any indication, it'll be very close. Hattie calls November *Mu'a*, which means grandmother in *Numu*, the Paiute language. November is teaching her about Native American traditions the same way she taught me."

"You list another person living at your domicile. Nagah Will. Is he Paiute too?"

"Yes. He came to live with us following the death of his grandfather. We've known him since he was a boy. Nagah is eighteen now and assists me in my veterinarian practice as well as copilots my plane. He has an extraordinary gift with animals. My hope is he'll go to college and on to vet school."

"I see."

As Mrs. Wilsey returned to the application and began writing on it, Gemma asked when we could meet the children.

"Right after we finish up here. Our policy is to preselect candidates based on your application and interview. Meeting prospective parents can be confusing for children and we want to avoid encouraging false hopes. Your first visit will be in a group setting and observational only."

"Meaning, no talking and engaging with them?" I said. "Or is it, you observe us observing them?"

"Both. Now, if you'll excuse me, I'll be right back."

Mrs. Wilsey was gone for a few minutes and then led us to a classroom where we stood with our backs against a wall. Five children who appeared to be nursery-school age were already there. A young woman supervised them as they colored, played with blocks, and looked at picture books. One boy with red hair and freckles kept stealing glances at us. When we didn't say anything to him, he stuck out his tongue. A girl whose glasses kept slipping down her pug nose carried a coloring book toward us.

"What color should I make the clouds?" she said, holding the book out to Gemma.

Before Gemma could respond, the young woman jumped up, took the little girl by the hand, and returned to the table. "Clouds are white or gray, Suzy. Sometimes black."

Five minutes later, Mrs. Wilsey ushered us outside. "Are you spending the night in Medford?"

"Yes, we have a motel room," I said.

"Then, if you'd like, we can meet again in the morning."

Gemma said. "Does that mean—"

"It means we'll continue our conversation if you're still interested."

"Of course, we are."

"Have a pleasant evening. I'll see you at nine." Mrs. Wilsey walked back to her office.

Gemma groaned. "I nearly jumped out of my skin when Suzy came up to us, I wanted to give her a hug so bad. And the redhead boy? When he stuck out his tongue for ignoring him, I thought I'd die. This is torture. I feel like a little girl looking through a pet-shop window hoping they'll let me take home a puppy."

I put my arm around her and we walked toward the parking lot. Our route took us across a blacktop striped with white lines outlining hopscotch and four square. Girls older than the ones we'd seen inside were skipping rope and jumping double Dutch. One was playing tetherball by herself. A group of older boys were huddled on the far side of the playground. I figured they were swapping baseball cards or dividing into dodge-ball teams.

When their voices grew heated, I took a closer look. They were surrounding two boys who'd squared off and were trading insults and shoves. One appeared two or three years older than the other. He was taller by a few inches and had at least twenty pounds on the smaller kid who I assumed was Native American because of his black hair and dark complexion. I looked for a playground monitor, but didn't see one. The pair's shoves turned into punches.

I fast-stepped across the blacktop as the smaller boy lowered his head and charged the bigger boy. He drove him into the wall of jeering boys, who pushed back.

"Slug him!" they shouted to the bigger boy.

The smaller kid was kicking as well as punching and giving a lot better than he was getting. His opponent had blood streaming from his nose and tears from his eyes. I pushed through the spectators to pull them apart. The smaller boy cursed me and it wasn't in English. I responded automatically, "*Dung lai di!*"

Snatching him by the back of his shirt, I pulled him away before he could land another blow. He wheeled around, cursed me again, and took a swing. I batted away his fist. He swore and took another. This time I grabbed his wrists and pinned them to his sides.

"*Dung lai di!* Stop it! *Day du. Da het.* Enough. It's over."

Still holding him, I barked at the others. "Take your buddy to the infirmary. He needs a bag of ice. Go on. Hup two. Show's over."

The bigger boy was pinching the bridge of his nose. "You dirty little gook. Just you wait."

I realized the kid hadn't cursed me in *Numu* or any of the other languages native to Oregon. It was Vietnamese and I'd responded out of habit with words I'd learned in country.

"*Ban co noi duoc tieng Anh khong?*" I said. "Do you speak English?"

"Why you care?" he said. His bottom lip quivered, but he wouldn't allow himself to cry.

"Because my *tieng Viet* is rusty. If I let go, will you promise to stay put."

"No."

"I'll give you points for honesty, but not manners." I kept hold of him. "I'm Nick. What's your name?"

"Let go." He tightened his jaw and his little body turned rigid.

"Come on, I told you mine. What's yours?"

"I tell, you let go?"

"Depends."

He mulled it over. "Johnny Da Den."

"Were you born in Vietnam?"

"You ask lot questions."

"Were you?"

"Saigon."

"Which neighborhood?"

"Tu Do."

"I've been there."

He sneered. "You go for boom-boom. All GI do."

I gave him another once over and it wasn't much of a stretch to conjure up a picture. His mother either grew up in Saigon or moved there from the countryside to find work after her village was destroyed. Tu Do Street was notorious for nightclubs filled with young girls catering to GIs. Many clung to a fantasy that one would take them back to the States. Given the curls in Johnny's hair, skin tone, and distinctive features, it was a safe bet his father was Black. Nearly a quarter of US combat troops that served in country were. That had been true for my squad as well.

I asked him how old he was.

"Let go. You said so."

"How old?"

He shrugged. "Dunno. Eight?"

"How long have you been in the States?"

He shrugged again.

"Did your mother name you Johnny or did they give it to you when you came here?"

"Always Johnny Da Den."

I scratched my memory. Johnny was what locals frequently called GIs. Da Den. *Da den*. Black skin. I remembered my radioman getting called that by farmers in a village we were searching for cached weapons. "It's no big thing, Sarge," DJ told me in his laconic way. "They only describing what I look like 'cause I got even more color than they do. I get called a helluva lot worse back home. So would they if they was living there, you know what I'm saying?"

Footsteps sounded behind us.

"Who's your friend?" Gemma said.

"Johnny."

Gemma crouched so she was eye level with the boy. "Hello Johnny, my name's Gemma. You have a little . . ." she ran her fingertips across her cheek. "Right here. Do you mind?" He tried to shirk but I held him fast. She took out a handkerchief, wetted it with her tongue, and then wiped drops of the bigger boy's blood off his cheek. "That's better."

I let go of him, but stayed close, ready to grab him if he started swinging.

"How old are you?" Gemma said

He shrugged. "Seven?"

"Have you lived here long?"

He nodded.

"What do you like to do? Play sports? Read? Color?"

"Nothing. I here til I go."

"And where would that be?"

"Any place. Boys here hate me. Everybody hate me. I *bui doi*."

"We don't hate you," Gemma said.

That made Johnny hesitate, but then he said, "You stink."

I went to grab him again, but Gemma's look held me off. "What makes you say that?"

His nose wrinkled. "I no lie. You stink."

"I think you mean to say 'smell.' What do I smell like?"

"Water buffalo. They pull cart."

Gemma laughed. "I see. Do you know what a horse is?"

"Cowboy ride. In cartoon."

"That's right. And cowgirls too. I smell like a horse because I'm a cowgirl and was with horses this morning. Feeding them. Brushing them. Moving them from the stable to the corral. Nick and I live on a ranch. Would you like to ride a horse?"

His chin dropped. "I no lucky. You lucky. All America lucky. Not Johnny Da Den. I dirty gook. I *bui doi*."

He ducked under my reach and ran across the blacktop and disappeared around the back of the building. I started to give chase, but Gemma called me back.

"Poor little guy, he's scared half to death. Chasing him will only frighten him more." Her head cocked. "What's a *bui doi*?"

"Dust child. It's what the locals call the Amerasian kids who got abandoned. They're not accepted and are forced to live on the streets and fend for themselves. There are no orphanages for the children of the dusty streets."

Gemma sucked in her breath. "You know who he reminds me of? The little mustang foal you rescued after its mother was poisoned. There's a lot of spirit under all that pain." When I didn't say anything, she said, "Who does Johnny remind you of?"

I swallowed. "Mostly I see little village kids crying outside their hooches as they went up in flames. I see DJ who died right beside me."

We stood on the hot blacktop looking at each other as the sound of girls singing jump-rope songs and the plunk-plunk of a tether ball became fainter and fainter and the faces of little Suzy and the redhead boy grew dimmer and dimmer. I'd seen that look of determination in the horse doctor's eyes before. It blazed no less fiercely right then.

"Are you sure about this?" I said.

Gemma nodded. "As sure as I am that a loving home has to be better than here for a little boy who's gone through what Johnny has."

"Come on, we'd better go."

"To the motel?"

"To Mrs. Wilsey's office. Why wait til morning?"

2

The sunbeams did their job and melted the frost on the windowpanes as Gemma and I got dressed and headed to breakfast. Pudge Warbler was already seated at the table working his way through a plate heaped with steak, eggs, and country-fried potatoes. A basket of frybread and a blue enamel coffee pot were in easy reach.

The old sheriff pointed his fork at us. "I told November I'm delivering a convict to the state pen today and be gone three days and she thinks no one can cook west of the Cascades. You think this is good and plenty, you should see the doggie bag of vittles she's packing."

I took a seat and poured myself a mug of coffee while Gemma pushed through the swinging door to the kitchen. "Who else is making the run to Salem with you?"

"Me, myself, and I."

"You don't have a deputy riding shotgun?"

His jowls shook. "Can't spare one. We're down a man since Edwards retired and I promoted Orville Nelson to chief deputy. Not the first time I've delivered a killer to the pen all by my lonesome."

The lawman took a bite and chewed. "This is a two birds, one stone deal. I got to be in Salem for a statewide county sheriff's meeting. The attorney general is up for reelection and needs a dog and pony show for the voters. Ordered all thirty-six of us front and center. The only excuse he'll accept for not showing up is a death certificate from our county coroner."

"But Dill McCaw is no run-of-the-mill offender. The jury found him guilty on all counts. Coldcocking the patron at the tavern where he was singing. Coldcocking the bartender when he tried to intervene. Lighting the tavern on fire to try and cover up what he'd done. The two men he knocked out were burned alive. So was a Burns fireman trying to put out the flames."

"And Dill will never see parole for it either. Not with his string of priors for assault and that missing record producer case up in Portland he's been linked to."

The old lawman swallowed some coffee. "Not to worry. I'll have him 'cuffed and shackled. I'm also bringing a gag in case he starts singing those godawful tunes of his and blathering about how he's a star and all the sweet young things who showed up at the courthouse every day to swoon over him are living proof. It's a long drive and a man's only got so much patience."

I asked him where he was overnighting.

"They got rooms lined up for us in a hotel near the capitol building, but budget being what it is these days, we got to buddy up. It'll be my luck to draw someone who snores like a grizzly for a roomie. Another reason I'm packing the gag." He dunked the frybread in his coffee.

The kitchen door swung open and Hattie galloped in, her little cowgirl boots clopping on the hardwood floor and her pigtails swinging. Her dog Jake was right behind, paws skidding and tail wagging. I gave the big mutt a pat and told him to lie down in the corner. He ducked under the table and sat in front of Hattie's chair.

"Morning, Daddy," Hattie said. "Morning, Grandpa. I'm starving."

"Worked up an appetite getting all your chores done, did you?" Pudge said. "What about those hands?"

She held them up for inspection. "Clean as a—"

He whistled on cue. "Good job. Where's Johnny?"

"Still washing up."

"Isn't he hungry too?"

"He fell in a cowpie and *Mu'a* said he has to change his pants before he can eat."

I asked if he was hurt.

"Not from falling down."

"Does that mean from something else?"

Hattie clapped a hand over her mouth. "I'm not supposed to say anything."

"But now you have. What happened?"

"Don't make me a tattletale, Daddy."

"You're not tattletaling, you're answering a question."

"Oh." She sucked in her breath and then blew it out in a long stream. "Johnny said a really bad word and then slugged a fence post and that made him say another and now his knuckles are bleeding and Mama is putting a bandage on them. So there."

Pudge clicked his cheeks. "Might be skinned knuckles will help teach him to rein in that temper of his."

"He's working on it," I said.

"I know that, son, but temper can be like spring in Harney County. If it comes in like a lion roaring with teeth and claws bared, it's likely to go out the same way. Speaking of, I woke up and saw the sun shining and the sky bluer than Gemma's mother's eyes and right away turned on the radio for the weather report to see if there were any surprises in store. Wasn't no surprise at all. It's going to snow right about the time I'll be driving over Santiam Pass." He shook his head. "Typical spring."

"Did you already switch out your snow tires?"

"Best thing about growing old is, I wasn't born yesterday."

The door to the kitchen swung open and Johnny came in, followed by Gemma and November. The Paiute healer was carrying a platter of bacon and eggs. Johnny kept his head down and one hand behind his back. He sat and quickly slipped his bandaged hand onto his lap.

"How are the horses this morning?" I asked him.

"Okay," he said.

"Give Sarah extra oats?"

"Uh-huh."

"It's important because she's still nursing her filly foal."

Hattie beamed. "My Shelly. As soon as she's old enough, I'm going to ride her."

"And, Johnny, now that you're feeding Wovoka, he'll let you ride him if I teach you," I said.

The boy shook his head. "Don't wanna."

"It's the best way to get around the ranch. Fun too."

"I said, don't wanna."

"Then when you're ready."

He scowled, but stayed mum. Gemma and November took seats and the heavy platter of food was passed family style. When it got to Johnny, he eyed it carefully, trying to figure out how to take hold of it while hiding his bandaged hand.

November tsked. "Do not be ashamed of a hurt hand. Only be ashamed if you do not learn not to hurt yourself again."

His head bowed lower. After a few moments, he reached for the platter with both hands.

Gemma asked Pudge when he was going to leave for Salem.

"As soon as the judge signs off on the transfer papers. I aim to be on the road no later than nine."

"Are you all packed?"

"Taking a pressed uniform to wear to the meeting and three days' worth of clean socks and skivvies."

"What if you have to stay over?"

"Don't plan to. Work will pile up higher than a snowdrift as it is." He gave Hattie and Johnny a wink. "I can't afford to be gone too long. These grandkids are sprouting up so fast, I might not recognize them if I was to stay a day longer."

Hattie giggled.

"What's your patient load looking like while I'm in Salem?" he asked Gemma.

"Heating up. I got a call this morning about a couple of troublesome pregnancies at the Triple Seven. Nagah and I are flying there right after breakfast."

"I wanna go too," Johnny said.

"And wouldn't I love to take you with me, but you know it's a school day."

"Don't wanna go school. Hate school."

It was becoming a common refrain, but Gemma and I were learning not to debate it with him. "Nick will drop you and Hattie off. If I'm back in time, I'll pick you up."

November harrumphed. "Better their own two feet carry them. Build strong heart. Strong backbone also. They will need them to walk their own path."

"True, but not today when I'm going to be on the other side of the county. I have enough to worry about." She was eyeing me as she said it.

We finished eating and I told the kids to grab their things and I'd meet them outside. I was setting a toolbox in the back of my pickup when Pudge walked out of the house cradling a Winchester and carrying an army-green ditty bag. His holstered .45 hung from a wide leather belt strapped around his ample waist.

"You got work to do on that old lineman's shack you call an office?" he said, tilting his chin at the toolbox.

"The stovepipe doesn't take to wind. After last night, I'll bet it's got more than a sailor's list to it. Probably lost a handful of roof shingles out of the deal too."

"One of these days your outfit's gonna hire a maintenance worker instead of making you wear all the hats. Any news about getting a new boss?"

"All I know is what was written on the letter HQ sent around announcing President Ford had appointed a new regional supervisor based in DC. Way down in the small print was a list of new district supervisors to go along with him. Ours is named L. Bloom and based in Portland, but I haven't heard from him yet. Don't recognize his name either. Probably a transfer from another region who'll be long on bureaucracy and short on field experience."

"Sounds like my boss."

"Before you go, I want to say thanks for calling Johnny your grandson. It means a lot."

"Johnny's a pistol, sure, but that's because he's a survivor. He had to be living on his own in the streets like he did, fighting with dogs, chickens, and rats over garbage scraps."

Pudge clicked his cheeks. "The things he saw, well, you and me, we both been to war, know firsthand what a living hell it is, but imagine being a little kid in one? The reason he's always drawing fighter planes and people getting shot is because he saw those things for real."

The old lawman put the ditty bag on the front seat of his new pickup, a white four-door four-by with a gold seven-point star decal on the front doors and SHERIFF painted in blue on the front fenders. He slid the Winchester into the gun rack, and then looked back.

"You get to be my age, you grow a soft spot about these

things. Between you and me and the fencepost, the night I cornered Dill McCaw in the alley behind the tavern, I had my forty-five out and he drew on me anyway. I could've shot him in the heart right then and there and wouldn't've missed. A clean shoot any way that anybody would've looked at it."

He pushed the short brim of his Stetson up. "But you know what? For a split second, I didn't see Dill or his pistol. I saw Johnny and little Hattie. Two things went through my mind. I wondered how much I'd miss them if Dill pulled his trigger first and I wondered if I'd change any if I killed him. If it'd make me feel any different when they sat on my lap or if they could tell I'd killed a man and feel different about me."

"But you fought at Iwo Jima and have been a sheriff a long time. It isn't like you never had to take a life defending your country or in the line of duty."

"That's true, son, but never as a grandpa."

"I'm glad you didn't let him shoot you, and I know Gemma is too."

"Likewise. The only thing I regret is how Bonnie LaRue wrote it up in the *Burns Herald*. She didn't mention that I shot the gun clean out of Dill's hand without giving him so much as a powder burn rather than drilling it and keeping him from ever being able to pluck that godawful guitar again."

"You know she did that to get your goat."

"And I reckon I deserve it. Hell hath no fury."

The flinty old lawman got behind the wheel and drove away. I watched as he turned from the ranch's drive onto the two-lane and headed for Burns to pick up the convicted killer. In all the years I'd known him, I couldn't recall a time when Pudge had expressed having a moment's hesitation.

I hoped for his sake, it wouldn't happen again. Ours too.

3

The old lineman's shack stood at the edge of No Mountain. It once sheltered watchmen for a short-lived railroad prior to becoming my office. Perched on a ladder while fixing the cockeyed stovepipe gave me a view of the entire town. It comprised a one-room schoolhouse where I'd dropped off Hattie and Johnny, the post office, and a block-long stretch of false-fronted commercial buildings that appeared to lean against each other for support.

A chain of black-capped buttes rose to the west, the Stinkingwater Mountains to the east, and an endless sea of sagebrush lapped at the base of snow-cloaked Steens Mountain to the south. I never grew tired of the view. It was both a window on and a gateway to the beauty and mystery of eastern Oregon. While I'd spent the last several years crisscrossing it for my job, I'd need more days than there were stars above to cover it all. Soul-stirring landscapes, gee-whiz geology, and unique wildlife aside, it was the high lonesome's spirit that captivated me most, for it hovered somewhere between the explicable and inexplicable, the earthly and unearthly.

Despite the stovepipe's wind-lashed crook, patina of rust,

and divots from hail, I was reluctant to replace it. A new pipe would draw better and cause less smoke to escape from the woodburning stove inside the shack, but I saw something in the original's ability to withstand whatever was thrown at it. Given what Gemma and I were going through, I had to wonder if our marriage would have the same kind of endurance.

I slipped a new pipe boot over it and was preparing to anchor the flashing to the roof when tires crunched gravel, a door slammed shut, and a woman's voice called up to me. "Is this the Fish and Wildlife Service's office?"

I had a nail between my lips, another pinched between my left thumb and forefinger, and a twenty-two-ounce hammer gripped in my right. I didn't take my eyes off the nailhead or remove the one from my mouth as I mumbled without looking down. "Yes, ma'am, but it's not a visitors center."

"I'm looking for a guide."

I swung the hammer and struck the nailhead square and lined up the next. "Stay on the two-lane and follow the signs to Malheur National Wildlife Refuge. There's usually a docent around who'll be happy to point out birds. I was there yesterday and saw colors galore, including a lazuli bunting. You see it, you'll think you're in the tropics. Self-guided nature trail maps are in a kiosk. They're free."

I hammered in the second nail.

"I don't want to walk a loop and a volunteer won't do. I need a ranger to take me where I want to go and show me what I need to find."

"Sorry, but I don't offer guide service."

"What if I ordered you to?"

"What the...?"

I looked down. The voice belonged to a young woman with tousled brown hair cut in a bob. She was wearing sunglasses and a khaki shirt. A badge was gleaming above her left breast. I shot a glance at the vehicle parked behind my rig. It had the same duck-and-fish emblem on the door as mine.

"That's right, Ranger Drake. I'm your new boss, District Supervisor Bloom." She cocked her head at the shack's door. "I left Portland at four in the morning and my thermos ran dry two hours ago. If you don't have fresh coffee in there, I may have to fire you."

I all but slid down the ladder fireman-style. By the time I wiped the soot off my hands and joined the new supervisor, she'd already found the coffee grounds and put a pot of water on the stove.

"I didn't know you were coming," I said.

"Surprise keeps people on their toes," she said.

Supervisor Bloom had taken off her sunglasses. Her eyes were as brown as a Van Morrison song. She looked to be in her mid-twenties, unusually young to hold such an important management position where promotions were typically rewarded for years on the job rather than the number of accomplishments.

"I read your personnel file," she said. "That's quite a record of policy offenses you've racked up. Not much for following the rules, are you?"

"I can explain. Well, a few of them, anyway."

"I'm not interested in what you did. I'm interested in what you'll do next. I'm big on people who show initiative, not so big on those who makes excuses."

The water boiled. She turned off the burner. "I don't see a percolator. How do you make coffee?"

"Allow me."

I poured grounds right into the pot and threw in a half a cup of cold water to sink them. She grimaced as she watched.

"Trust me, you'll like it," I said.

"I'll be the judge of that. By the way, where's your partner?"

"You mean Loq?"

"Unless there's another ranger assigned to this territory that I don't know about. Is he back?"

"We patrol a dozen refuges between us and not all get radio reception. Sometimes we go days without talking."

"Back from Hollywood is the question. That's right, I know all about the movie that was filmed here last year and how Loq got roped into being an actor. I even saw it. Not bad, if you like Westerns, which I don't particularly. Don't like the way they portray Indians, and certainly not the way they portray women."

"Loq's been back at work since the end of fall. Last we spoke, he was hot on the heels of a gang of poachers operating in the Upper Klamath Basin complex. He'll catch them, if he hasn't already. You can count on it."

"My, my. You two are quite the pair, aren't you? Always have each other's back. His personnel record is as rule-flaunting as your own."

I wasn't about to answer that and so I asked her how she took her coffee.

"Strong and black," she said.

It was the first and only mark in her favor so far. If it was going to be the last, I realized working for her was going to be a rough go. I filled two mugs and placed them on the rickety wooden table that served as my desk. She promptly sat in the chair I usually took. I remained standing.

The new supervisor picked up a mug, pursed her lips, and blew on it. She wasn't wearing any lipstick. No makeup either. Her only jewelry was a field watch and a choker of polished turquoise beads that peeked beneath the open collar of her uniform. She took a sip and then another.

"That's quite good. What do you call the way you made it?"

"Cowboy coffee. You're not from the west, are you?"

Her tousled brown hair framed a face that was tanned but creaseless. "No. Maine."

"Is that where you were before being assigned to Oregon?" When she nodded, I said, "I didn't know Fish and Wildlife had an office there."

"I was working for the state. Maine Department of Inland Fisheries and Wildlife."

"If you don't mind my asking, Supervisor Bloom, did you apply for the job in Portland or did the feds poach you?"

"Does it matter?" She drank some more coffee, gave another approving nod. "While I am your boss, I prefer to be on a first-name basis with people I work with in the field. It's a different story back in the office. I'm Liz."

"Nick," I said. "And of course, I'll guide you. Depending on how much time you have, we could start at the Malheur and then go on to Hart Mountain National Antelope Refuge. The pronghorns there are starting to calve. I know where the main herds bed down this time of year."

"I'm interested in the area east of here."

"You mean the Deer Flat refuge along the Snake River? Sure, it's about a two-hour drive to the Idaho line. I'll hook up the skiff's trailer and we can put in south of Nyssa and tour the different islands. The water's tricky this time of year with all the snowmelt, but the outboard's plenty powerful and can handle it."

"Not there. The Snake River area south of Boise. More specifically, the Bruneau River beyond where the two meet."

"But that's mostly BLM land. There's no national wildlife refuge there."

"Precisely. It's why I need to go."

"Can you tell me why or is this one of those deals where Washington is planning on establishing a new refuge and they don't want to tip their hand to keep land speculators from driving up the price per acre?"

"You have a suspicious mind."

"I'm a ranger. I bust bad guys."

The smile reappeared. "The Bureau of Land Management has its eye on naming a stretch of the Snake River near Swan Falls Dam where birds of prey gather as a National Conservation Area. A local by name of Morley Nelson who's made quite a name for himself is pushing for it. Years ago he got the Idaho legislature to pass a law protecting raptors and recently he's been working with power companies to keep their transmission lines from electrocuting bald eagles."

"I met Morley. He's a solid guy. A World War Two vet. Earned a Purple Heart."

"Like you did. It's in your file. You and Loq were both hired through a special program for returning Vietnam veterans."

"Morley is pushing sixty, but you wouldn't know it by the way he rappels down the sides of sheer canyon walls to band raptors, or braves claws and beaks to rescue injured birds that he rehabilitates. John Denver worked with him on a television documentary that aired on ABC a few years back. Morley speaks peregrine."

Liz laughed. It was a good laugh. Not too loud, not too long. Not forced or self-conscious either.

"I like that, speaks peregrine. I saw that show. 'The Eagle and the Hawk.' It made a real impression on me. In fact, it's one of the reasons why I wanted this job. Why I've dedicated myself to creating wildlife refuges for raptors."

She started humming, then sang some of the lyrics from the show's theme song about being an eagle, being a hawk, about people who see them sharing in the freedom when they fly.

"Do you remember that song?" she said.

I nodded and could hear Denver's voice as he crooned about

dancing on the west wind and touching the mountaintops and sailing over the canyons and up to the stars.

"You're not going to sing it?"

"Not a chance."

"Don't tell me you don't even sing in the shower?"

I took another sip of coffee instead of answering.

Liz groaned in disappointment, but then said, "The fact is, the bald eagle and peregrine falcon are protected by the Endangered Species Act. Fish and Wildlife Service is in charge of administering that law, not the BLM. We can't relinquish our authority, and one way to ensure that is to establish more wildlife refuges."

"And you think a good place to start is along the Bruneau River?"

"I do. I need to go there and document threatened and endangered species that depend on it for survival to prove my point. The people upstairs need convincing."

"That part of the country is extremely rugged and most of it roadless. I know a four-wheel-drive track that leads to an overlook where you can look down and see the river flowing through Bruneau Canyon. It'll take the best part of a day to reach it."

Liz shook her head. "Driving above the river and looking down won't get the job done. I need to be *on* it. Hiking it and logging wildlife along the way. I brought my camping gear. How soon can we leave?"

"Whoa! That'll take some planning and even more doing. The Bruneau is one hundred fifty miles long. There's no marked trail along the water to speak of, only a ten-mile deer path up on the rim above a section of the canyon."

"Have you hiked it?"

I nodded. "It's a real knee-scraper."

"Then we'll go by boat."

"Not by the skiff trailered outside, we won't. The river's a minefield of boulders and chutes. It's too narrow in spots and too shallow in others."

"I also saw you have a canoe. We can take it. I did a lot of canoeing in Maine. I'm a good paddler."

"That canoe is aluminum. It'd get flattened like a beer can within the first mile."

"And you know this because you've floated it?"

"You don't float the Bruneau, you run parts and portage what you can't. Few people take it on. It's remote and hard to access. And then there are all the rapids, rocks, and drops. The main obstacle is water level. It's only runnable several weeks out of the year because it's either a torrent from all the snow melting in the Jarbidge Mountains or there's not enough water because, well, it flows through the high lonesome."

I waved at the window. "Summers here are long, hot, and dry. Except when the wind blows. Then they're long, cold, and dry."

"What weeks is it runnable?"

"Usually in the first half of spring."

"But that's right now."

"Seasons don't abide by calendars around here. A lot of snow fell this winter and the runoff is epic. The Bruneau is likely to stay at flood stage for weeks."

Liz turned on the smile again. "I've found that for every likely, there's an unlikely. Look outside. The sky is blue. It's warm enough for you to be up on the roof in shirtsleeves. I'm familiar with changeable weather. Maine could switch from rainclouds to clouds of black flies in a day."

"It's mosquitos here in Harney County, and a cloud doesn't quite describe them. More like a blizzard."

Annoyance flashed across her face. "What I'm saying is, I've learned you have to prepare for both eventualities and get on with it. Otherwise, you're left standing still while the world passes you by. I've never done that and I'm not about to start.

Not with having this new job and not with seeing an opportunity to create a new wildlife refuge to protect endangered species."

I drank coffee to stall for time while trying to come up with another argument for why we should wait. Liz didn't give me much of a chance. "You said people do run it. In what?"

"Rafts and kayaks."

She leaned forward. I detected a trace of patchouli. "You have a skiff and a canoe. What about a raft or a kayak?"

"I don't have either."

"Does that mean you've never run a river before?"

"I've run plenty. Oregon is awash in whitewater. I've rowed rafts on the Deschutes, McKenzie, and Rogue. Kayaked the Middle Fork of the Salmon in Idaho too. Now that was big water. But the Bruneau is altogether different."

"Good, you're an expert. Where can we get our hands on a raft or a couple of kayaks?"

Fine, I thought. If my words couldn't convince her, a look down from the Bruneau Canyon Overlook at a raging snow-swollen river where knife-edged boulders churned a frothing cauldron of whitewater would. If it didn't, well, that would also tell me what kind of boss I'd be working for. That is, if we were both lucky enough to survive running it.

"I might know a guy," I said.

"What are we waiting for? Take me to him."

4

Blackpowder Smith wore a pair of half-frame reading glasses perched on the end of his nose as he compared a shelfful of cans to a list on a clipboard. He looked up when the bell on the front door of his combination dry-goods store and tavern jingled.

"Why, howdy there, young fella. Caught me in the middle of taking inventory. I'm running low on vegetables and calculating how many cases to order given everyone's spring garden is gonna be a month late. Who's your friend?"

"This is my new boss, District Supervisor Liz Bloom. She's headquartered at Fish and Wildlife's office in Portland."

The old codger grinned. "A pleasure to make your acquaintance. If there's anything you want or need to know about Harney County, I'm your man. I not only own this establishment, but I'm the mayor of No Mountain, head of the chamber of commerce, and chief of the volunteer fire department."

He tapped the crown of his black cowboy hat that was encircled with a snakeskin band. "I also write a little verse, if you care to hear some. I've been called the Bard of the High Desert."

"Nice to meet you, Blackpowder. Nick tells me you can help us procure a raft or some kayaks."

"I'd be happy to. Are you planning to float the Blitzen or the Silvies to look for birds?"

She glanced at me for an explanation.

"The Donner und Blitzen River drains Steens Mountain to the south and flows north through the Malheur Refuge into Malheur Lake. The Silvies flows south from the Aldrich Mountains north of here. It splits into two forks, east and west. Both empty into the lake."

"They don't flow into rivers that reach the Pacific like the Snake does via the Columbia?"

"No. Think of Harney Basin as a bathtub and Malheur Lake as the drain at the bottom."

"That's unusual."

"Like everything else in the high lonesome."

Liz turned to Blackpowder. "We're going to run the Bruneau River."

The store owner's eyes grew wide behind the half-frame glasses.

"Are you sure you want to do that, miss? It is miss, isn't it? I don't see a wedding band."

"You're very observant," she said.

"Pays to be. By the way, I ain't hitched myself." He cackled. "Back to the Bruneau. It's more than dangerous. It's downright deadly. Last fall, two fishermen set out to float a stretch after a heavy rain. When they were overdue getting home, their wives called Owyhee County Sheriff's."

Blackpowder rarely grimaced, but didn't hold back now. "That triggered Search and Rescue, but the boys had to turn back with only the fishermen's rig they'd left at the put-in to show for all their effort. Couldn't make much progress along that devil of a river, not with the weather turning bad, which it did in a big way and stayed that way all winter. They sent up a helicopter too, but nobody spotted nothing down in the pitch-dark canyon."

He tucked the clipboard under his arm. "The pair are presumed drowned. If not that, then they surely froze stiff. The search for their bodies will resume in, oh, I'd say, three, four weeks' time. That's when the water level will likely drop enough to get a raft down it safely. Not that the river is ever safe."

"That's tragic," Liz said.

"The real tragedy is it wouldn't've happened in the first place if they'd listened to common sense instead of dreaming of trophy trout." He untucked the clipboard. "So, you need a raft or a couple of kayaks in about three, four weeks. That gives me plenty of time to round them up. I'll make some calls and let Nick know when I got 'em."

"Not in three weeks. Right away."

"But—"

"I work for the federal government, and this job can't wait."

Blackpowder stroked his white billy-goat beard. "I savvy that. It was the same when I worked for the government, courtesy of the US Navy. When Uncle Sam wanted something done, he wanted it done yesterday, like escorting convoys across the Atlantic in WW Two, which I did. Damn the torpedoes and full speed ahead. I'll put the call out on my grapevine pronto."

"I'd also appreciate it if you kept our destination between us."

"You can count on me. Loose lips sink ships. I found that out during the war too. Not once, but twice."

I told him we were also going to need a week's worth of supplies. "I brought a list."

Blackpowder read through it. "Looks like you're packing

grub for three. Am I to assume our favorite member of the Klamath Nation is goin' with you?"

"But he doesn't know it yet."

"Can't think of nobody better I'd want to shoot rapids with. Loq's stronger than that outboard you got strapped to the back of your skiff."

"Call me at the ranch, okay? We're heading there now. The supervisor is going to stay with us since we have a spare room for the next couple of nights."

His hat waggled up and down. "That's right, Pudge left for Salem today. He told me he was goin' give Dill McCaw a lift to his new home. Can't say I feel sorry for that young man spending the rest of his born days behind bars. I knew the bartender he killed. A good man. Left a wife and a little one."

"My father-in-law is the sheriff," I said to Liz. "He's taking a convicted murderer to the state penitentiary."

She shook hands with Blackpowder. "I'm looking forward to your call telling us you have our boats."

"Certainly. But can I offer a friendly piece of advice? It's something my daddy told me when I left home as a young whippersnapper. He pressed a ten-dollar gold piece in my hand and said, 'Take care of it, son, because a fool and his money are easily parted. Even more important, take care of yourself, because a fool and his life are easily departed.'"

I got my boss out of there before Blackpowder started cackling again. We walked back to the lineman's shack. As we neared it, I could hear Gemma's voice reverberating on the police band radio in my rig.

"Nick, do you read? Over."

I made fast work down the gravel drive and picked up the mike. "I'm here. What's up? Over."

"Where are you?"

"Parked out front of my office. Why?"

"Nagah and I have our hands full here. A breech. A prolapse. A case of dystocia. And that's for starters. We're going to try to get home by suppertime, but no guarantees. Can you pick up the kids?"

"Sure. By the way, we have a guest staying the night."

"Really, who?"

"The new district supervisor."

"Did you know he was coming and forget to tell me or did he show up unannounced?"

"It was a bit of a surprise. And it's she, not he."

Static sounded. "What's she like?"

"Determined."

"Has she been with the service a long time?"

"No, she's new."

"Meaning she's young. Is she pretty?"

"I hadn't noticed."

Gemma snorted. "It's about time Fish and Wildlife joined the twentieth century and hired women supervisors."

"I couldn't agree with you more," Liz said as she came up behind me.

"Is that her?" Gemma said.

"Yes, I'm Liz Bloom," she said before I could.

"Hello, I'm Gemma. If I get home tonight, we can meet properly."

"I'm looking forward to it."

"Radio from the air when you got an ETA so I can light the strip for you," I said. "Over and out." I recradled the mike.

Liz said, "Right answer."

"What?"

"Saying you hadn't noticed." The smile twitched before I could respond. "I take it your wife is a veterinarian. And you have kids too? I don't recall reading that in your file, only the list of policy infractions."

"I wasn't a husband or father when I hired on as a ranger. Guess I forgot to update my paperwork."

"We'd better get a move on if you don't want to leave your children standing on the curb. Your wife doesn't sound like the kind of woman who'd appreciate that."

We drove caravan style. As I pulled up to the schoolhouse, the front door swung open and a wave of kids rushed out. Hattie and Johnny beelined straight for my pickup and clambered into the front seat.

I eased back onto the road, checked the mirror to make sure Liz was following, and made the short drive to the turn-off to the ranch. As we approached the cattle guard, Hattie raised her boots. "Lift your feet, Johnny. You don't want them caught in the rails and break an ankle." She giggled as we clattered over.

Liz parked right behind. "Who's that lady?" Hattie asked when we got out.

"That's Miss Bloom, my new boss. She's going to have supper with us and spend the night. Come on, I'll introduce you. You too, Johnny."

"I don't wanna," he said.

"It's not an option. It's called manners. Come on."

Hattie skipped right up to Liz. "Hi. I'm Hattie Drake and I have a pony named Shelly. Do you want to see her?"

"I would," Liz said.

"And this is my son, Johnny," I said.

"Hullo," he said, looking at his feet instead of her.

"Hi Johnny. You don't have to be shy. I don't bite."

Hattie laughed. "You're funny."

"Sometimes. How old are you?"

"Five. I just had my birthday."

"Congratulations. Did you have a party?"

"Uh-huh. And I got Shelly as a present. Which is short for Shell Flower. Which is English for a beautiful Paiute princess named *Thocmentony*. But white people call her Sarah Winnemucca. See, Sarah is my mama's horse's name and Sarah's Shelly's mama."

"I think I followed all that."

Johnny scowled. "I don't call her Sarah Winnemucca 'cause I not white."

Liz's expression didn't change. "Yes, your skin is a beautiful shade of, I'd say, closer to hot cocoa than coffee."

"Johnny was born in Vietnam," I said, "but he lives with us now and we're glad he does."

The boy spun and ran to the house, sprinting up the wooden steps to the front porch. The screen door slammed behind him.

"He's in a bad mood because a girl made fun of him," Hattie said. "I wanted to pull her hair, Daddy, but I know I'm not supposed to."

"Why don't you go in and change and then you can introduce Liz to Shelly. Maybe we can go for a ride before supper."

Hattie hotfooted it to the house.

"Johnny started living here last summer and it's been a difficult adjustment for him," I said. "For all of us." I stopped myself, wishing I hadn't said the last part.

Liz pretended not to notice. "Did you know his parents when you served in Vietnam?"

"No."

"Is he part of President Ford's airlift that's been all over the news?"

"Johnny got here before then and it wasn't sanctioned or government-sponsored like Operation Babylift is now. I've been able to piece together his journey. It's hair-raising and filled with danger and chance at every turn. It's hard to imagine a little boy was able to do it, much less survive it. If we have time someday, I'll tell you about it."

"Perhaps when we're floating down a lazy stretch of the Bruneau or around the campfire one night."

Thinking of that made me realize I'd have to tell Gemma I'd need to be away for a week. With everything going on with Johnny and her job, it wasn't going to be an easy conversation. Not by a longshot.

5

The sun sank behind the Cascades and the last hour of daylight was tinting the sky lilac before it plunged into deep purple. Liz Bloom was sitting on the top rail of the corral watching Hattie astride Sarah as I led the mare around with a halter lead rope. A musical hum sounded overhead and then turned into an unmusical roar. Jake's hackles stood as he raised his muzzle and howled. Gemma's single-engine plane zoomed in from the east.

"Mama and Nagah are home," Hattie said.

"Just in time," I said. "We won't have to light the airstrip after all."

The plane circled overhead and the wings waggled. Hattie waved back. Then it lined up for a touchdown on the dirt runway not far from the corral and stables.

"Can I ride over by myself?" Hattie said. "I want to show Mama I can do it."

"All right, but you need to wait until the plane's finished taxiing and the propellor stops spinning. Keep Sarah at a walk and no galloping."

When the plane came to a halt and the engine was off, I

unfastened the lead rope and opened the corral gate. Hattie kicked with her bootheels, but didn't need to give Sarah any encouragement. Nor did she have to do any reining. The mare could've made the short trip blindfolded. Jake trotted right alongside.

Nagah Will had been behind the stick. He hopped out, blocked the wheels, and fastened the tie-downs. Gemma exited on the passenger side, took one look at Hattie and cheered. "Yippie-ki-yay, girl. Come on over and give your mama a lift. These old bones are weary."

If Gemma was really as tired as she professed, it was impossible to tell. She vaulted up behind Hattie, clucked her tongue, and Sarah broke into a brisk trot back to the corral with Jake having to break into a wolf-like lope to keep up. The horse doctor guided the mare with her knees and they went straight in, bypassed me, and came to a stop in front of Liz's perch on the top rail. That put the two women at eye level.

After sizing each other up, Gemma finally said, "Welcome to our ranch."

"I'm glad to be here. You have a beautiful family."

"Thank you. Do you have kids?"

Liz's tousled hair crested like waves across her cheeks when she shook her head. "Too busy with work, both where I was before and now the new job here. Maybe one day when things slow down. And if I meet the right man, of course."

"Things never slow down, only speed up. And as for the right man? Take it from me, they're only right about things half the time."

"That often?"

"Good one. You'll have to excuse me. I need a shower in the worst way and a change of clothes. Nagah and I have had our arms up to our shoulders in cow vaginas all day."

She slid off the back of Sarah, reached up and swung Hattie

out of the saddle, and carried the little girl squealing and laughing to the house.

"Come on, Sarah," I called to the mare. "I'll get you unsaddled."

As the cutting horse ambled toward me, Liz said, "How did you and Gemma meet?"

"Awkwardly."

"How's that?"

"I was new to Harney County and her father asked me to help him find a missing girl. He'd heard I had tracking experience from leading long-range reconnaissance patrols in Vietnam. Gemma's very protective of her dad and warned me I'd better stay on my toes around him or I'd have her to answer to."

"And did you?"

"You bet. Still do."

"Did you find the girl?"

I hesitated. "At the Hart Mountain refuge, but not before she'd been murdered and buried in a gully. She wasn't the only victim."

Liz shuddered. "That's horrible, but in a way, you and Gemma met because of it."

"I wouldn't put it that way."

"What I meant is, Gemma's lucky because in finding them, she found quite a catch."

She was looking at me with a hard-to-read smile as if challenging me to say something back, but the ground beneath my boots felt more than a little slippery, and it wasn't from fresh horse droppings. I slipped the reins over Sarah's head.

"I better tend to her. Don't want to be late for supper. November doesn't like it if anyone is. She's particular that way. See you there."

I led the mare into the stable and didn't look back. By the time I finished unsaddling and brushing her, Liz was gone. The sky was darkening, and a chilling of the air would surely come. Once I told Gemma about the Bruneau, I knew the bedroom windowpanes wouldn't be the only things with frost on them.

Everyone but Liz was already seated by the time I washed up and joined them at the table.

"Did anyone tell Liz supper's on?" I said.

Gemma gestured at her father's office down the hall that doubled as a sheriff's substation. "She said she needed to call her secretary and catch up on a lot of important business. Do you know how many people she oversees?"

"I'm not exactly sure, but it's got to be growing because of all the added work that came with the Endangered Species Act."

"Something tells me Liz believes she can handle whatever's thrown at her."

I put my napkin on my lap. "Should we start without her?"

November harrumphed. "We will give her two minutes, but not a second more. I do not want the cornbread to grow any colder than it already has."

To pass the time, I asked Nagah if the air currents they encountered while flying over the Stinkingwaters were stronger than usual.

"As long as I don't fight them, they don't bother the plane," he said in his quiet way. "Watching eagles soar on them taught me that."

Nagah had cleaned up after work too. He wore a folded red bandana as a headband even though his long hair hung in a tight single braid down his back. The bandana had belonged to his late grandfather, my old friend Tuhudda Will. It was more than a way for Nagah to pay homage to him. The bandana was a touchstone that linked him to the old ways of the Paiute people that Tuhudda had come to embody both in life and now from the spirit world. Nagah had vowed to his grandfather he would carry on the tradition.

"Do you have to go back to the Triple Seven tomorrow?" I asked Gemma.

"Yes, and then on to the Rocking H too." It was the largest ranch in the county and owned by her ex-husband.

I started thinking of how to broach the subject of my having to leave for a week when Liz joined us. As soon as she was seated, November bowed her head and said a blessing. After she finished, she nodded to Gemma to begin passing the food.

"What language was that?" Liz asked.

"*Numu*," November said.

"November is a revered elder among the *Wadadökadö* band of the Northern Paiute," I explained. "She's a healer and dancer."

"What does the name of your band mean?" Liz asked her.

"Wada Root and Grass-seed Eaters. Many bands are known by the names of their main source of food. Hare Eaters. Sagebrush Eaters. Salmon-Caught-in-Traps Eaters."

"Indians lived where I was working in Maine too. They were members of the Penobscot tribe."

"The People of Where the White Rocks Extend Out. That is what they call themselves in the Algonquin language."

"Yes. Do you know any Penobscot people?"

"My own eyes have not seen them, but I have been told their old ones wove beautiful baskets from sweet grass and made canoes. The skin of each came from a single piece of bark peeled from the white birch tree. They say the canoes were very swift and very strong."

Liz turned to me. "Too bad we don't have one of those, Nick. We could run the Bruneau in it instead of having to rely on Blackpowder to find us a raft or kayaks."

"Excuse me?" Gemma said.

"We're running the Bruneau for a special project of mine. It's why I'm here. Didn't Nick tell you?"

Gemma aimed her eyes at me. "And when are you embarking on this special project?"

"I only learned about it today. I was going to tell—"

"Tomorrow," Liz said. "I called Blackpowder Smith when I was in your father's office. He told me he found a raft for us. He's already gathered the food and other supplies on the list Nick gave him."

"He did, did he?" Gemma said.

Gimlets, I thought to myself. Not the cocktail, but the nickname of the last ground combat unit to leave Vietnam. My squad had fought alongside them a couple of times. Third Battalion, Twenty-First Infantry. They were named for the gimlet, a tool used to bore through rock. That's what they did. Right through enemy lines. And that's what Gemma's eyes were doing to me right now.

November pushed her plate away. "The Bruneau is forbidden. It is not a river of water, but a river of death."

"Why is that?" Liz said.

"Because of *Tsa-ahu-bitts*."

"Is that another Paiute word?"

"It is *Newe*, what the Shoshone people call themselves in their language. My husband is *Newe*."

"Does he live here on the ranch too?"

"No. Shoots While Running and my daughter Breathes Like Gentle Wind dwell in the spirit world."

I explained to Liz that they had drowned in the Snake River fifty years ago when the bus they were taking to visit family on the Shoshone reservation in Idaho went off a bridge.

Liz frowned and then said to November, "What does *Tsa-ahu-bitts* mean?"

The old healer crossed her arms. "It is the name of a demon who lives in the land where the Jarbidge and Bruneau rivers join together. Jarbidge was how white men looking for gold tried to pronounce *Tsa-ahu-bitts*. First Tsawhawbitts, then Jahabich, then Jarbidge. The demon takes many forms and devours anyone who dares enter the canyons or walks the mountainsides or drinks and fishes from the rivers."

"Oh, it's an Indian legend. I love those. I know this old timer who lives in a cabin along the Kennebec River. He knows all the Penobscot ones, like an evil cannibal named *Giwakwa* who lives in the ice. Another is about a giant lake monster called *Aglebemu*. In the old days, parents would tell the legends to the children to keep them from playing on frozen ponds and breaking through the ice or paddling canoes without permission."

November's tsk was sharp. "There is truth in every legend. *Si-Te-Cah* were evil giants with hair the color of flames who warred against *Numu* long ago. A band of warriors finally trapped them in a cave near Lovelock and sealed them inside. Many years passed and the people began to think it was only a story and stopped believing in *Si-Te-Cah*. But one day miners working in the cave uncovered the remains of giants that had become mummified as they lay beneath the guano dropped by bats hanging from the cave's ceiling."

The old healer rocked in her chair. "All legends have a reason for being told. Some to save lives, some to explain how things came to be, and some to share traditions among a people to bind them together for all time. If a people forget their legends, they become no people at all."

"I can tell you about something that sounds like a legend, but isn't," Gemma said. "It's gruesome and taking place right now but doesn't seem to have any explanation."

"What is it?" Liz asked.

"Nagah and I started hearing about it a while back when we were making our rounds. It was happening on ranches in the southeast corner of Malheur County near where it borders

Idaho and Nevada. We finally saw it for ourselves today at the Triple Seven."

She sipped some water. "There were a half-dozen dead cows in a field. All that was left of them were skin and bones. No innards."

"They probably died last summer and dried out in the heat," I said. "Then whatever was left was hidden by snow and couldn't be seen until now when it melted."

"You'd think so, but the strange thing is, the cattle had been released to graze in that field recently. What little remains of them is relatively fresh."

"Could be rustlers, I suppose. Instead of taking live beeves like they usually do, they're butchering them on site."

"That's what the rancher thought at first, but there aren't any tire-tread marks, footprints, or horseshoe tracks."

"Okay, then it has to be a mountain lion or maybe a big black bear coming out of hibernation. Maybe more than one. It can't be a grizzly. The last one of those was killed in Oregon in the thirties and a wolf hasn't been seen in the state since the forties."

"It wasn't a bear or a mountain lion," Gemma said. "They would've left paw prints or scat. There aren't any ants or flies around the bodies either. Even the turkey vultures have left them alone."

"Mama, you're scaring me," Hattie said. "I'm going to have nightmares."

I looked over at Johnny. He was hunkering over his plate and clutching his knife and fork as if they were weapons.

"I know a friendly giant legend," Nagah said quickly. "You will like it, little sister and brother. Long ago, Beaver was much bigger than he is now. He was as big as a mountain. Beaver was always hungry, so hungry that he ate all the trees in the land around here and turned it into the desert it is now.

"Beaver had to go in search of new forests so he wouldn't

starve. He sniffed and smelled fresh trees growing on the other side of the mountains and set off to find them. Away he went, dragging his big, heavy tail behind. As he walked, his tail plowed the Earth so wide and so deep that when it stormed, all the rain fell into it and all the rivers that gathered did too. Beaver continued walking and left a trail behind until he reached the tall trees that grow beside the ocean. And that is how the Snake River and Columbia River came to be."

Hattie clapped her hands. "I like that legend."

The phone rang in Pudge's office. "I'll get it," Liz said. "It'll be my secretary."

As she stepped away, the rest of us started in on our meals except for November who started rocking in her chair, muttering in *Numu*.

Liz came right back.

"Wrong number?" I said.

"No, it's a man named Orville Nelson. He says he's a sheriff's deputy and needs to talk to Gemma. Something about her father being stuck in a snowstorm."

6

THE TWO-LANE

When Pudge Warbler left the ranch that morning, he sped to Burns and parked his new rig in front of a squat pink stucco building housing the Harney County Sheriff's Department.

"What in tarnation!" the old lawman thundered as he searched his desk for the signed form remanding Dill McCaw over to the state penitentiary.

The words had barely left his lips when rubber wheels skidding on linoleum screeched and a wheelchair that resembled a dragster shot into his office.

"Good morning, Sheriff," Chief Deputy Nelson said cheerfully.

"What's so good about it, Orville? Looks like the judge forgot to punch Dill's ticket to the big house."

"It is only a slight delay, sir. The judge's regular aide came down with the flu yesterday and went home early. The form is being typed as we speak and you will have a signed copy within the hour."

"An hour! That's gonna put me in Salem behind schedule. Call prison intake and let 'em know I'll be arriving late. I don't want to find a 'Closed' sign when I get there and have to check into the hotel with a suitcase in one hand and a killer 'cuffed to the other."

"You could always delay until tomorrow."

"Nope, can't miss the AG's meeting. Looks like I'm gonna be exercising the lawman's late-for-supper privilege and use the lights and siren to make up for lost time."

"It would be ill-advised to speed over the mountains, sir. I checked the weather on my computer and also radioed the State Police. They are already reporting snow flurries and icy road conditions."

"I'll be okay as long as they don't get lily-livered and close the pass. What else you got?"

"Bonnie LaRue called. The *Herald* is running a story about Dill McCaw's last day in Harney County. She wants a quote."

"Be my guest. 'Bout time the voters get used to seeing your name in print. Lord knows they've seen enough of mine over the past three decades."

"I will write up a statement and run it by you for approval."

"Son, if I trust you enough to be my second-in-command, I surely trust you can handle Bonnie LaRue. And a heckuva lot better than I've done, especially after she was widowed."

"Affirmative, sir. One other thing."

"It better not be a reminder about packing my toothbrush. Gemma already checked on how many skivvies I'm taking."

"It is about the group of young women who attended Dill McCaw's trial. A source tells me they are planning a demonstration today to protest his transfer to Salem."

"They must've plunked themselves around the corner on the front steps of the courthouse because I didn't see anybody on our side when I pulled up."

"My source did not provide details of the location or nature of the protest."

"This source of yours, is he another one of your G-men friends?"

The young lawman had once hoped to be an FBI agent until a cattle rustler's bullet to the back dashed his dreams. Since then, he'd cultivated ties within the agency.

"He is a confidential informant I have developed who lives here in Burns. One of the young women is an ex-girlfriend."

"And your snitch is jealous of the attention she's been paying to a caterwauling guitar picker and this is his way of getting back at her?"

"Revenge and self-preservation are always motivations for my CIs. I have learned leveraging those impulses can produce tangible results."

"Give him a call back and see if he's come up with any more of your tangi. . . uh, tangerines. I don't want to be running a gauntlet when I walk Dill out to my rig. They start chucking rotten tomatoes at me, I'll have to drive back home to get a clean uniform. I can't afford another delay."

"Right away."

Orville wheeled around and scooted out. Pudge thumbed through a pile of mail and faxes. Forty minutes later Orville rolled back in waving a piece of paper. "Here is the remand form. The ink on the judge's signature is barely dry."

Pudge slapped his short-brim Stetson back on and hitched his gun belt. "I'll collect Dill myself. Any word on protestors?"

"I have not been able to reach my CI."

"Then send a couple of deputies out front in case. Make sure they play on the department's softball team. I need guys who can catch."

Pudge galumphed up to the second-floor cells. Dill McCaw was dressed in jailhouse denims and sitting on his bunk. He was already handcuffed and shackled.

"Stand up, Dill. Time to go."

"How do you expect me to walk with these leg irons?"

The old lawman squinted at the killer. Dill had narrow hips and rubbery lips. His long, wavy hair fell to the tops of his shoulders. Then Pudge pictured the fireman who'd died trying to put out the blaze. They'd bent elbows together at the VFW on many occasions.

"Slowly," he said. "You don't want to trip going down the stairs and break that pretty face of yours before you get your prison mugshot taken."

"You're a mean old bastard. I should've shot you in the alley when I had the chance."

"You'll have plenty of time to contemplate your shoulda, woulda, couldas. Get a move on."

"What about my belongings?"

"What about 'em?"

"I got a right to take them with me. That guitar is a Gibson. I paid two hundred bucks for it. My black leather jacket and matching boots are my signature. They're collector items."

"My deputy is checking them out of the property room and putting them in the back of my rig. They'll get logged into the property room at the state pen during your intake and be waiting for you when you get released." Pudge gave it a couple of beats. "But with three life sentences stacked back-to-back, the only way that's gonna happen is when they wheel you out toes up."

Pudge marched the prisoner down the stairs. Orville was waiting at the front door.

"The coast is clear, sir. Not a demonstrator in sight."

Another deputy was standing beside Pudge's four-door pickup. "I put his property in the back, Sheriff."

The deputy opened the rear passenger door, sat Dill on the bench seat, and fastened a chain linking the handcuffs and ankle shackles to an eyebolt welded to the floor.

"Give it a yank," Pudge said. "I don't want him kicking the back of the front seat or reaching over and making a grab for my neck."

Satisfied the prisoner was secured, he said, "Mind the store while I'm gone, Orville. It's yours now."

Pudge got in, adjusted the rearview mirror to make sure he could keep an eye on the prisoner, and fired the ignition. As he steered west through Burns, he looked for protestors and checked the side mirrors for following cars. After passing through the neighboring town of Hines where westbound Highway 20 narrowed from four lanes to two, Pudge put the pedal to the metal and watched miles and miles of sagebrush hurtle by.

The killer started humming, then whistling, and then broke into a song about a stranger rolling into a town full of broken dreams and lonely women with razorblades in their eyes. His voice was a mishmash of blues, folk, country, and rock. Pudge gritted his teeth. It was going to be a long ride no matter how fast he pushed it unless he put the kibosh on the one-man juke box in the back seat.

"Say, Dill, if you're as good a musician as you think you are, why'd you throw it all away?"

The dark lyrics kept coming as resolutely as thunderheads. The refrain made Pudge's fillings ache. "You left a hole in my chest where my heart used to beat. No heart, no heartache. No heart, no heartbreak. Got no heart. Got no hope."

Pudge was about to order him to shut it when Dill stopped singing and said, "A dude thought I was making eyes at his girl. He didn't know what makes a star a star is a talent for making every woman listening to you believe you're singing only for her."

"And you had to explain that to him by breaking a bottle across his head?"

"It was self-defense. I've heard harmonicas make more sense than that court-appointed lawyer they give me. I told him to let me take the stand, but he wouldn't do it. I would've gotten off if I'd been able to tell my side to the jury. There were six women on it. I got a way of reaching into their hearts and souls."

"What could you say that they hadn't already heard from all the witnesses?"

"How the dude charged the stage when I was in the middle of a song and said he was going to shove the microphone stand where the sun don't shine. How when the dude made a grab for it, I couldn't risk breaking my picking hand since it's my livelihood. How I had to use the bottle of Jack set on a stool next to me to protect myself. It's another one of my signatures. The Jack on the stool."

"You could've walked away in those signature boots of yours."

"I sing about men who stand tall. Men who know how to unlock a woman's desires with a whisper in their ear. I had my reputation to think about, what my fans expect of me."

"You think anyone is gonna hold you in high regard after killing him, the bartender, and then setting them on fire which caused a fireman to lose his life in the line of duty?"

"For starters, the fire wasn't intentional. The bottle of Jack broke and splashed them both with Old Number Seven. I keep a lit cigarette in an ashtray on the stool too. Curling smoke is another one of my signatures. It got knocked over and lit the Jack."

"The jury didn't see it that way."

"They would've if I'd been allowed to testify. If I'd been out to kill him, I would've shot him. I always go on stage strapping. I put my gun on the stool. It's part of my—"

"Signature. I get it."

"Go ahead and poke fun, but you know what? My fame is

only going to grow after a stint in the can. Look at Chuck Berry, Merle Haggard, Keith Richards. They got even more fans coming to hear them play and big record deals to go with it."

Pudge groaned. "You must've been dropped on your head as a baby. None of them killed nobody or got sentenced to life. The only people ever gonna hear you sing are fellow prisoners when you're in the shower. Word of advice, Dill? Someone asks you to pass the bar of soap, don't drop it."

They crossed into Deschutes County and reached the outskirts of Bend. The two-lane became four lanes with stoplights again. The old lawman was unused to traffic. Metro Bend had forty thousand people living in it, ten times that of Burns. All of them seemed to be on the road at once. He glanced at the odometer, added the miles left to Salem, and then did a quick calculation of the size of his gas tank and the four-by's mileage. He could make it on a single tank if he drove the speed limit, but he had no intention of doing that.

The sheriff bypassed the first couple of gas stations because cars were at every pump; he didn't want looky-loos staring at his prisoner. But the light changed red at a busy intersection and Pudge brought the pickup to a stop.

"Eyes straight ahead," he barked when he glanced in the rearview mirror and saw Dill eyeing the car idling beside them. Kids were in the backseat staring at him.

The light switched green and the cars began to move. Two blocks later, he caught another red light. A blue Honda sedan was next to him. Two girls who appeared to be high schoolers were in the front bucket seats and two more rode in the rear. The girls were all looking in his direction. Only they weren't looking at him. They were staring at Dill who'd pressed his face against the glass and was kissing it. The girls closest to his rig rolled down their windows and blew kisses back. One of the two in the backseat pulled up her sweater and flashed Dill.

Pudge hit the lights and siren, pulled into the oncoming lane, and weaved around cars. He spotted an opening in the cross traffic at the intersection and punched it. Dill laughed the whole way.

The sheriff cut to a parallel street and continued west. He kept watch for the blue Honda. When he reached the outskirts of town, he got back on Highway 20 and continued west. The further Bend withdrew in the rearview, the thinner the traffic became. Before long it was only his rig, a few long-haul truckers, and the occasional passenger vehicle. He didn't see a blue Honda behind him.

The two-lane began to climb toward the chain of snow-draped volcanoes that comprised the Cascade Range. Thick stands of yellow-bark ponderosa pine lined both sides of the blacktop, growing so close together in spots that it was like driving through a steep-walled tunnel with low-hanging clouds forming an impenetrable ceiling. When Pudge reached the town of Sisters, he pulled into a gas station. The façade resembled an Old West trading post, complete with a wooden Indian out front.

"Fill 'er up?" the pump jockey said.

"All the way," Pudge said.

"Want me to get the windshield for you? It's snowing up ahead and visibility's worse than the three blind mice's."

"But the pass is still open, right?"

"So far so good until a citizen spins out or a trucker jackknifes. Then it'll be all she wrote. Good for me, but bad for anyone in a hurry. I make time and a half when I drive the tow truck." Gold fillings flashed when he grinned.

Dill piped up. "I gotta take a leak."

"Wiggle your toes," Pudge said. "We'll be in Salem in two hours."

"Take me to the can or I'll piss your back seat. You won't be able to hang enough Christmas trees on your mirror to cover it up."

Pudge leaned out the window and asked where the restrooms were.

"Around back," the pump jockey said as he squeegeed the windshield.

"Enough room to park by them?"

"Plenty."

When the tank was full and he paid up, Pudge drove to the rear of the building and stopped in front of the door signed 'Men's.' He got out to make sure it was empty. As he started to turn the knob, the door yanked inward. A burly man with a grease-stained yellow Caterpillar ballcap filled the doorway. He took in Pudge's uniform and then his gaze settled on the sheriff's meaty right hand resting on the butt of his holstered .45.

"You got me, officer. Guilty as sin. I forgot to flush." He chuckled and walked out.

Pudge stepped in, looked around, and then returned to get Dill. "I'll uncuff you so you can do your business. Try anything and I'll shoot whatever's in your hand like I did last time. And I mean, *whatever*. Understood?"

He walked him to the can, unlocked the bracelet around the prisoner's right hand, and waited while Dill stood in front of the urinal and unzipped.

"I can't go with you watching," Dill said.

"Get used to it. Your privacy days are over. Should've considered that when you started swinging that bottle."

"Ah, jeez, Sheriff. Haven't you ever done something in the heat of the moment? I'd change it if I could, but I can't. All I'm asking for is a little mercy. Didn't they teach you about forgiveness in Sunday School?"

"They did."

"What if I promise to earn yours. I'll do something to make

up for what I done. I know I'm going to hit it big, sell a lot of records and concert tickets too. I'll donate all the money to the families of those men. You want a piece, say the word. I'll give you whatever you want. Let me walk and it's yours. I swear."

"You'd do that for me, huh?"

"I would."

"Okay, listen up, because here's what I want."

"Now we're talking. Name it. Anything."

"Are you listening?"

"All ears."

"Good." Pudge turned on the faucet. "Running water, Dill. Listen to it. Works like a charm. You got one minute to finish bleeding the snake."

Back on the road, Pudge said, "Here on out, you don't say another word, don't hum, don't whistle, don't sing. The two-lane gets real tricky up ahead. The snow'll be coming down hard. The wind'll be blowing hard. The ice slicking the road'll be hard. You distract me and we crash, I'll likely be able to crawl out before that full tank of gas bursts into flames. You?"

The sheriff clicked his cheek. "Whoosh. Like my friend the fireman and the two others you burned alive."

The highway climbed steeply as it wound toward a high pass that had been carved between the icy crest of Mount Washington and the jagged peaks of Three Fingered Jack. Wind blasted over cinder cones and whipped the snow across lifeless fields of lava as swirling flurries turned the highway into a cloudy white ribbon.

Pudge shifted the four-by into low as he passed a big rig pulled off to the side. The driver had clambered out. It was the burly man wearing the grease-stained yellow Caterpillar ballcap. He no longer looked jolly as he contemplated wrestling with frozen tire chains. A station wagon fishtailed and then finally pulled over to chain up too. The sheriff kept going, thinking slow but steady wins the race.

He passed the turnoff to Black Butte Ranch and figured he'd be over the top in another twenty minutes when twirling gumball lights up ahead made him swear. An Oregon State Police cruiser was blocking the lane. A trooper wearing a blue Smokey Bear hat and matching parka stood beside it waving a flashlight.

Pudge eased the pickup to a stop. "What's the problem, Troop?"

"Harney County Sheriff's, huh? What brings you this way?"

"Transporting a prisoner to Salem."

"What did he do?"

"Murdered three men."

When the trooper's brush moustache twitched, the ice crystals on it glinted with the reflection of the gumball lights. "Got a road closure up ahead due to a slide. A trucker reported it. Saw it in his side mirror. If he'd been a couple seconds later, it would've caught him and swept him over the side. Snow. Boulders. A real mess."

"Can my rig get around or through it?"

"Only if it's got wings. We're already stopping traffic down at Sisters. Anybody between there and here, I'm to send up a hundred yards to the Camp Sherman cutoff where they can turn around and head back down to wait it out."

"How long you figure that'll be?"

"Hard to say. A crew is on its way up from Bend and another that's stationed at Santiam Junction is already mustering to attack it from the west side. Both crews will work toward each other to get at least one lane open. Once they do, we'll flag traffic through in batches."

"If the slide is between the pass and Santiam Junction, what about catching Highway Two Forty-Two out of Sisters to the One Twenty-Six and taking it up to the junction?"

"Sure. If it was summertime. Two Forty-Two rarely opens before June and the only thing rare about this year are the way I grill my ribeyes."

"I can't go down to Sisters and wait. That would mean crawling all the way back up here in a slow line of cars and big rigs and then playing onesie-twosie waiting to get waved through. I need to be at the head of the line going west to get this convict tucked in his bunk tonight. Any place up ahead I can wait it out so I'll be first?"

"My orders are to turn everyone around, but seeing you're a fellow officer, there's a lodge on Turtle Lake just shy of the closure. It's closed until late spring, but the owner lives there year-round to keep the pipes from freezing. He's getting up there age-wise and keeps a small crew on hand to get things ready for the season."

"Sounds like it'll do the trick. I'll be able to hear the heavy machinery clearing the road and know when it's my time to get a jump on everyone waiting in Sisters. Maybe the owner's even got a pot of hot coffee on."

"You can try rousing him on your radio to let him know you're coming, but reception's real spotty up there because the lake is in a canyon right below the summit. It's called turtle 'cause it's shaped like one, not 'cause any live in it. Freezes solid."

"Thanks, Troop."

"Take her easy, Sheriff."

Pudge pulled around the OSP patrol car and picked up the radio's mike and called his office.

"You set a land speed record if you are already in Salem, sir," Orville said when the call was patched through to his desk.

"Wishful thinking is for people who bet on racehorses. I'm stuck at the pass for a spell because of a slide. Gonna wait it out at the lodge at Turtle Lake. Call the state pen and tell them I'll be there, but I can't say exactly when."

"Yes, sir. Please keep me posted."

"Probably won't be until after I get over the pass because of radio reception up there. Do me another favor and call Gemma and let her know what's what. I don't want her to get a bee in her bonnet if she tries to reach me and can't."

"Affirmative. Over and out."

Pudge cradled the mike and kept driving. He finally spotted a wooden sign with spears of icicles hanging from the bottom. Snow salted the front, but he could make out the words "Turtle Lake." He turned off the two-lane.

A toboggan run of a curving narrow road led down to a two-story lodge made of peeled logs and continued around the frozen shore of an ice-covered lake. A boathouse and a dock that listed drunkenly to one side stood just past the lodge. Pudge pulled in beside a bright orange Sno-Cat parked out front. The boxy vehicle sat up high on tank treads.

The sheriff turned to Dill McCaw and jabbed a stubby finger at him. "We're going inside this lodge until they clear the pass. I expect you to mind your P's and Q's. The cuffs and shackles stay on."

"I'll freeze walking to the front door. I need my jacket."

"All right, I'll get it out of the back."

Raps on the driver's-side window made Pudge turn around.

"What the Sam Hill?" he said as he stared into the twin eyes of a double-barreled shotgun pressed against the glass.

7

Liz Bloom said she was turning in early after supper in order to be ready to leave for the Bruneau River first thing in the morning. November and Nagah said goodnight too. Gemma and I put Hattie and Johnny to bed and then went to our bedroom and closed the door.

"You're not worried about Pudge being stuck on Santiam Pass, are you?" I said as I sat on the bed and pulled off my boots.

"Of course not, but I'm glad Orville called to let me know. The only thing I'm worried about is you trying to run that river. You know it's foolhardy this time of year."

"I'm hoping Liz realizes that when we stop at the canyon overlook. She'll see for herself what it's like at flood stage."

"Who's the one who always says hope isn't a strategy?"

"What would you have me do? She's my boss."

"You're not in the military anymore. You don't have to follow orders that can get you killed."

"We've had this discussion before."

"And it bears repeating. You have more responsibilities than ever. We both do."

"I don't need to be reminded of that. I know exactly what they are."

"Could've fooled me, running off on some wild adventure with a pretty young woman the first chance you get."

"This is work, and you know it."

"Listen to you." Red spots flared on Gemma's cheeks, matching the sting in her voice.

"I am. I'm also listening to you and I can't believe what I'm hearing."

"I'm only saying what's true. You and I are out of synch. The kids, work, us, all of it."

"We're going through a rough patch is all. Like November says, a life with no twists and turns is not a life but a dream."

"It never used to be like this between us."

"But it is now." I took a deep breath. "All we have to do is agree we'll handle whatever gets thrown at us. A kid scarred by war. A boss with a hare-brained scheme. A pasture filled with cows all dropping calves at the same time."

"And why are you so sure we'll be able to? You're not even going to be here."

The truth was, I wasn't convinced. Things seemed to be coming at us all at once and from all directions. It reminded me of combat when everything got speeded up so all you could do was react. Mistakes got made. People got hurt. People got killed. You either accepted it and moved on or joined the fallen.

"We're not the first to go through this," I said. "Your dad? He figured out a way when your mom got sick and died and left him with a five-year-old. From everything I've heard, you were no angel. But Pudge didn't quit his job. He couldn't. He found a way."

"He did, but he also didn't go adventuring with a beautiful boss."

"How many times do I got to say it? I don't have a choice. This is work."

"There's always a choice."

"And there's always bills to pay and kids to raise and horses to tend to. Come on. It's not like I'm asking you not to do your job."

"Better not."

"See? Exactly. We can't let all the stuff coming at us get in the way."

"But it is."

She was right, and I didn't want to admit it.

"It's late," I said. "We both have early starts. We can talk about this when I get back."

"Fine," she said.

"Yeah, fine."

We traded stares as we tried to calm down. Gemma broke the silence. "Promise me you'll be careful on the river for the kids' sake."

"I don't think we're going to run it."

"You'll run it."

"What makes you so sure?"

"Liz. You called her determined. I call her impulsive. She wouldn't put your life at risk if she weren't."

"Lots of officers in 'Nam did that. They didn't think they had a choice."

"There's always a choice. Real leadership is knowing the difference between the right one and the wrong one. Pudge taught me that."

"Loq will be there too. When I finally reached him after supper, he said he'd meet us in the little town of Bruneau. We'll drive up to the canyon overlook and have our looksee. It'll be two against one if Liz orders us on a suicide mission."

"Neither one of you will be able to say no. Liz is young, sexy, and ambitious."

"Sounds like the woman I fell in love with a few years ago."

Gemma's eyes did the gimlet thing again. "Don't compare her to me. You need to be careful. When Liz sees something she wants, she'll do whatever it takes to get it, no matter who gets hurt in the process. Trust me. I know the type."

"All this time together, you've never been jealous. Why all of a sudden now?"

She touched the corner of her eyelid. "It's not jealousy, it's intuition."

"Women's intuition?"

"Is there any other kind? Watch yourself, hotshot. Whitewater and *Tsa-ahu-bitts* won't be the only dangers you'll encounter on the Bruneau."

8

The fourteen-foot-long Avon Redshank raft was the color of a Navy destroyer and had a yellow four-inch-wide rub strake around its perimeter. Its owner dropped it off at Blackpowder's store deflated and rolled up. I packed it into the bed of my pickup along with life jackets, fishing gear, extra ammo, and duffle bags stuffed with clothes and camping equipment. The old codger had even packed food for us in an expedition-size metal ice chest along with a Coleman stove and a gallon can of kerosene. It all went into the back of my rig too. The raft's aluminum frame and nine-foot-long oars got strapped on top.

Liz Bloom spoke little after we pulled out of No Mountain and headed east on Highway 20. She studied maps and made notes on them with a number two pencil. I didn't say much either until we reached Nyssa and started across the bridge over the Snake River.

"That's Idaho on the other side."

"Is this the same bridge where November's husband and daughter's bus crashed?" she said.

"That one was replaced years ago, but it's the same spot."

"She never remarried?"

I shook my head. "For November, the spirit world is very real. She talks with Shoots While Running and Gentle Wind and looks forward to the day she joins them there."

"She's not afraid of death?"

"November isn't afraid of anything."

"Except for *Tsa-ahu-bitts*. She definitely seemed afraid of him."

"That wasn't fear. It was respect and understanding."

I knew that because of what November had said to me when I was leaving the ranch that morning. She'd followed me out to my pickup and pressed a fringed sheath made of tanned deerskin into my hands.

"Take this. It belonged to Shoots While Running whose father gave it to him as his father had given it to him and his father before him back to Chief Washakie, the great Shoshone warrior."

I gripped the antler handle and unsheathed the knife. The pointed six-inch blade was double-edged like a dagger and made of hand-knapped obsidian. "It's beautiful."

"And very sharp."

Even though I knew it was an insult in Paiute culture to refuse a gift, I sheathed the dagger and told her I couldn't take it. "It's an heirloom and too precious. I might lose it if we run the river and flip the raft in the rapids."

"That is why you must take it. The knife can protect you since you are going where *Tsa-ahu-bitts* dwells. He is evil and can take many forms. Know this, it takes a demon to stop a demon. If you must become one, do not forget who you really are or you will remain a demon forever."

I glanced at Liz. "November is what some people would call a medicine woman. She sees things. Feels things. Travels to places both in her mind and . . . Well, I can't really explain it, but

I've learned since moving to the high lonesome and living among a people who've called it home for more than ten thousand years, it's best to accept things rather than question them."

"I didn't take you for someone who believes in the supernatural."

"Spend enough time down here and you might wind up surprising yourself about what you do and don't believe in."

We crossed the bridge over the wide river and made our way southeast through the towns of Nampa and Kuna to a spot along the Snake River Canyon a couple of miles from the Swan Falls Dam. I pulled off the road and parked.

"This is where I first met Morley Nelson. I have a hunch if BLM creates a national conservation area, this will be at the center of it. Come on, I'll show you why."

We followed a trail to the rim. Liz gasped. "If I took another step, I'd be walking on air."

"Maybe for a split second, but then you'd be falling five hundred feet to the rocks below. If we were further north at Hells Canyon, it'd be over a mile to the bottom. Last year, Evel Knievel tried jumping it on a souped-up motorcycle."

"I saw it on the news. It was crazy. He fell short, but lived to tell the tale. Takes all kinds."

"Keep your eyes open. It won't be long now."

Seconds later, a falcon zoomed by.

Liz rocked back on her heels and grabbed my arm to keep her balance. "Wow! Was that a peregrine?"

"Prairie falcon. They're about the same size and look pretty similar, only browner. A peregrine has slightly longer wings and a dark hood. It's faster too."

"Have you seen peregrines here before?"

"Up close and personal. When Morley Nelson invited me to join him here, I thought it was going to be a simple meet and greet, but he showed up with two assistants and climbing gear.

They'd gotten word that a female peregrine had been killed by a car near where we parked. Morley wanted to see if she'd left any chicks. In spring, hundreds of pairs of raptors build nests in the canyon walls along this stretch of the river."

"Did you find them?"

"It took some doing. I volunteered to climb down the side to help him look. I'd learned how to rappel in basic training. He asked me if I was sure. I said I was. He said okay, but I'd probably wish I'd worn my brown pants."

"Are those specially made for rock climbing?"

"It was his way of warning me it was going to be scary."

"I don't understand."

"Brown because it would hide the shit when it got scared out of me."

Liz laughed.

I told her how we donned climbing harnesses and the two assistants belayed us as we stepped backward off the rim and rappelled part way down the face. My job was to guard Morley from the dead mother's mate and any protective aunts and uncles by waving my arms so they'd dive-bomb me and not him while he searched crevices.

"Morley found the nest," I said. "Three white balls of fluff with black masks were in it. They were starving and screeching for their mama and slashing and stabbing with beaks as sharp as scissors. He spoke some peregrine and pulled them out one by one and stuck them in a satchel and back up we climbed."

Liz's face glowed with excitement. "I would've loved doing that."

We watched an aerial parade of raptors for an hour while flocks of ravens berated us with caws. Peregrines joined prairie falcons along with three different species of hawks. First a golden eagle and then a bald eagle soaring majestically overhead were the showstoppers.

"Time to go," I said. "Loq will be waiting for us."

We continued heading southeast to the blink-and-miss-it town of Bruneau. I spotted a white Ford that matched my rig parked alongside an irrigation canal. The nose of a red kayak was poking out of the pickup's bed.

Loq was wearing jeans and a Fish and Wildlife uniform shirt with the sleeves cut off despite the cold weather. His long mohawk rippled when he nodded at us and then he sized up Liz. His face didn't gave away what he thought about her. Finally, he hooked a thumb at the canal that carried water from the Bruneau River to the surrounding potato and alfalfa fields.

"It's called Buckaroo Ditch," he said to Liz. "Did you know that's an Indian word?"

"Is this a test?" she said.

"It's a question."

"No, it's a trick question. Okay, I'll play along. Buckaroo is a bastardization of the word *vaquero* which is what Indians native to old Mexico who became cowboys were called by their rich landowner bosses. *Vaca* is Spanish for 'cow.'"

When Loq didn't acknowledge her answer, Liz said, "You know I'm right. Okay, I have a question for you. Why did your people let a tribe from the Columbia River Plateau name you Klamath when you'd always called yourself *Maklak* in your language? *Maklak* meaning 'the people.'"

It was one of the few times I ever saw Loq look surprised. He quickly blinked it away and said, "You're younger than I expected. Did you get this job because you're a senator's daughter?"

"I've heard that one before. You need to try harder if you're testing to find out if I have a thin skin. By the way, you're a lot older than I expected. You looked younger in that movie. They put a lot of makeup and a woman's wig on you, didn't they?"

Loq gave a hard stare. She returned it. The Klamath was the first to break it off, and he did so with a grin.

"As long as you never say the Great White Father in Washington sent you like my last boss did, maybe we'll work together just fine."

"We'll do better than fine. We'll do great." She stuck out her hand. "Call me Liz."

After they shook, she pointed down the irrigation ditch. "What's that big body of water we're looking at?"

I explained it was the backed-up mouth of the Bruneau River from its confluence with the Snake twelve miles away. "An old earth-filled hydroelectric dam named C. J. Strike brings both rivers to a near standstill. The impoundment on the Snake is three times longer than this one."

Loq cupped his ear. "That sound you hear are the tears my Shoshone brothers and sisters are still shedding. That dam and all the others on the Snake River stopped the salmon from making the journey they'd made since the Great Creator put them here. Now the Shoshone must buy salmon at a supermarket."

"Maybe salmon will get protection from the Endangered Species Act one of these days and those dams will come down," Liz said, "but until then, our focus is on protecting the species already listed. That's why we're here and that's why we must prove the Bruneau needs to become a national wildlife refuge."

She ran her hand over the nose of the red kayak. "I'm glad you brought this. Is it yours?"

"A neighbor's in Chiloquin."

"Is he *Maklak* too?"

"No, he's a hippie. He likes to float rivers and fly fish. He's good at both."

"Are you any good at kayaking?"

"We'll see," Loq said.

"Because I read that using a kayak to scout rapids before running a raft down them can come in handy."

"We'll see," he said again.

Liz asked me how far it was to the put-in.

"A long way on a very rough track, but before we drive all the way out there, let's go to the canyon overlook and see what we're dealing with."

"It won't change my mind," she said.

It was my turn to say it and so I did. "We'll see."

9

We followed a dirt road across sagebrush scrub and grasslands for nine miles to a spot that had been marked on my map with a red dot and labeled "Take-out." It didn't mean a burger joint. Nothing was around but high lonesome as far as the eye could see.

I parked the rig and Liz walked to the river's edge. "I canoed on rougher water on the Kennebec. This doesn't look scary at all."

"Don't let the Bruneau fool you," I said. "We're below the canyon here and the big elevation drop is still upriver. Calm water and road access are the reason why this spot is used as the end point for river trips. We'll leave Loq's rig here for our shuttle. That is, if we even need one."

Loq transferred the kayak to my pickup along with his government-issued Winchester .30-30 and a green duffle bag that he'd been issued by the US Marine Corps. He opened the passenger door. "You want middle or shotgun?"

"We'll take turns," Liz said and slid in beside me.

The Bruneau Canyon Overlook was another ten miles upriver. The road got rougher with every spin of the knobby tires, dropping into and climbing out of gullies. The silhouette of the Jarbidge Mountains loomed on the horizon. Clouds clustered around the highest peaks A recent rain had left the potholes full of mud. Chunks shot up and thudded against the pickup's wheel wells as we bounced through them.

We pulled into a crude parking lot marked by a weather-beaten sign. The wind was whistling in a high-pitched alto as we got out. I turned my shoulder into it and tucked my head to keep from being blown backward while walking to the rim. Liz used me as a windbreak as she followed close behind.

Huddling at the edge, we looked down. Slashes of whitewater-streaked dark water and waves taller than the lineman's shack crested over boulders and slammed down with such force we could sense their concussions despite the eight-hundred-foot-thick layer of rock beneath our feet.

"It's a lot deeper and narrower than where we were watching peregrines," Liz said appreciatively. "All the rainbow bands of color remind me of the Grand Canyon."

I told her we were looking at a very different kind of rock. "The Colorado River cuts through layers of sedimentary sandstone and limestone, but the Bruneau is sawing through old volcanic flows of igneous basalt and rhyolite. They're twice as hard as limestone on the Mohs scale."

"The Mohs scale?" she teased. "Maybe you should be working for the US Geological Survey instead of Fish and Wildlife."

Loq played dot-to-dot with the rapids below and counted the seconds between them out loud. I asked if he thought the river was runnable.

"It's moving so fast in this stretch, there's no time to line up for each rapid. Get turned broadside, you'll flip. Then it'll be try and grab the chicken line and get dragged the rest of the way down unless the raft wraps or gets sucked into a hole."

Liz asked what a chicken line was.

"Technically, it's called the perimeter line," I said. "It's a rope tied to D-rings around the outside of the raft. It comes in handy for clutching onto something when the rapids get scary. If you get bucked off, it's something to grab hold of to stay with the raft."

"I won't fall out," she said.

I started reeling off the names of other lines to keep from telling her that if we ran what we were looking at, it'd be a miracle if any of us didn't get dunked, or drowned.

"Throw lines are used for hauling the raft ashore and tying off. Static lines are for emergencies like pulling a raft off a rock if it gets wrapped. We have a bag of hardware including carabiners and pulleys to help with that."

She asked how big I thought the rapids were.

"Very," I said. "Whitewater is ranked from Class One to Five. This time of year, the Bruneau has plenty of fours and fives."

"What about running it in the kayak? Won't that be easier?"

Loq answered before I could. "Maybe easier for slaloming around rocks, but the paddler better know how to roll like my Inuit brothers and sisters do."

"You mean an Eskimo roll. I practiced that on a lake in Maine. It's all about using your shoulders and the paddle for leverage to re-right yourself after you capsize." She mimicked the maneuver.

Loq didn't point out there was a big difference between a calm lake and a roaring, boulder-strewn river. "The Bruneau is angry," he said. "If we want to know why, we'll have to go down to the water and ask."

"Seeing it now, Liz, what do you think?" I said.

"Since we've come this far, let's continue to the put-in and make camp. We can sleep on it and make a decision in the morning. If nothing else, it'll give us a chance to hike around and look for endangered species."

Driving to the put-in was easier said than done. The dirt road got a lot rougher and the sky soon turned as dark as the water that had been rushing through the canyon. I had to stop a few times to wipe the mud from the headlights in order to make out the curves and dips in the narrow track that grew increasingly more faint from lack of use, proof that all but the most determined eventually turned around.

We reached the Bruneau's confluence with the Jarbidge River after midnight. The pickup's headlights revealed rolling grasslands studded with sagebrush and junipers. We parked on a relatively flat spot to make camp. The colliding rivers rumbled like thunder while I unloaded the red kayak and aluminum raft frame and set them on the ground so I could get to our gear stored beneath. Loq went in search of wood for a fire. Liz waved off my offer to pitch a tent.

"A sleeping bag rolled out on an EnsoLite pad is fine with me. If it starts to rain, we can pile into the pickup. Whose turn is it to cook dinner? I'm famished."

"November's. I packed her version of C-rations for tonight."

Loq was gone longer than it should've taken to gather wood. When he finally returned with an armful of kindling and logs, he stayed mum. He lit a fire and we sat in its warmth and glow while we ate our ready-to-eats. I thought of Pudge and the to-go bag of food November had provided him. The pass over the Santiam had surely been cleared that morning and the old lawman would've checked Dill McCaw into the state pen and was now fast asleep in a hotel bed. I chuckled recalling how he'd groused about drawing a snorer as a roommate. Pudge's own night music rattled the rafters at the ranch house and was as regular as the old grandfather clock ticking and chiming in the living room.

Liz polished off a wing and drumstick of cold fried chicken and made short work of a bowl of chokecherry pudding, a favorite Paiute dessert. "My compliments to November. Now, if you gentlemen will excuse me, my mummy bag calls."

We bid her good night. Nylon rustled and then a zipper zipped. Her flashlight flicked off. Loq added more sticks to the fire and set a pot of water on a flat rock to boil.

"Do you want some of November's herbal tea?" I said.

"Coffee. Need to stay awake. I'll take first watch."

"Why, did you see something when you were collecting wood?"

"Caught a whiff of it." He motioned toward the Jarbidge River branch of the confluence. "The further upriver I walked, the stronger the smell got."

I noticed he was still strapping his Smith and Wesson .357 magnum. His lever-action rifle was propped against a big rock within easy reach.

"Was it mountain lion or bear?"

"I never found any tracks."

"What did it smell like?"

Loq stared into the fire and then up at the night sky. His nostrils flared. "Like a kill box three days later when no one's come to collect their dead."

It had been years since I rode the Freedom Bird home, but I could still recall the stench of enemy KIAs left on a battlefield beneath a tropical sun. It was something I'd never forget no matter how long I lived.

"I'll make coffee for both of us. We'll stand watch together and then go look for it at first light."

When the coffee was ready, I handed him a mugful. He took a sip, and then said, "What do you think?"

I drank some. "Coffee always tastes better around a campfire."

"I meant about Liz."

"She knows what she wants, that's for sure, but how to get it is a different story. Why, what do you think?"

"Time will tell. She doesn't lack for self-confidence, but the elders taught me it's more important to have confidence in others."

"Tribe before self," I said.

"Might come a time we have to help her learn that. If we wind up running the Bruneau, we definitely will."

"You sound like Gemma. She told me to watch out. Among a lot of other things."

Loq drank some coffee. "I take it it's not getting any easier with Johnny."

"Sometimes it feels like a forced march. Other times a battle where you already know there aren't going to be any winners. It's been pretty hard on all of us."

"You're talking about your marriage, huh?"

I shrugged.

"But you don't have quit in you," he said.

"Neither does Gemma. But I'd be lying if I said I don't mind being away for a bit."

"Away from Johnny or—"

"Let's leave it at just away."

Loq drank some more coffee as he mulled that over. "Careful, brother, or you might get used to it."

10

The cloud cover dropped low during the night, so low that even sitting close to the fire, the sleeping bag draped over my shoulders was slick with dew by the time dawn broke.

"You ready?" I whispered to keep from waking Liz.

Loq grunted. "Point or sweep?"

"I'll take point. We'll go up a hundred yards. If we don't see anything, we come right back. Make breakfast, drink coffee. Estimate how many cubic feet per second the Bruneau is flowing over flood stage, and then convince our boss that discretion is the better part of valor."

"And how did that work out for you when you were in country?"

"Charlie didn't always give us a choice."

"Marines never took it even when he did. Let's move out."

We followed the Jarbidge River upstream. It was narrower, rockier, and the water ran clearer than the Bruneau whose turbidity had earned it the name "brown water" in the language of French fur trappers.

I carried my 12 gauge at port arms, occasionally shouldering it to sweep the area whenever the hairs on the back of my neck stood up. Every so often I'd stop to listen and sniff. I never turned around to see where Loq was. He moved with the stealth of a wolf.

Forty yards. Fifty yards. Sixty yards. I counted off our paces and calculated the distance. Nothing. Nothing smelled. Nothing moved. Nothing flew.

We reached one hundred yards. I started to turn around. Maybe it was a breeze, maybe the change in direction, but I caught a whiff of something and it sure wasn't sagebrush. I sniffed deeper. A fetid mix of fruit, feces, mothballs, and garlic soured my nostrils.

I pointed my shotgun. "One o'clock. Smells like a corpse." Loq drew abreast of me, but kept ten feet apart so we wouldn't be a single target. "Can you smell it?"

"It's not as strong as last night, but something's dead in that stand of junipers. Can't see through them, so we'll have to go through them."

"Gimlets," I muttered. "Okay, let's pincer it. I'll take right."

We crept onward, keeping our long guns pressed against our shoulders. My route took me up a slope and into the trees. I used the barrel of my shotgun to push branches out of the way. The cloud cover was lower in the thicket and reduced visibility to a few feet. I halted, sniffed, and then kept my mouth closed to keep the foul odor from settling on my tongue.

A giant figure suddenly loomed in the mist. "Halt!" I barked.

It didn't answer. I readied to let loose a blast of buckshot. "Halt!"

No response. I took a couple of steps and peered into the swirling gray. The giant wasn't about to move. Not then. Not ever. Near the top of a twelve-foot-tall mountain juniper, a headless body dangled, skewered through its torso by a needleless limb. The rest of the tree's branches had been snapped off at the trunk. A second headless body hung from a nearby tree.

My first thought was the two missing fishermen.

Loq stepped out of the mist and prodded one of the corpses with his .30-30. "Elk. They've been gutted and headed."

"It's out of season for elk hunting. We're dealing with poachers or trophy hunters unafraid to break the law."

"If humans did this."

"Why do you say *if*?"

"No boot tracks. No rope burns on the trunks from hauling the bodies up the trees to stake them on those limbs."

I examined the ground for animal tracks.

"Don't bother," Loq said. "No bear or mountain lion could've carried a thousand-pound elk clenched between its teeth up one of these trunks without leaving claw marks."

I told him about what Gemma and Nagah had seen at the Triple Seven and the absence of animal and human tracks there too. "Ranches in Malheur County have also reported gutted livestock with nothing left behind but skin and bones. That's not very far from here as the raven flies."

"Then it must be *Tsa-ahu-bitts*."

"You know about the Shoshone man-eating giant?"

"We all do. If not *Tsa-ahu-bitts*, then by our own demons in our own tongues. For *Maklak*, it was the monster who lived at *Ska'mdi*. That's our word for Klamath Marsh. There's a cauldron where the water always boils and can't move downriver. The demon who lives there will eat anyone or anything who trespasses."

"We've patrolled the marsh refuge together lots of times, but this is the first you've ever mentioned a monster. How come?"

"And give you an excuse not to come and help me out?"

"Funny. Well, I don't know a thing about evil spirits, but since Rocky Mountain elk don't climb trees, and I've yet to see an eagle big enough to pick one up and then drop it from the sky, I have to stick with humans having done this. We need to stop them from killing out of season again. The Jarbidge-Bruneau may not be a national wildlife refuge, but we're still duty-bound to enforce hunting regulations. Agreed?"

Before Loq could respond, terrified cries echoed from the campsite. We took off running, crashing through the juniper branches and hurdling over shrubs.

One look took it all in. Liz had carried the red kayak down to the river to paddle around a backwater created by the confluence of the two rivers. The pool of flatwater was actually an eddy and it quickly spun her into the main channel. Fast-moving water caught the kayak and reeled her into the Bruneau's grasp.

"Help," she shouted as she paddled furiously for shore.

"She's not going to make it," I yelled to Loq. "She'll carom off those rocks and go tail-first down the next chute. We have to grab her."

We ran alongside, but soon ran out of riverbank when towering hoodoos, rock spires, blocked our way. I laid my shotgun down, pulled off my jacket, and started to kick off my boots.

Loq's fingers dug into my shoulder. "Stop. You can't swim fast enough to catch her."

"I have to try."

"But not that way. The current is pulling her toward the far side. There's a notch in the overhanging bank. Liz sees it and is aiming for it."

"Even if she makes it, the current's too powerful for her to paddle back upriver."

"We'll get her in the raft."

"We won't be able to row back upriver either or tow it. With that overhang, there's no bank to walk on."

Loq looked down his high cheekbones. "So much for discretion. It's time for real valor now."

The red kayak slammed into the notch and was pinned against the bank. I picked up my 12 gauge, aimed at the sky, pulled the trigger, pumped in another shell, and fired again. Liz looked back at us. I pointed to camp, pantomimed rowing a raft, and then back at her. She waved her kayak paddle to signal she understood.

Loq and I hustled. We inflated the raft with foot pumps, strapped the aluminum frame on top, and carried it down to the river's edge. After loading our gear, I put on a pair of well-worn roper gloves with the fingertips cut off, slipped the oars into the oarlocks, and we shoved off. I sat on the big metal ice chest positioned mid-raft between the thwarts and grabbed the oars while Loq knelt in the front.

Water shot over the bow as I steered down the first set of rapids and angled for the opposite side. It only took a minute to travel a couple hundred feet.

"Slow. Slower!" Loq said. "Don't ram her."

I braced my feet against the forward thwart for leverage and switched from pushing the oars to pulling them to my chest. The water was deeper and slower upriver of the notch. We held.

Loq picked up a throw bag that contained a coil of nylon line inside it. One end dangled out and was attached to the chicken line by a carabiner. He held the throw bag up. "Catch," he yelled and lofted it at Liz.

The line uncoiled out of the bag as it flew. Loq's toss was perfect. She caught it and held on. I pulled both oars harder, backed the raft away from the notch, and then pivoted the bow into the current. The throw line twanged as the slack tightened and the red kayak popped loose without capsizing. It followed right behind.

The overhanging bank turned into steep walls punctuated

by the spiraling hoodoos. We shot down the rapids and surfed into a deep pool at the bottom of a chute. I held us steady while Loq reeled in the kayak. Liz drew abreast of the raft. I was expecting to see terror and gratitude on her face.

She flashed a grin of triumph and guile instead. "Looks like we're going to run the Bruneau after all."

Right then I knew what kind of boss I had.

11

As soon as Liz and Loq switched spots, he paddled ahead to scout rapids. Liz had little time to get comfortable on the forward thwart. The relentless current carried us out of the deep pool. More hoodoos rose dizzyingly to scrape the underbelly of scattered clouds while the ever-steepening canyon walls revealed no ravines leading up and out. A series of stomach-dropping rapids demanded my full attention and scotched any conversation. Liz and I wouldn't have been able to hear each other anyway over the slam-bam of waves smacking against boulders.

Despite my roping-turned-rowing gloves, my palms burned and wrists ached as I pushed and then pulled the oars to steer a course clear of rocks to prevent the raft from becoming wrapped or knocked broadside. The riverbank on either side offered no safe harbor; it was still weeks away from emerging from its watery grave.

The Bruneau finally rounded a bend and the whitewater took a break. I pulled the oar blades up and let the raft glide as I gulped air to oxygenate blood for its return trip to my heart.

Despite the cool temperature, my shirt dripped with sweat beneath the lifejacket.

Liz turned around. Water droplets speckled her face and enhanced the shine of excitement. She pushed her wet hair behind her ears except for a wayward lock pasted to her forehead.

"That was wild! The wildest ride ever. I want to try rowing. The next set of rapids, okay? How far do you think we went?"

Her words tumbled out in a breathless rush that reminded me of Hattie when she tried to string too many thoughts together at once.

Liz didn't wait for an answer. "Let's see, it's, what did you say, the run is forty-three miles from put-in to take-out? If we cover ten, eleven miles a day, that's four full days. We're sure to see peregrine and bald eagle nests in the canyon walls like we did on the Snake. I'll keep a sighting log with mileage markers for proof."

I blew out a lungful of carbon dioxide. "Tell me, Liz, and no bullshit either, was taking the kayak back at camp your way of forcing us to run the river?"

She didn't quail. "Would've you and Loq done it otherwise?"

"You could've gotten yourself killed. You could've gotten us killed. You could still get us killed."

"But we didn't drown. Everything worked out fine. It's all going to work out fine. I had to do it because it's the only way there'll ever be a wildlife refuge here. You'll see."

"Next time—if there ever is going to be a next time—try asking first. Loq and I might surprise you."

Her eyes flashed, her tongue darted, but then she closed her lips before speaking. The raft started drifting out of the deep pool.

"I'm sorry. I shouldn't have done that, but being a woman in this job isn't easy. I don't mean the physical and mental parts—I can handle those—it's other people's expectations that I won't handle something or can't. It's mostly men who think that, but, surprise, surprise, some women do too."

Liz's chin jutted. "I've always fought against that. Always will. I don't expect you to understand that."

"Maybe not completely, but I know Gemma faces the same thing. A lot of ranchers balked when she hung out her shingle. She told them they had two choices: let their stock die or let her save them. I'd like to think Hattie won't have to deal with it too, but I know she will."

I put the oar blades back in the water. "Here's something I hope you can try to understand. I learned it while in combat. It wasn't always clear who the enemy was. NVA regulars. Viet Cong. Villagers forced to hide weapons. Corrupt officials. Brass looking out for their own ass."

I started to row as the current started us spinning. "I finally discovered who was the most dangerous enemy of all."

"I imagine it was either LBJ or Nixon who kept escalating the war for their own political purposes."

"It was me. I started believing I was invincible. But then I led my men into an ambush and they were all killed. I got hooked on heroin because of the guilt and ended up in a locked ward at Walter Reed. The VC didn't do that to me. I did."

Strands of wet hair fell loose from behind her ears. Liz tucked them back. "I get your point, Nick. It won't happen again. Trust me."

"Another thing I learned in 'Nam? Trust is earned."

The raft picked up more speed and any sunlight dancing on the water disappeared as clouds filled the sky over the canyon and turned the water darker than its usual brown.

Better tighten your life jacket and grab hold of something," I said. "Looks like a major washboard up ahead."

I stood up to pick a route. The starboard side was tempting

as it ran along the inside of a bend and held deeper water and fewer rapids, but the swollen current could also push the raft up onto the canyon wall and cause it to flip.

I took my seat on the ice chest and steered toward a channel on the port side that funneled into a steep flume. The raft hesitated at the top as it crested a boil created by an enormous underwater boulder. Then the bow tilted and gravity took over. Whoosh! We were in it right then, and when the oars started clacking against rocks, I raised the blades to keep them from splintering.

With limited steering, we were at the flume's mercy, pinballing off rocks and bucking up and down. A boulder the shape and shine of a breaching whale's back rose at the bottom. Water boiled around all sides and dirty foam ringed its base. Naked limbs from the trunk of a juniper deadfall poked like gnarled fingers waiting to grab anything trying to pass.

Port or starboard? Port or starboard? My mind reeled on which way to steer around, but there was no time to second guess. I jammed the blades down and chose starboard toward an opening no wider than the raft. The oars shuddered as they struck bottom and the sting ran up their shafts to my forearms. Curses rang in my ears as I swept the oars back and then dug them in again.

The whale came up fast and I gave another push to slide past it, but just when I thought we were clear, the whirlpool at the end of the flume picked us up and flung us back. The force drove the raft sideways up the big rock.

"High side!" I yelled. "High side. Put all your weight on it."

Liz threw herself on the port side tube as I let go of the oars and bellyflopped onto it too. I reached across to push us back down before the raft flipped. Seconds passed. A minute. We were teetering between ten and eleven o'clock—we'd flip at twelve. The raft seemed frozen in place, frozen in time. Water was pouring over the starboard tube and weighing us down.

"Push harder!" I yelled. "Harder!"

I gritted my teeth and shoved. The raft started to slip sternward. I gave one more shove and then scrambled back to my seat, grabbed the oars, and hauled them to my chest.

Liz screamed something, but I couldn't make out the words. And then, wham! The raft popped loose and we were pulled backward through the whirlpool and spat into a deep pool. I spun us around so we were bow first again. Liz wasn't straddling the tube, bow, or forward thwart. I glanced back at the whale. She wasn't clinging to it or hadn't scrambled up it. I looked down into the water. She wasn't behind me, on either side, or ahead.

"Liz!" I shouted. "Liz!"

Something groaned. Something splashed. Fingers reached over the top of the forward thwart. A face appeared next. Liz was lying prone on the swamped floor where she'd been thrown. I reached across and gave her a hand as she scrambled onto her knees and then sat on the thwart facing me so she could look back at what we'd come through.

"Wow! The way you rowed us through that, a regular Robert Mitchum, aren't you?"

"What?"

"The movie he was in with Marilyn Monroe. *River of No Return*. You didn't see it?"

"Must've missed it."

"Too bad. It was exciting, but what we just came down? Definitely Class Five brown pants."

That got a grin. "Technically, it was class four. The fives are still ahead."

"Bring 'em on," she cheered.

12

The temperature dropped. The wind picked up. The soaking we'd gotten intensified the chill factor. I stayed warm by rowing. Although Liz was busy bailing the raft, the sound of her teeth chattering was akin to oar blades dragging across rocks. Loq was somewhere ahead, how far, I didn't know. But when we rounded a bend and a curl of smoke beckoned downriver, I picked up the pace.

Loq had beached the kayak and draped his lifejacket over one end of the double-bladed paddle sticking upright from the cockpit. It was an impossible-to-miss "Welcome" sign. I steered for it and nosed the Avon's bow onto shore. He grabbed the perimeter line and held fast as Liz scrambled over the tube.

"Go for a swim?" he said.

Her scoff rang with indignation. "Heck no. I never got bucked off." She marched straight to the campfire and hugged herself, standing as close to the flames as she could take it.

"We got pushed up a rock that looked like a whale and had to high side it," I said. "The raft took on a lot of water. It could've gone either way."

"That beast caught me by surprise too," Loq said. "We'll

need to stick together from here on out and use the kayak as a sweeper as well as for scouting. We can portage the big rapids if there's enough riverbank to walk on. Can't risk losing the raft. Three of us won't fit in a kayak."

I tied a line around a boulder to secure the Avon. "This is the first landing spot I've seen for a pull-out. Have you explored it?"

"Only a little. It has the feel of a box canyon. The bottom thirty feet or so of the walls have been polished smooth by the river over the years. There's a couple of breaks in them higher up that look like drainages from a plateau up top. Right along the river here it is fairly level but then it slopes up over there." He pointed inland downriver.

"Are you thinking what I'm thinking, make it our first night's camp even though there's still some daylight left?"

"Bird in the hand."

"Let's get some hot coffee and food before setting up. We can take a looksee afterward. I don't need another sleepless night because of a stinking dead elk hanging from a tree."

"Or anything else."

We carried cooking gear to the campfire, lit the kerosene stove, and put water onto boil. Liz and I changed into dry clothes and hung our wet ones on a line stretched between an upright oar and the kayak paddle.

The coffee worked wonders. So did a snack of thick slices of sharp cheddar and smoked salmon sandwiched between hunks of November's homemade bread.

"The river's running high, but trout still need to eat," I said. "Maybe I can catch a couple for supper."

"Which species live here?" Liz asked between bites of an apple.

"Rainbow and redband trout. Mountain whitefish too."

"And the tastiest is?"

"The one you catch."

"Does that mean you want to spend the night here?"

"We don't know how far down the next pull-out might be and we don't want to be searching for one in the dark."

"If you think that's best." Liz turned to Loq. "I told Nick I was sorry the way I got you both on the river."

He looked over his coffee mug. "How the journey began isn't important. How it ends is. We have our work cut out to get there."

"You can count on me."

"I already am."

Liz declined my offer of a tent again. "If you want one, go right ahead. I'd like to take advantage of sleeping under the stars."

"I'll pitch one for insurance. I don't like the look of those clouds. And then there's the wind. It's growing teeth."

I unrolled one of the two backpacking tents, fitted the collapsible poles, and staked it with a rain fly over it.

"Loq and I are going to take a walk around. Do you want to join us or are you good staying here?"

"I'll go. Maybe we can get up high and look for nests."

I pulled my service revolver out of my gear bag and strapped it on. Loq did the same. Our long guns were wrapped in oil cloth in a waterproof bag. I retrieved those too.

"What's with all the artillery?" Liz said.

Loq grunted. "We don't like surprises."

"Me neither." She reached into her gear bag and pulled out a government-issued .38 Special. "Make sure your badges are clearly visible."

We filed out of the campsite and headed into the box canyon. Loq took point and I swept. The ground was rockier than our first campsite and the sagebrush and brittlebush scrubbier. The right side was gouged by a creek bed. The water rushing down it seemed anxious to join the Bruneau.

The ground began to climb and the canyon walls grew closer together. The lowest part was slickrock. Loq was walking twenty or so yards ahead. He began switchbacking up a slope blanketed with scree. The loose footing made for tough going.

When we reached the top, a fairly level expanse of scrub and grassland rolled toward the rear wall of the canyon. Loq held up and we joined him.

"You were right about it being a box," I said. "It's hundreds of feet up to the rim. I see those ravines you were talking about. In a heavy downpour they'd produce three-story-high waterfalls over the sheer walls at the bottom."

Liz scanned the cliff face with her binoculars. "There are lots of crevices raptors could nest in up high, but I don't see any."

"The mamas and papas are very skilled at camouflaging them and we wouldn't be able to spot hatchlings anyway. They won't be peeking over the edge for a few more weeks."

"You'd think we'd see adults hunting like we did at the Snake River. They're not called birds of prey for nothing."

"You're right. This is unusual."

Loq started taking deep breaths through his nostrils.

"What is it?" I said.

"Same as before."

I started sniffing too.

"What's going on?" Liz said.

"When you went for your paddle this morning, we were tracking down the source of a stink Loq smelled when he was getting firewood last night. It turned out to be two dead elk that had been hung and dressed out."

"Butchered by hunters?"

"They're called poachers out of season."

"Do you think they've been poaching here too?"

"One way to find out," Loq said. "Look lively."

We followed as he led the way. After a few minutes, he held up his hand and halted.

"Smells like a killing field coming from the other side of the creek."

"We can use those rocks as a bridge," I said.

We hopped from rock to rock and then Loq started slow-stepping as we neared a maze-like field of tawny slabs that had sheared off the cliff and plummeted to the canyon floor. He waved me to approach it from up canyon.

I touched Liz's shoulder. "Best come with me."

We crept single-file around blocks the size of pickups. The route took us to a clearing close to the base of the cliff. Fresh carcasses and old hides and bones littered the ground. It was as if herds of deer had done a lemming off the top.

"It's like one of those African elephant graveyards you see in *National Geographic*," Liz said. "The old bulls and matriarchs go to a special place to die."

"I've never heard of deer doing that. Never seen it before either."

Loq joined us. "There's not only deer here." He pointed to the curling horns of a bighorn sheep and an elk with his rack still intact.

"A trophy hunter wouldn't have left that," I said. "The bull has to be a three hundred pointer."

Liz asked what that meant.

"Hunters use a scoring system based on a mathematical formula multiplying the number of points on the antlers, the length and beam of the rack, and so on."

"It's like the pair we found this morning only it still has its head," Loq said. His eyes were crisscrossing the breadth of the canyon as he spoke.

I looked at my field watch. "It'll be dark soon. Want to keep going?"

Loq answered with his feet. Liz and I followed him deeper into the canyon.

Ten minutes later he crouched to examine the ground.

"Tracks?" I said.

"No hoof, paw, or footprints, but something lay or fell here and then was dragged. See?"

The furrow gouging the rocky ground made me think of Nagah's story about the giant beaver's tail. "Let's find out."

The drag mark ran out before we spotted any sign of hide, hair, or blood. It was as if whatever had made it suddenly up and flew away. While Loq and I walked intersecting circles trying to pick up the trail again, Liz scanned the canyon walls for raptor nests.

"I see something," she said. "It's a cave at the back of the canyon."

I raised my binoculars. "Near the ground?"

"About ten, twelve feet above it."

"Got it. Looks like the entrance of a lava tube. The Pacific Northwest is riddled with them from all the volcanic eruptions millions of years ago. They can be pretty extensive. The Ape Cave at Mount St. Helens is over two miles long."

"There's something sticking out of it in the bottom left corner. See it? It's gray and roundish. Wait, there's two of them."

"Looks like the stump ends of two tree trunks lying side-by-side."

"Strange place for trees," Loq said.

"Must be deadfalls that got washed in there from a time when the Bruneau flooded a lot higher than it is now. Here, take a look."

He pressed the field glasses to his eyes. "The river didn't stick them in there. They've been cut. It's a ladder."

"You're right. I can see the first rung," Liz said. "But if the ladder is in the cave, that means whoever pulled it up is still in there. We need to check it out. They could be sick or injured and need help."

Loq and I exchanged glances. "We'll come at it from two angles," he said. "Stay low, stay behind something. They have the high ground."

"And you have the rifle to cover me," I said. "I'll get in close and call up to them."

"Whoever's there already made us."

"All the more reason your aim better be true when I show myself."

"Hold on!" Liz said. "That doesn't sound safe."

"Neither does spending the night back at camp not knowing who we're sharing the canyon with or trying to find another pull-out in the dark."

"Do you think it's poachers?"

"Most likely."

She asked Loq what he thought.

"Knowing is always better than guessing, and both are better than hoping."

I could hear Pudge Warbler saying the exact same thing. Maxims like that had served him well in World War II and throughout his long career as a lawman. Words to live by, I thought, as I went to find out who or what was hiding in the cave.

13

THE LAKE LODGE

The double-barreled shotgun rapping on Pudge Warbler's pickup window was snugged against the shoulder of an old man wearing a red-and-black plaid wool cap with the ear flaps down. He hadn't shaved for a few days and the white stubble on his face was collecting snow. His black eyes darted like fleeing swallows silhouetted against a rheumy sky.

"Roll your window down," the old man croaked, his voice raspy from breathing the freezing air.

While the sheriff kept his eyes fixed on the gunman's, he patted around and found the butt of the holstered .45 that he kept on the seat beside him while driving.

"Can't with your shotgun pressed against it," he said. "I'm likely to jar it and get two loads of birdshot for my efforts."

The old man licked his cracked lips. It was a mistake in the cold. The saliva would freeze and widen the splits.

"All righty. No funny business." He took one step back but kept his fingers on both triggers as he aimed the twin barrels at the sheriff's face.

Pudge lowered the window with his left hand while sliding

the gun out of its holster with his right and holding it on his lap. He took in the old man's misbuttoned barn jacket and what appeared to be pajama bottoms. A pair of bedroom slippers were on his feet.

"You look in need of assistance, sir. Can I help you?"

"You really a lawman?"

"Been one so long I stopped counting the years the same time I stopped counting the gray hairs sprouting beneath my hat. I'm the sheriff of Harney County."

"Harney, huh? Don't like it there much. Not enough lakes and mountains for my tastes." His eyes kept darting.

"We got our share. Say, it's pretty cold and snowy. You want to tell me what you need?"

The old man looked past Pudge at Dill McCaw.

"What'd he do?"

"Broke the law. Why he's riding with me."

"You arrested him?"

The sheriff nodded.

"Good, 'cause that's what I need you to do for me."

"Arrest you?"

"Not me, you dang fool. Them."

"Who's them?"

"The sonsofbitches stealing me blind, that's who. They made me a prisoner in my own place. Gonna kill me if I don't tell 'em where I got the gold hid. Not that there is any, mind you."

"Your place?"

"This lodge. Turtle Lake. I own it. Free and clear."

"The ones you say holding you captive, how many are there?"

"Two. Man and a girl. Backstabber and a sweet talker. They're quite the pair. Hired the both of 'em to work for me to get this place ready for opening and this is the thanks I get. Your radio work? Best call for backup. Mine's broke. Backstabber snapped the antenna off and threw it in the lake."

Someone was walking toward them from the two-story lodge, but Pudge couldn't make out much with all the snow blowing around. He tightened his grip on the .45. When the person drew closer, he saw it was a young woman dressed in a bulky winter coat. Snow was gathering on her shoulders and powder-blue ski cap. Her cheeks were rosy.

She raised a mitten, waved hello at Pudge, and then said, "Come back inside, Wilmot. You're going to freeze to death out here. Come on now." Her voice was singsong, like calling to a child or a pet dog.

The old man started to wheel toward her, his fingers still on both triggers. Pudge stabbed his hand out the open window and grabbed the shotgun by its side-by-side barrels and shoved them skyward. Two metal clicks sounded at the same time the woman called out, "It's not loaded!"

Pudge wrenched the shotgun from the old man's hands anyway and tossed it in the snow.

"You damn fool!" Wilmot screeched. "Now she'll kill the both of us."

The sheriff had the door open and was out of the front seat by the time the words left the old man's cracked lips. He was still gripping the .45, but kept it at his side as he eyed the young woman.

She wore a rueful smile. "Sorry. Wilmot carries that old dinosaur around like a teddy bear. He's . . . well, it's gotten hard on him living up here."

"He shouldn't be loose with a gun of any kind anywhere. Gonna get himself shot."

"It's my fault. He wandered off when I turned my back in the kitchen making him coffee." She looked at Wilmot and then smiled at Pudge. "Would you like to come in for a cup?"

When he hesitated, she said, "My name's Christina, but everyone calls me Tina."

"Pleased to meet you, Tina. I'm Sheriff Warbler."

"What about your passenger? Would he like a cup too? I have homemade biscuits hot out of the oven."

"He's a prisoner, ma'am. Where I go, he goes. Wilmot said your radio's down and so you probably haven't heard. The road's closed at the pass from a slide. State trooper told me I should wait it out here while they get it back open. Could be a couple hours or so."

"Is he sending more motorists our way too? We're not open for business yet."

"No, they're getting turned around and sent back to Sisters."

Relief crossed her face and she made a whooshing sound. "For a moment there I thought I was going to have to scramble and make a lot more coffee and biscuits. Come on in. You're welcome to wait inside where it's warm."

The flaps on Wilmot's red-and-black plaid hat waggled as he jutted his grizzled face into Pudge's. "Don't say I didn't warn you. She's gonna sweet-talk the life right out of you. And whatever you do, don't turn your back on her fancy man. You'll get a blade between your shoulders sure as Sunday."

Tina shook her head and put her arm around the old man. "You know you're the only one I'm sweet on, Wilmot."

As she guided him back to the lodge, Pudge said, "I'll be right along."

Pudge returned to the pickup and tried the radio. Every channel was static.

"She's like a Christmas present, ain't she?" Dill McCaw said.

"Offering hot coffee and biscuits for stranded motorists is only being neighborly," Pudge said and tried the radio again.

"I meant under all that gift wrapping she's wearing. Mm-hmm."

"Remember what I said about P's and Q's, Dill? Don't make me turn them into S's and W's."

"What's that stand for, 'soap and water'? You going to wash my mouth out for saying out loud what any man be thinking?"

"Smith and Wesson. The brand of leather sap I carry in my back pocket to knock manners into foulmouthed cretins like you."

"You are one mean bastard, Sheriff Warbler."

"Keep trying me and you'll find out I'm only getting started."

Pudge opened the back door and removed the chain linking Dill's handcuffs and shackles to the eyebolt welded to the floor. He yanked the prisoner out and redid the handcuffs so they were now behind his back. Then he draped Dill's black leather jacket over his shoulders and frogmarched him to the lodge. He pushed him against the door while he twisted the knob to open it.

The entranceway was a mudroom with benches on both sides for guests to sit on while they took off their boots and hung their jackets on a row of hooks above. Pudge removed neither his jacket and boots nor Dill's. He also didn't take off his prisoner's handcuffs and shackles.

They passed from the mudroom into the lobby. Its floor was made of wide wood planks and the walls were knotty pine. The stone fireplace had a hint of quartz glinting in it. Pudge had been expecting a blast of welcoming heat, but the logs smoldering on the hearth were almost down to coals. A motley collection of stuffed chairs and couches were arranged in a half circle in front of it under the fixed gaze of two glass-eyed deer heads and a trio of mounted rainbow trout. The curtains on all the windows were drawn and a pair of flickering hurricane lamps set on tables provided the only light. Books pulled from shelves cluttered the floor.

"We're in here," Tina's singsong voice called from behind a swinging door.

Pudge used Dill as a door opener again and followed him through. Tina had taken off her jacket and ski cap and was standing next to a stove. She wore a frilly apron over a pink sweater. A silver moon with a winking eye hung on a thin chain around her neck.

The oven's door was open and its heat bathed Wilmot, who was sitting directly in front of it. Melting snow puddled around his slippers and dripped from the hems of his pajama bottoms. His arms were clutched to his chest and he was muttering. "My shotgun. She won't let me have it no more. It's gonna rust out there."

"Don't worry about it, Wilmot. I'll go out and get it later," Tina said. "Let me tend to the sheriff first." She gave Pudge a bright smile. "Have a seat. Make yourself at home."

He pulled out a chair and steered Dill into it before sitting down himself. Pudge looked around and noticed the sink was full of dirty dishes. The counter next to it too. Tina took a stainless-steel percolator off the stovetop and poured two cups of coffee and set them on the kitchen table followed by a plate of biscuits. Their bottoms were burned.

"That's all they gimme," Wilmot said. "Bread and water. Trying to starve me."

Tina sighed. "Now, Wilmot. You know I feed you proper." She gave Pudge a see-what-I-have-to-put-up-with look. "Sometimes we get so busy working to get the lodge ready, we're late on driving down the mountain to pick up his favorite desserts. He has a powerful sweet tooth."

Pudge wondered why she didn't offer cream and sugar. He sipped the coffee. It was pretty light on the grounds.

"When you say we, does that mean you and your husband?" he said.

"Uh-huh. Caleb. He's working in the boathouse today. It was in a bad state when we got here and needed lots of repairs."

"That's a damn lie!" Wilmot shouted. "It was shipshape like everything else until you two started stripping it." He switched his glare to Pudge. "Fixtures, hardware, copper pipes, you name it, they pry it off the walls and load it in a truck for resale. He's over there stealing the outboards from my boats. Why you gotta arrest the both of them. Damn thieves."

"You know that's not true," Tina said to the old man. She made an exaggerated frown. "It's also very hurtful considering how hard Caleb and I've been working here, and without you giving us a paycheck yet."

"That's a hoot! Pay you while you're robbing me."

Dill said to Tina, "Could you help me out here, doll? I'm sure your coffee is as delicious as you smell, but I can't drink it with my hands 'cuffed behind my back." He chinned at the cup. "Hold it to my lips so I can get a swallow otherwise I'm gonna have to lap it like a kitten." He gave his rubbery lips a once-around with his tongue.

"Knock it off," Pudge said.

"Just being neighborly like you said."

The sheriff took the cup and held it to Dill's mouth. The killer took a sip while eyeing Tina.

"Mm-hmm," he said after he swallowed. "I knew she was gonna be tasty."

"What's your name?" Tina said.

"Dill McCaw. You've probably heard of me."

He started humming and then broke into his song about a stranger and a town full of broken dreams and lonely women. He kept time by tapping his foot and making the shackles jingle.

"You're the singer!" she said. "I didn't recognize you without your guitar and—"

"Bottle of Jack and lit cigarette. My signatures."

"I heard you play, oh, it must've been last summer, maybe the year before. Up in The Dalles. A tavern there."

"Hardly a joint in Oregon I ain't sung at."

Tina chinned at his shackles. The silver moon with a winking eye around her neck caught the light and shined. "Mind if I ask what's going on?"

"A man like me makes other men feel uncomfortable about themselves. Weak and puny and scared I'm gonna take their woman from them because they know I know how to make her wet by singing to her, make her cry for more."

"Can it, Dill," Pudge said. "Don't listen to him, ma'am. He's a killer. Murdered three men in Burns. A court of law found him guilty on all counts and I'm taking him to the state penitentiary."

She reached for her necklace. "Oh my goodness."

Wilmot hooted again. "Lordy, now I got three killers under my roof."

The kitchen door swung open. A black-bearded man wearing a dirty ball cap and heavy wool shirt jacket held the door open with a steel-toed work boot. A hammer hung from a loop of the toolbelt buckled around his waist. His half-lidded eyes surveyed the room, then stopped on Pudge.

"Hi hon," Tina said quickly. "The pass is closed and the sheriff is waiting for it to reopen. It's only him and his prisoner. Everybody else on the highway got turned back."

"Any coffee left?" he said.

"Uh-huh. Let me pour you a cup."

Caleb came the rest of the way into the kitchen, but made no move to sit down. "You're not Deschutes County," he said to Pudge.

"Nope. Harney County."

Tina scurried over and handed him a cup. He took it but didn't drink.

"What brings you up this way?"

"Taking this prisoner to the state pen in Salem."

"That's Dill McCaw, hon," Tina said. "He's a rock star."

Caleb said, "Sometimes it takes them quite a spell to reopen the pass. Won't they wonder why you're late?"

Pudge swallowed the rest of his coffee. He wished it were stronger. The heat coming from the open oven door was making him drowsy after the hard drive in the snow. "They know where I'm at."

"Do we gotta worry about him?" Caleb pointed his cup at Dill.

"He's under restraints. I've never lost a prisoner yet."

"Good to know. Being up here away from everyone, Tina and me, we don't want to have to worry about anything."

"And Wilmot?" Pudge said.

"What about him?"

The sheriff kept looking at Caleb. "You don't want him to worry either, right?"

Lips tightened behind the black beard for a second. "'Course not."

"The only thing you gotta worry about is if the sheriff takes me to prison," Dill said. "That way you won't get rich."

"What are you talking about?" Caleb said.

"Ask Tina. She called it. I'm a bigtime recording artist. Help me get loose and I'll sign my royalties over to you. Every time someone buys one of my records, you'll get paid. The checks will roll in for the rest of your life. Beats freezing your ass off in the middle of nowheresville."

"I told you to shut it," Pudge said. He stifled a yawn. What he wouldn't give for a quick nap in one of those stuffed chairs in the quiet of the lobby.

Dill grinned. "Come on, sheriff, you can't blame me for trying."

"You can try, but you're wasting your time," Caleb said. "Tina and me, we're no lawbreakers."

Dill started singing again and keeping time with his foot and jingling shackles. "You left a hole in my chest where my heart used to beat. No heart, no heartache. No heart, no heartbreak. Got no heart. Got no hope."

"More coffee, hon?" Tina said.

"Sure," Caleb said and held out his cup.

"Let me top off the sheriff first."

She picked up the stainless-steel percolator and stepped toward Pudge as he swallowed another yawn. By the time it registered on him that Caleb had yet to take a sip of his, Tina pitched the coffee at his face. He managed to duck so the brim of his Stetson deflected most of the hot black wave coming at him, but the crown didn't deflect the hammer that Caleb yanked from his toolbelt and brought down on his skull.

14

Liz Bloom's joke that I should be working for the USGS because I knew the Mohs scale of hardness for classifying minerals missed an important mantra in wildlife fieldwork: know the rock, know the plant, know the critter. The symbiosis between geology and biology taught me a lot about high lonesome peculiarities, such as how the magma that created a lava tube was full of magnetic minerals.

But a force stronger than magnetism was pulling me toward the mysterious opening in the box canyon alongside the Bruneau River. It was the power of curiosity. Who made the ladder out of juniper-tree trunks? Was he still inside? Was he hurt, hungry, hostile, or dead? Was it a missing person or a malevolent poacher? Was it man or beast?

My keenness to find those answers was the same that had driven me in Vietnam to track the enemy and locate downed airmen and captured GIs. The Army scouts who joined me on patrol shared my curiosity. We saw our job as searching for truth because knowledge was a formidable weapon. It could help a platoon avoid an ambush, orchestrate a counterattack, and rescue a fellow soldier.

After a few missions, the regulars in my squad got tiger tattoos at an ink parlor on Tu Do Street, the same Saigon neighborhood where Johnny Da Den had lived. I asked DJ what was with the tats. "It's no big thing, Sarge," the radioman answered. "The big cat reminds us that curiosity eventually kills him, but it ain't til the tenth time that it kills him for good."

Twenty yards from the lava tube's yawning maw, I halted and glanced around. A shallow hollow that was no deeper than a chrome moon hubcap was all the cover I could hope for if someone started shooting.

I breathed in, held it, and then slowly breathed out. "Hello the cave! Fish and Wildlife. Do you need assistance?"

The words echoed through the canyon. Since I couldn't think of anything else to say, I shouted them again.

The final echo drifted away unanswered. I raised my binoculars and zeroed in on the opening. A hole created by scattering clouds allowed rays from the drooping sun to illuminate a few feet inside the entrance. In addition to the handmade ladder, I could see something heaped in a pile. Was it a body? Was it human or an animal that had been hauled up for eating?

Someone or something made a sudden movement from behind the pile. A silhouette inched toward the opening, but stopped short of the sunbeams.

"Hey there," I said. "Just checking to see if you need any help. The river's running high and want to make sure you're not marooned."

I got no response.

"I have food to share if you're hungry, a first-aid kit if you're injured."

The silhouette moved again. It pulled something off the heap, and retreated into blackness. I gave a sideways glance at the hubcap-deep hollow and debated whether it was time to dive for it.

Then the figure reappeared and stepped into the light. It was a large man. A mountain of a man. A mountain man. He was dressed like he'd stepped straight out of the frontier era, right down to a long bearskin coat and a cap made from a skinned badger whose masked face was perched right above his own. I was relieved to see the giant wasn't holding a flintlock rifle or a weapon of any kind.

"How many are ya?" he snarled through a thick, long beard.

"Three," I said. "I'm Nick Drake. What's your name?"

Even from where I stood, I could see that his eyes were red-rimmed. I assumed it was the result of living in a cave that trapped smoke from a campfire.

"Jasper."

"Like the semiprecious stones this area is known for?"

The man and the badger's masked face moved up and down. It had red eyes too, no doubt polished jaspers that had been glued on after the creature was skinned, tanned, and turned into a cap.

"Do you live here or were you traveling down the river and get trapped by high water?"

"Ain't trapped nowhere. Everywhere's home."

"You mean you live off the land?"

"And the air and water."

I rejected asking him about the bone pile. If he was also responsible for the two kills back at the Jarbidge-Bruneau confluence, then he either had a boat of some kind or knew a trail in and out of the box canyon. Lava was a natural gimlet and maybe it had bored a shaft straight through the cliffs that he used as an underground passageway. If there were such a tunnel, it'd be a lifesaver to know about it.

Liz arrived and whispered, "Oh my god. He's got to be at least seven feet tall and three-hundred-fifty pounds. Maybe four hundred. Ever since I moved to Oregon, people have been telling me about Bigfoot. I thought it was like the Easter Bunny, but, well, that couldn't be him, could it?"

"Not unless you believe in cryptids."

"What?"

"Hominid creatures like Sasquatch, Yeti, Yowie. Most cultures have one that people swear is real. In Vietnam, it was *Batutut*. Lot of strung-out GIs fired their weapons at what they swore was a hairy wild man living in the forest."

"Of course I don't believe in that stuff, but, well, that fur coat he's wearing... It is a coat, right?"

"Bearskin. He says his name is Jasper and he's not hurt or lost."

"Hello, Jasper," she called out. "I'm Liz Bloom with the US Fish and Wildlife Service."

The brawny mountain man ignored her. His gaze was fixed on Loq who'd appeared silently and stood off to our right. "Be ya *Newe*?" he growled.

"*Maklak*," Loq said.

"*Newe, Numu, Maklak*, ya'll have the same blood."

"Everyone shares something if you go back far enough. My people have lived by *Giiwas* ever since the creator made us. It's a sacred place."

"That's Crater Lake," I whispered to Liz.

Jasper scowled. "Ya a long way from home, *Maklak*."

"I've been further." He was holding the Winchester at his side. The barrel was pointed at the ground, but I knew a round was chambered. "What about you?"

"What about me?"

"Where are you a long way from?"

"Nowhere, 'cause I live everywhere."

"How long have you been living in that cave?" Liz said.

"What's it to ya, missy?"

Liz bristled. "Because the pile of dead animals over there

makes it my business. Killing animals out of hunting season is against the law. So is killing more than an annual hunting license permits. You do have a license, don't you?"

"Who says I kilt 'em?"

"If not you, then who?" she fired right back. "We could see your cave from where we found the carcasses. That means you can see where they died. Maybe you saw who butchered them."

"*Who? Who?*" Jasper flapped his arms while screeching the words like an owl. He followed with a loud guffaw that rolled down from the lava tube and filled the box canyon. The echo bounced off the cliff faces and drowned out the thrum of the Bruneau. "Who says they're dead, missy?"

"I do. We all saw them."

"And can ya also see the monster that lies beneath your bed? The goblin hiding in your closet waiting for ya to open the door? Can ya see the demon that dwells in your soul? Can ya, missy? Can ya?"

"I'm not anyone's missy, Mister! I'm Fish and Wildlife District Supervisor Liz Bloom and I can arrest you for breaking the law."

"Ya welcome to try." He belly-laughed and turned his back as he prepared to retreat into the cave.

"He's batshit," she said.

"I see you, *Tsa-ahu-bitts*," Loq called out. "I smell you. Those clothes you wear can't mask you. That voice won't hide you. You reek of death. I know you, *Tsa-ahu-bitts,* and I don't fear you."

Jasper spun around. His red-rimmed eyes locked on Loq. So did the badger's. After a long minute, he roared. "Ya no brave warrior, *Maklak*. Ya no braver than missy there. Ya gonna arrest me? Fight me? Shoot me? Go ahead and try. I'll be waiting for ya." His belly laugh was even louder this time.

The bearskin-clad mountain man seemed to melt away as a

cloud blew in front of the sunbeams and turned the maw of the lava tube even blacker.

"What should we do now?" Liz said.

"Unless we want to stand on each other's shoulders and climb up there, not much we can do," I said. "To prove Jasper killed all those animals, we'd need to go back to the bone pile and conduct field autopsies to come up with evidence. Even then, we'd have to link a weapon to him."

Loq crouched and balanced the Winchester across his knees. He picked up a handful of dirt, sniffed it, rubbed it between his palms, and then let it sprinkle back to the earth. His murmurs turned into a song and though I knew more *Numu* than *Maklak* thanks to November's patient teaching, I could make out the words for birds that never stopped flying and an ancient people walking through a boundless forest and a river that flowed back into itself.

"He's a trickster," Loq finally said. "He's Coyote. Raven. He can look like whatever he wants, whenever he needs. Dress up in the clothes of a mountain man he trapped a hundred years ago. Wear the moccasins of a *Newe* warrior he devoured. The dress of a pioneer woman whose wagon went off the Oregon Trail."

Liz rolled her brown eyes. "The reason we're not seeing any peregrines or eagles around here is because he killed them too. I don't care if he's a cryptid or a demon or an antisocial crackpot. I still intend to make this a wildlife refuge to protect endangered species and that means we either have to put him behind bars or in a padded cell."

"What we have to do is get back to camp right now," I said. "We didn't bring flashlights and it's going to get dark soon. We don't want to be stumbling down the hill and risk breaking a leg. We can decide what to do about Jasper when we get there. Come on. Let's go."

Liz hesitated. Loq stood. He raised a palm and blew the dust on it toward the cave and then started walking back the way we came.

"That's it? That's all we're going to do?" Liz said.

"It's all we can do right now. Jasper has the high ground. Until he doesn't, he can make all the rules he wants."

"Fine. But I don't like it. Not one bit."

Not one bit, but two, I thought. I didn't like the idea of him being *Tsa-ahu-bitts* at all.

15

Scarlet was streaking the clouds when we arrived at camp.

"Red sky at night, sailor's delight," Liz said, her mood having turned more cheerful with each step we took away from Jasper and the lava tube. "It's what we say Down East. I loved sailing from one little harbor to the next. Each was as pretty as a painting."

"There's still enough light for fishing," I said. "It's cold, but trout could be rising."

"Give me some line before you go," Loq said.

I handed him a spool of monofilament, presuming he was going to use it to stake out a trip wire. "Forewarned is forearmed."

Pulling on a pair of waders, I grabbed my fishing gear and walked down to the water's edge. No insects buzzed the air and no exoskeletons littered the ground. With nothing to match a fly to, I selected a bead-headed nymph and tied it to a length of tippet that I'd surgeon-knotted to the end of the leader nail-knotted to the fly line on my reel.

The bank was edged by a narrow, knee-deep gravel bench

that extended a few feet into the river before dropping away. I waded onto it, careful to keep close to shore and away from the rush of whitewater, and began casting toward the top of a riffle that emptied into a pool. After letting the fly drift, I retrieved it and casted again.

I moved downstream a few steps after the third cast and started the rotation over again to cover a new stretch of water. On the third drift, I felt a tug. I raised the rod tip at a forty-five-degree angle while pulling down on the fly line with my free hand. The hook set and the tip bent like a dowser's divining rod. The trout made a downstream run and then suddenly U-turned and ran straight back at me. I reeled to pick up the slack, ready to give the fish more line should it reverse course again. Red like the streaks overhead flashed as a rainbow launched himself out of the water in an attempt to shake the hook. He splashed back down and I let him fight the rod tip. When he grew closer, I guided him into my net.

The fourteen-inch buck wasn't a trophy, but his body was firm and I could all but hear the skin crackling as it cooked over an open flame. I removed the hook, slid the fish into a creel, and started casting again as I worked my way downriver.

Along with birdwatching and sketching wildlife, fly fishing had become a way to connect more deeply with nature. Wading in a river, feeling the water rush around my legs, and listening to a duet of birdsong and the fly line singing as it arced overhead were balms for the soul. I wanted to introduce Johnny to fishing as soon as he was open to trying it. Like horseback riding, it might help him forget his traumatic upbringing and free him from his belief he would always be a *bui doi*.

I caught a second rainbow that was a twin to the first. Catch a third and we'd all have our own trout for supper. I moved downstream a few steps and cast again.

The pulse from a tug shot up the fly line and I reflexively

raised the rod tip. It took a nosedive and I dug in my heels to keep from being yanked face-first into the drink. When the fish didn't make a run in either direction, I decided the line had wrapped around a rock or the hook had snagged the bottom. I started wading downstream. If I got the angle right, I could dislodge the hook.

The line entered the middle of the pool. I closed in on it, pulling the rod left, then right, then up. The hook stayed stuck. Before snapping the tippet and losing a fly that had already proven to be a winner, I waded closer for a looksee. The tiny brass bead-head flashed less than an arm's length down, its tiny hook imbedded in a sunken log. I slid the line between thumb and forefinger down to the fly. I was up to my bicep in cold water when I felt the bristly body of the imitation nymph. Pulling on it dislodged the log. Water swirled and it bobbed to the surface.

Only it wasn't a log.

If I gave a startled shout, I didn't hear it. Loq must've, because suddenly he was knee-deep in the river next to me.

"What's wrong?" Then he looked down. "Must be one of the missing fishermen. Or at least what's left of him."

The human torso hooked to the end of my fly line was wearing a fishing vest. Hair washed back and forth around a blanched face whose skin was the consistency of an onion that had been left in a boiling pot too long. His eyeballs had either been eaten by crayfish or sucked out by lampreys. Otherwise, the freezing water had done a good job at preserving him. If his detached legs were still in the pool, I wasn't about to dive down looking for them.

"Let's get him to shore," I said.

Loq didn't need my help dragging half a man to shore. He grabbed him by the front of the fishing vest and carried him like a suitcase. Water dripped but no blood did; it had long drained out.

Once he was on dry ground, we could see the jagged edges of the wound that ran just beneath his hips.

"He's been ripped in two," Loq said. "The last time I saw something like this was after a fellow leatherneck stepped on a landmine."

"It's possible he fell out of the boat and was swept headfirst downriver. His feet could've gotten wedged between rocks and the force of the current pulled his femurs out of the hip sockets and tore his legs off."

Loq's long mohawk rippled. "Dead animals on shore. Dead fishermen in the water. The only thing they have in common besides being dead is being next to who or whatever is living in that cave. His buddy probably ended up like this too."

"I was giving it some thought on the walk back to camp. The box canyon becomes an island when the river is at flood stage. Any animals that came here to graze before then are stuck until the river drops low enough for them to ford back across because the lowest part of the cliff walls are too sheer to climb. Jasper says he's lived all over this area. He'd know this spot has a dry cave and a built-in meat locker. Not a bad place to spend the winter."

"If you're right, then he has a powerful appetite for innards since they were missing on all those animals, including the ones who still had meat on the bone."

"I thought about that too. When you were in Saigon, did you ever visit Cho Lon? It means 'big market.'"

Loq's mohawk rippled. "Once. We were tracking down an arms merchant supplying the VC. Why?"

"When I was there, I saw stalls selling more than ginseng and cabbage. There were glass jars full of organs and baskets packed with monkey paws. One stall was set up like a pharmacy. A different part for whatever ailed you. Some real exotic stuff too. Tiger penises. Bear gallbladders. Powdered rhino horn. How they got them, who knows, but you remember how it was in 'Nam. The war didn't stop stuff flowing down the Ho Chi Minh Trail, be it machine guns or yak butter."

"What's Cho Lon have to do with the Bruneau River?"

"It could be Jasper is more than a live-off-the-land mountain man. Maybe he's a poacher of exotic organs. He gathers and stores them in the cave all winter and then takes them downriver where he meets a buyer. Maybe he's not the only one doing it. Maybe that's what's going on in Malheur and Harney County too."

"I heard about that, but it's cattle that have been found skinned and gutted there. Beef organs are as common as hamburgers."

"True, but a Red Angus kidney could be mixed with an elk's. Double the organ. Double the profit."

"You did a lot of thinking on that walk. Did you also give any thought of how we're going to pass the night without winding up like the fisherman here or how we're going to get through all the Class Five rapids ahead without drowning?"

I offered a grin. "I was leaving that up to you since you're native to this part of the world and scouting the route."

"White man exploitation all over again. You need me to be your Sacagawea, okay, but what are we going to do about him?" He chinned at the torso.

"Two choices. Bury him and mark the spot on a map so his loved ones can come fetch him when the river gets lower, or pack him out."

"I vote for burial. We have enough going on without having to worry about a dead body rolling around the raft when we're bouncing through whitewater."

"Agreed."

"And Liz, do we tell her?"

"Tell but don't show. You and I've seen bodies like this

before. It doesn't do anyone any good to have to see one if they don't have to."

We searched the fishing vest and pockets of a flannel shirt under it for ID, but there wasn't any. Loq carried him to a spot next to a juniper that looked like it would stay dry even if the river rose another six feet. We piled rocks over it to protect it from scavengers and planted branches at the head and foot to mark the spot, not that there were any feet.

"Do you want to say a few words?" Loq said when we were finished.

"What I've been forced to say way too often since moving to the high lonesome." I looked down at the cairn and then up at the sky. "I hope your death was swift. If it was by accident, don't spend eternity blaming yourself. If it was by the hands of another, I'll help find your killer so your family gets justice."

Loq picked up a handful of earth, rubbed it between his palms, and let it sprinkle over the rocks. "We both know this was no accident."

"What do you want to do, march back to the cave and strongarm Jasper into confessing? He still has the high ground whether he's a flesh-eating demon or a homicidal organ poacher."

"So?"

"So, getting down the river alive has to be our top priority. We can't put Liz in the middle of a firefight."

"She seemed ready to take him on."

"Seeming and being able to are miles apart. I say we get down the river and call for backup. A lot of it. The Bruneau isn't going to drop much in the next three days and that means Jasper isn't going anywhere unless he's got a boat or a tunnel through the mountains."

"Or he's a giant and can step right over the river."

"More the reason we need to get backup, including air

support. Blackpowder told me Owyhee County Sheriff's has a helicopter."

Loq looked at the makeshift crypt. "Better be a Huey Cobra. If Jasper is what I think he is, nothing less than an attack chopper with fifty-calibers will do."

16

Liz had made herself useful while we were burying the body. Wood was stacked next to the campfire, the cooking equipment and foodstuff were laid out, and a pot of water boiled away on the Coleman stove. She was sitting cross-legged on a tarp, writing in a journal. The gloves she wore didn't seem to impede her penmanship.

"Have any luck?" she said.

"I got a couple," I said.

"Do you need help cleaning them?"

"No thanks. Already done. How does trout and wild rice sound for supper?"

"Tasty and healthy. Blackpowder packed cans of vegetables and cling peaches for us. Let's have those too." She smiled. "I like river rafting. The meals are a lot better than backpacking where all you have is what you can carry. Eating trail mix and freeze-dried mac and cheese gets old fast."

It was time to snatch her good mood away. "Listen, when I was fishing, my fly snagged something. It turned out to be one of the missing fishermen. He's been dead for quite some time."

"Oh no!" Despite a knit wool cap pulled low and a puffy down jacket zipped up to her chin, she shivered.

"We pulled his body out of the river and covered it with rocks to protect it from scavengers. I'll mark the location on our map so when we get downriver we can alert the county sheriff's department."

"Any sign of the other fisherman?"

I shook my head. "We have no way of knowing where this one entered the water. It could be anywhere upriver and the current swept his body down here."

"But the other man could still be up there somewhere. Maybe even alive."

"That's unlikely given the snow this winter. Even so, there's nothing we can do about it now. There isn't a trail to hike back upriver because of high water and rowing against the current is out of the question. There's always a chance he stayed with their boat and is somewhere below us."

"It doesn't feel right not being able to do anything."

"Alerting the sheriff's department is doing something. They'll be able to retrieve the body and his family won't have to go through life wondering what happened to him."

Liz looked down at her journal, nodded to herself, and then back at me. "When you told me not to bullshit you about taking the kayak, I answered you straight up. I'm asking you to do the same right now. Do you think Jasper killed him?"

"I don't know, but we have to assume he did. We'll stay on high alert all night. Loq set a trip wire. We'll keep the fire going and sleep in shifts one at a time with two awake, armed, and standing guard."

"Do you think that's necessary?"

"I'd rather look back at this someday and admit I overreacted than never be able to look back at all."

Liz unzipped her jacket so she could clear her .38 from its holster. "Count me in for first watch."

As wild rice slow-cooked in a pot on the Coleman stove, Loq fashioned juniper branches into a grilling basket with the skinning knife he always wore. He placed the two trout into it and positioned them over the campfire that provided the only light once darkness consumed the scarlet streaks and clouds blocked any stardust.

The wind grew stronger and we danced the campfire two-step to keep the smoke out of our eyes. I remembered how it used to be camping with Gemma. I'd tell her how smoke followed beauty and would slow-dance her right to the sleeping bags we always zipped together. Those were the days and I pondered what life would be like if we couldn't recreate them.

After supper, we drank tea brewed with herbs and wildflowers November had picked and dried.

Liz said, "It's going to be a long night. We need to do something to help pass the time. What'll it be, twenty questions or truth or dare?"

Loq looked down his high cheekbones. "The only games I know involve fast horses and leg wrestling." He grabbed his Winchester. "I'm going to walk the perimeter." In a blink, he was gone.

Liz pointed her mug at me. "That leaves you and me, Nick. Story time it is. You said you'd tell me about your son Johnny's escape from Vietnam. Let's have it."

Chamomile and spearmint. That was what I breathed in when I held the hot tea close to my lips. It was a lot better smell than the dead elk back at the put-in or the skin-and-bone pile by Jasper's cave.

"Everything I know is what I learned by reading Johnny's records from the orphanage and talking with GIs I tracked down through a veterans group, including a warrant officer who knew him and his mother. Johnny has given me a broad brush about a few things, but mostly he keeps the details buried deep because of what he went through. It's as if he's suffering combat fatigue."

"Like you did," she said. "I read your personnel file, remember?"

"I'd like to think I'm over it, but maybe you never are completely."

I stared into the campfire and sipped some tea. Johnny and I'd both been changed forever by the war. But I was a grown man and he was a little boy. I had a place to come home to, access to shrinks and nurses at Walter Reed, and the freedom to start a new life. Johnny had none of those things.

Gemma and I were trying to change that for him, but like the Vietnam War itself, good intentions were never enough and mistaken ones triggered catastrophe. The only map we had to go by was the one charted by our own hearts: give Johnny a safe place to live, plenty of love, and time to heal. Failure wasn't an option because it wasn't just him who'd suffer. We all would. Hattie, November, Nagah, Pudge, Gemma, and me. Even Jake the dog.

"Johnny was younger than Hattie is now when his mother was killed," I began, as the flames warmed and the wood crackled and the embers glowed. Liz leaned forward and hung on every word.

∼

HIS MOTHER'S name was Thien, which meant "heavenly" in English. She was only seventeen when she had him. Up until her death, Thien and Johnny shared a bed in a ramshackle bunkhouse attached to the back of a boom-boom club that opened onto hustling, bustling Tu Do Street. It was the only home he'd ever known.

Their cramped quarters were little bigger than the single, swayback bed. Colorful bedspreads strung on a clothesline served as walls between their room and those of the other girls who were indentured to the boom-boom club's owner. He kept eighty percent of their earnings for rent and charged them the remainder for meals.

A box filled with Thien's and Johnny's meager belongings was stored beneath the bed. Next to it was a flattened piece of cardboard and a blanket. Whenever Thien brought home a "special friend," she'd whistle before drawing open the curtain. Johnny would dive under the bed as she'd trained him. He'd curl up on the piece of cardboard, pull the blanket over him, clamp his eyes shut, and put his fingers in his ears.

Eventually, he grew brave enough to peek out from beneath the blanket. He could see lace-up boots and green uniforms on the floor. Most were usually strewn about. Some were neatly folded. Many were sweat-soaked and mud-caked. A few were neatly pressed and had names and insignias on them.

One time a special friend had placed a pack of cigarettes and a silver lighter on top of his folded uniform. A fire-breathing red dragon's head was embossed on the shiny metal. It fascinated Johnny and he couldn't resist reaching out to touch it. As soon as he did, a thick, white hand clamped his wrist and yanked him out from under the bed. The hand pulled him straight up so that he was staring into the square face of a man with yellow hair and eyes the color of the sky in the morning before the steam of the jungle and the exhaust of motorbikes painted it dirty gray.

"Well, lookee here! You're the biggest cockroach I've seen in Saigon yet." The man's laugh made his face turn red. He dangled Johnny over Thien. "I take it he's yours."

Thien made a grab for him, but the man held him higher. "Now, now, sweet thang. Don't fret. I'm not gonna hurt him. I only wanna take a look at him."

He gave a whistle of surprise. "Mighty fine son you got, but if I'm not mistaken, it appears you've been entertaining some of our soul-brother soldiers. Not that I got any brook with them. They've saved my sorry white ass more than once." He followed that with another laugh.

The square-faced man lowered Johnny back to the floor. "You like my Zippo, kid? Go on, take it. Consider it a gift from your new uncle. I plan to be your mama's number one customer since I'm gonna be around plenty now that they put me in charge of the motor pool here in town."

His name was Chief Warrant Officer Jim Craig, but the men who worked for him called him Chief Gimcrack because of an oft-shouted rant whenever he discovered a repair that didn't meet his exacting standards: "What lazy bumbleass did this? The work's gimcrackery. Our boys depend on a deuce-and-a-half whose wheels won't fall off. Fix it right or you'll be riding to the next battle strapped to the front bumper."

Jim Craig hailed from a small town in Alabama but had no intention of returning there. Nor to the good ol' US of A either. He was a military lifer who preferred living overseas, ideally in a warzone where the starched collars were few and far between.

"Over here, I'm king," he'd crow over boilermakers at the boom-boom club. "Got me a fine-looking gal who doesn't measure a man by the size of his paycheck or screwdriver. Back home? Best I could hope for is pumping gas at the Gulf station to pay the bills for a passel of snotnoses and a wife meaner than a cottonmouth."

He'd shake his square head, down his drink, and then buy another round for the house before grabbing Thien's slender wrist and taking her to the curtained room out back where he'd toss Johnny a 10 *xu* coin to go play in the street for an hour.

Johnny soon learned that Uncle Jim wasn't the only GI who'd pay him. It seemed all the American soldiers were rich.

While arriving at the rooms they'd give him *xu* coins to fetch bottles of beer, shine their boots, or run across the street to buy packs of L&Ms and Kools. A few even offered him 500 *dong* bills to procure marijuana from the streetcorner boys. They also taught Johnny a few choice words in English, getting a kick out of him parroting GI slang and acronyms such as SNAFU and BOHICA.

Johnny kept his money in a discarded tobacco tin that he hid in the box beneath the bed. He always kept the silver lighter with the fire-breathing red dragon's head on it that Jim Craig had given him in his pocket because he never wanted to lose it. He liked to flick open the silver base lid and thumb the spark wheel and rub his fingertip on the dragon's head crest with the words "Orient Express" stamped beneath. It was the motto of the Seventh Transportation Battalion.

Thien also hid the tips Jim Craig and other special friends gave her. She had to because the club owner would take them. He considered everything his, from the girls' bodies down to the last *xu* they made.

Duong Pham was his name and he had a penchant for colorful silk shirts and white linen slacks. He wore his longish hair slicked back with scented oil. In addition to a ferret's smile and a hair-trigger temper, he kept a razor-edged butterfly knife tucked inside his ankle-high leather boot. More than one of his girls had felt its blade when they tried to withhold tips.

Pham had learned French during the French Indochina War when the boom-boom club catered to Foreign Legion soldiers fighting the *Viet Minh*. He quickly picked up English when the French pulled out and Americans took their place. He liked the GIs better. They drank more, screwed more, and tipped more. He was making lots of money. Enough to pay for bribes to corrupt officials, a swanky apartment where he lived with his wife and kids, and champagne and Chanel No. 5 for his young mistress.

It happened during the two weeks Jim Craig was dispatched to Cam Rahn Bay to oversee readying a new shipment of Commando armored personnel carriers made by Cadillac. Thien and Johnny had taken a rare opportunity to go out for *banh pia* sold from a cart on the street. After enjoying the sweet mooncakes, mother and son returned to their room. When Thien pushed through the curtain, she shrieked. Duong Pham was sitting on the bed. Next to him was Johnny's tobacco tin. It was open and coins and bills were spilling out. Her own roll of *dong* and dollar bills was fanned on the bedspread.

"You have been stealing from me," Pham hissed, his beady eyes darting above his ferret smile.

Before Thien could say a word, Johnny rushed to snatch back his tobacco tin. The pimp struck with stunning speed. Silver flashed as metal clicked and swished. Before Thien could shriek again, Pham had one arm clenched around Johnny's chest and the blade of the butterfly knife pressed against his throat.

"Let him go," Thien cried. "Keep the money. All my fault. Sorry. So sorry." She started bowing.

Pham's lips twisted. "Of course I will, because the money is mine anyway. But there is a price for theft."

He pressed the blade. Blood oozed on either side. Johnny cried out.

Thien shrieked. "Cut me, not him. He is only a baby. Please. So sorry." She kept bowing.

"If I cut you, then customers will pay me less. You are worth money. The boy is worth nothing."

"I have more money. I have lots of tips. Please. I will show you. Let my baby go."

Pham hesitated, but greed won out. "Where?"

"In the mattress. Sewn inside."

"You little bitch. Show me."

"You are sitting on it."

Pham hesitated again. Greed won out again. He flung Johnny aside and stood. Thien leapt on him, her fingernails scratching for his eyes. But this time, Pham didn't waver. He struck with serpent speed once more and plunged the butterfly knife into her heart.

Johnny screamed in the slang he'd learned from American soldiers. "Broken arrow! Broken arrow! Gooks in wire!"

The GI call to arms that the base was being overrun alerted a special friend in the next cubicle. Suddenly, the curtain swished open and a young man wearing green boxer shorts and a tiger tattooed on his bicep followed his outstretched US Army .45 into the room. He didn't falter one blink. The first round burrowed into Duong Pham's forehead, the second in his throat when his head snapped back.

When the smoke cleared, the soldier spit. "Foxtrot 'Nam. Even the cathouses are FUBAR."

∽

LIZ'S EYES had been riveted on me as she listened, but I suddenly stopped talking. "Go on," she said. "What happened next?"

"Shh," I whispered.

"What?"

"Shh. I heard something. We're not alone."

"It's only Loq coming back. I want to know what Johnny did after Pham killed Thien and the soldier shot him."

My head was rotating now, trying to get a bead on whatever or whoever was watching us. "It's not Loq," I whispered. "He never makes a sound. He'd be sitting beside you before you even knew he was there."

I was looking past her, keeping my eyes away from the firelight. Letting them adjust to the darkness. A shrub moved, but not by wind. A dark shape was trying to hide behind it.

"I got to take a leak," I said loudly. "Put some more wood on the fire, would you?"

"But—"

I cut Liz off with a glance.

"Oh," she said. "Okay."

I stood. Stretched. Feigned yawning. And then walked into the darkness, slipping the .357 from my holster as I went. Three tours leading reconnaissance patrols had trained me well for walking silently. I circled our campsite, my wrists crisscrossed in front of me, my sidearm gripped in my right hand, an unlit flashlight in the left.

My recon route took me behind the shrub where I'd spotted the dark shape. It was now silhouetted by the glow of the fire. I'd already made up my mind to shoot first and ask questions later. The dead animals. The dead fishermen. Jasper was not to be trusted. I closed in.

The dark shape still hadn't heard or sensed me. Something about it was off. It had neither the height nor bulk of the monstrous mountain man. I thumbed on the flashlight. The shape turned around. The beam illuminated a hollow-eyed man wearing a fishing vest that draped his emaciated frame.

"At last!" he cried. "I'm saved."

17

Scurvy. Rickets. Frostbite. Malnutrition.

The lost-now-found fisherman appeared to be suffering from all of them. He huddled next to the campfire with our spare sleeping bag wrapped around him. The back of his hands were covered with scratches and scabs. He clutched a mug of soup that he shakingly brought to chapped lips. The metal rim clanged against his few remaining teeth.

I tried to be sympathetic as I watched him, but mostly I was suspicious. The odds of him having survived were off the charts.

"You still haven't told us your name," I said.

"J-j-jerry," he stammered.

"With a J or a G?"

"J-j-j. Short for J-j-jeremiah."

I tried to remember if Blackpowder told us the names of the two lost fishermen. If he had, I couldn't recall them. "Got a last name to go with that?"

Sunken eyes darted behind the mug. "J-j-johnson."

"Jeremiah Johnson. Like the famous frontiersman. Any relation?"

His filthy, tangled hair shook back and forth. "Been the butt of j-j-jokes all my life."

"I'm Nick Drake and she's Liz Bloom. We're with Fish and Wildlife."

"Can I have some more soup?"

"There's still a little left in the pot," Liz said. "Here, let me pour it."

He held the mug out like a street beggar. The fingernails that weren't broken were long and curved and blackened with dirt caked under them.

I asked him when was the last time he ate.

"What day is it?"

I told him. "You've been here since November. The fact you made it through the winter is a miracle."

"Day to day," Jerry mumbled. "Told myself get through the day and I might see my wife again."

"I'm sure she'll be thrilled to know you're alive," Liz said.

"What about your friend?" I said.

His eyes seemed to sink even deeper into his gaunt face. Soup dripped from his scraggly beard. "Friend?"

"Your buddy. The report was two fishermen went missing."

"Owen."

"That a first or last name?"

"I'm not sure. Always called him Owen. Only Owen. Everybody did."

"Okay, what happened to Only Owen?"

He sniveled. "Died."

"How?"

"Don't want to talk about it."

"We need to know," I said. "For the report."

"Report?"

"The report we'll have to file with Owyhee County Sheriff's when we get you out of here. There's always paperwork."

"Paperwork?"

"Makes the world go around. What happened to him?"

"Drowned. He was thrown in the river. I couldn't help him. Nearly got killed myself."

"Did your boat capsize or was it a slip and fall from the bank or when he was wading?" If Only Owen had been wearing waders, maybe they were still on his missing legs.

Jerry slurped more soup. "Rain came out of nowhere. By the bucket. River rose fast. Our dory hit a rock. Hull splintered. It went down and we went out."

He held out the mug again. It was empty.

"You put in on the Bruneau in a dory?"

"Better for fishing from than a raft. Can stand while casting."

"I assume that was upriver and you got washed down here."

He waved the mug. "Got anything else?"

"We have a bag of jerky," I said.

Wrinkles creased hollow cheeks. "Tired of meat. What about sugar? Candy? Anything sweet."

"We have those cans of cling peaches." Liz said to me.

"Go ahead," I said, making no move from my stance by the fire to get it myself.

I wasn't about to take my eyes or gun off Jeremiah "Jerry" Johnson, much less turn my back on him. When I'd brought him to the campfire, I did so at the point of my Smith and Wesson. This wasn't the time to change tactics. Not until Loq got back, wherever he might be. It wasn't like him to have missed spotting someone spying on our camp. Even if he hiked back up the box canyon like I assumed he had, his sixth sense would've picked up on the presence of a stranger now sitting beside our fire.

Liz rummaged through our stores and came back with the peaches. She opened it with the can-opening blade on her Swiss Army knife. Seeing it reminded me of the P-38 openers that came with C-rations in 'Nam. A lot of grunts called the tiny hinged blade a "John Wayne" because of its toughness and durability. I still had one I used at the old lineman's shack for opening tin cans of coffee.

Jerry was salivating as he watched Liz open the peaches.

"Were you able to salvage any of your gear when your dory went down?" I said.

"Only what we had in our pockets."

"You and Owen couldn't stick together when you went in the drink?"

He didn't look at me, only at the can. "I wore a life jacket. Owen didn't. Said it got in the way when he was casting."

"It's lucky you didn't freeze when you washed up on shore, it being November and you soaking wet and half-drowned."

"I lit a fire."

"How?"

"What's it matter?"

Liz got the can open and was about to hand it to him, but I waved her off. "For the report. The one the sheriff will want."

He reached for the peaches.

"Hold it," I said. "You want a peach, you answer a question. Simple as that."

His stare switched from the can to me. I could see the snarl on his lips which he tried to cover by licking them.

"I struck two rocks together."

"I've had to do that myself. Hard enough to do with dry wood. When everything's wet..."

I let it hang and chinned to Liz to spear a slice of peach and offer it to him. He pinched it off the blade of her knife and slurped it. It reminded me of old pictures from the 1930s when swallowing goldfish was a fad along with seeing how many people could stuff themselves into a telephone booth. Those were the days, not a care in the world. Not like right now on the

Bruneau. Maybe Loq was right. Maybe Jasper was a shapeshifter and had assumed the body of the presumed-dead fisherman with a famous mountain man's name slurping peaches.

"What did you do for shelter all these months?" I said.

"Caves. The canyon's riddled with them. Like Swiss cheese."

I nodded to Liz. She gave him another peach slice. He did the swallowing goldfish thing again.

"And food?" I said. "Your fishing gear and all your stuff having gone down with the ship and all."

I got the snarling look again. "I thought good Samaritans were supposed to be nice."

"We come in all stripes. How did you feed yourself?" I pictured the drumsticks of cold chicken we'd eaten and then Only Owen's missing legs. Maybe the current hadn't pulled them off.

"Scavenged. Whatever I could find."

Liz gave him another peach slice.

I didn't wait for it to slither down his throat. "From Jasper's bone pile or did he feed you in exchange for doing his bidding?"

I'd never seen a goldfish fly, but the peach did when Jerry spit it out.

"So, you do know Jasper. Not exactly a nice Samaritan either, is he? How come you didn't mention him?"

Jerry started wheezing and then alternated between cowering and glaring. "Because I didn't want to scare you. Have you shove off in the middle of the night and not take me with you."

"Why do you think we'd do that? We already met Jasper, spoke to him. We haven't bolted yet."

"You should've. He's the devil, is what he is. He killed Owen. The only reason he hasn't killed me is because he thinks he already did."

"Why did he kill Owen?"

"I told you. He's the devil. He kills whatever he sees, whatever he wants. Fish. Lizards. Birds. Animals. Men."

Liz was breathing heavily now, but she didn't gasp or cry out. I noticed she'd put the half-eaten can of cling peaches on the ground and was holding her sidearm on her lap.

"How did you avoid him?"

"Sleep by day, scavenge by night."

"From the big pile of animals he killed."

Jerry's head went up and down.

"How does he kill them, with a gun, traps?"

"Every which way. Club. Spear. His bare hands."

"How did he kill Owen?"

"Picked him up off the riverbank by his ankles when we washed up and slammed him on the edge of a jagged rock and then swung him round and round until Owen tore in half and his body went into the river."

"And you?"

"He picked me up the same way and was going to slam me too, but my boots came off in his hands and I went flying. I hit the river and swam underwater and hid behind a boulder."

I looked at his feet. Strips of bark were wrapped to his soles with lengths of dry grass.

"You won't leave me, will you?" Jerry whined. "Promise? I'll pay you anything you want. I'm not a rich man but I got a little plumbing business back in Boise and a house with not much of a mortgage. It's yours. All of it. Just take me with you. Don't leave me here. I don't want him to get me. Kill me. Like he did Owen and all those animals."

The flames abruptly switched direction as if something was blocking the wind. I swung my gun toward it, my finger about to yank the trigger.

Loq stepped out of the darkness. Mud darkened his face for

camouflage. He held his long skinning knife in one hand, his sidearm in the other. His rifle hung from a strap over his shoulder. He gave Jerry a sideways glance before speaking.

"*Tsa-ahu-bitts* is on the move."

18

As I looked across the campfire at Liz Bloom and Jerry Johnson, I thought of the drill instructor I had in basic training. A textbook hardass, he'd earned his combat stripes in Korea and had zero tolerance for shaved-heads who displayed ignorance, weakness, or, worst of all, cowardice. His tried-and-true tactic for bending us to his will was to order us on a ten-mile run shouldering full rucksacks followed by an hour on the obstacle course and then standing at full attention in the blazing sun while he lectured us about Walter Bradford Cannon.

Dr. Cannon, Sgt. Hardass bellowed, was a pointy-headed professor of physiology at Harvard who'd come up with an even more pointy-headed theory called fight-or-flight. According to the rock-jawed DI, that's when animals facing threat of attack underwent a biochemical reaction flooding their bloodstream with adrenaline and prompting them to put up their dukes or run like pansies.

After making it abundantly clear we were animals, Sgt. Hardass roared, "But in this man's Army there is only one reaction, and it's fight like hell!" Without taking a breath, he let loose with a second full-throated fusillade against another of the good Dr. Cannon's theories. Called "voodoo death," it was when an animal got so scared it dropped dead.

"But in this man's Army," Sgt. Hardass screamed, "the only thing you better be afraid of when you're in the jungle defending the American Way is me coming after you if I hear you turned tail. It won't be fear that kills you, it'll be my own two hands around your goddamned neck!"

Loq's news about Jasper had definitely unleashed adrenaline in all of us. How we reacted to it would determine whether we lived or died, either by defending ourselves against the killer or by jumping in the raft and trying to run the flood-swollen Bruneau in the dead of night.

Looking at the open can of cling peaches and then Jerry, Loq said, "Who's he?"

"The other fisherman," I said. "His name's Jerry Johnson, short for Jeremiah. Like the famous frontiersman."

Loq spit. "Infamous, you mean. Liver-Eating Johnson butchered Indians by the hundreds."

"I'm not related. I swear," Jerry whined. He was quaking in his grass and bark shoes.

"We'll see about that."

Loq turned back to me. "Are you sure he's not a *sko'gs*?" he said, using his native tongue for ghost.

"I'm betwixt and between," I said. "He slurped down a can of soup followed by those peaches and I don't know if they eat in the spirit world. He also said Jasper tore his fishing partner Only Owen in half and tried to do the same to him but loose boots saved him. We know he's telling the truth about his buddy since we buried what's left of him under a pile of rocks."

"You found Owen?" Jerry said.

"He didn't have any legs?" Liz said.

"I don't trust him," Loq said. "There's his name and then

there's *Tsa-ahu-bitts* dressed up like a mountain man."

"I thought the same thing. Why I still haven't taken my gun off him. I give it a better than even chance he survived because Jasper let him take scraps from the bone pile."

I turned back to Jerry. "What else can you tell us about Jasper?"

"Nothing. He killed Owen. He tried to kill me. He kills animals."

"It's only the two of you living here?"

"Except for the animals. And there's not many of them left alive. They'll all be dead by the time the river drops. And if we don't get out of here right now, we will be too."

"What's he do with the parts he takes from the ones he butchers?"

Jerry started shaking even harder. "Eats some on the spot. Takes the rest up to his cave."

"How?"

"Carries it up the ladder."

"Have you ever gone inside?"

His head swung back and forth. "Why would I do that?"

"Maybe he took you. Maybe to steal something. Maybe to try and kill him in his sleep."

"I couldn't do that."

"Why not?"

"He'd catch me."

"Does he ever leave the canyon, either by boat or by walking?"

"If he has a boat, I've never seen it. If there was a trail, I'd've found it and left first chance I got. The bottom of the canyon walls are too steep to climb. Need a ladder even taller than what he's got to reach the first place to get a handhold. Either that or if someone had climbed down from the top and left a rope hanging. No one has. I've looked."

"Have you ever seen him wearing anything besides that long bearskin coat and badger cap?"

"I don't think it's a coat. I think it's his own skin. He's a monster, I tell you."

"He's *Tsa-ahu-bitts*, all right," Loq said.

"What makes you say that?" I said.

"From what I saw when I was doing recon in the box canyon after supper."

"What was it?" Liz said.

"Something I've never seen before, not even in a sweat lodge with tribal elders or the time I attended a peyote ceremony with a Kiowa brother at the Native American Church in Oklahoma."

Loq breathed deeply through his nose. "Animal spirits. They came running from the skin-and-bone pile. Deer, elk, bighorn, antelope. Mountain lions and bobcats too." He nodded toward the sky. "They glowed like stars, but I could see right through them."

"I've seen them too," Jerry whimpered. "I thought it was because I was starving. Like a mirage or something."

"Could be the result of another one of Doctor Cannon's theories," I said.

"Who's he?" Loq said.

"Doesn't matter. What does is, we've all seen Jasper, seen what he's done. We got to do something and do it now."

"Run!" Jerry cried.

"That's what he wants. No, not wants, needs. Jasper, *Tsa-ahu-bitts*, Tsawhawbitts, Jahabich, Jarbidge, whatever you choose to call him, whoever or whatever he is, he's a hunter. He likes the chase as much as the killing. I've seen it before."

Loq grunted. "We can set a trap. Lure him here and spring it. You and me, we'll be the jaws on either side." He waved his knife and pistol.

"Wait a second," Liz said, jumping to her feet, kicking over the can of peaches. Heavy syrup spilled onto the ground. "You're talking about setting up an ambush and killing him. That's murder. We're sworn law-enforcement officers, not executioners. We couldn't live with ourselves if we did that."

"We might not live if we don't," Loq said.

November's warning echoed in my head. It takes a demon to stop a demon. "Liz is right. We can't just open fire on him. We have to try and capture him."

Loq glared at me. "And then do what with him? Tie him up and put him in the raft with us and the *sko'gs*?"

The gaunt fisherman's sunken eyes suddenly bulged. "You got to kill him now. You put him in your raft, he'll find a way to kill us all. I won't ride with him."

"I'm the superior officer here," Liz said. "We try to arrest him. If we succeed, then we'll figure out how to transport him."

"Fair enough," I said. "Let's set a trap."

"Who's going to be the bait?" Loq said as he looked back and forth at Liz and Jerry.

I asked Liz if she'd gone through more than basic weapons training.

Her knit cap nodded. "When I was a state wildlife officer and again with my new job."

"Have you ever pulled your gun on a violator?"

"Once. In Maine. I was at a state park and a man leapt from behind a tree and attacked me. Turned out he was the Backwoods Rapist. That's what local authorities had been calling him. They'd been trying to catch him for months."

"Did you put him down?" Loq said.

Liz returned his stare without a blink. "Do you have a girlfriend, sister, mother? Do you know what it's like to have someone threaten you with his . . ." Her face grimaced with disgust. "It was me or him and I made the choice it wasn't going to be me."

"Jasper already knows Jerry's with us," I said. "He either sent him or senses it. Only one person by the campfire will make him suspicious. It has to be two. Jerry and me."

The fisherman moaned and Liz started to protest, but it was our best shot at trapping the monster whether he was the human kind or something else.

"We need a back door if Jasper somehow turns the tables on us," I said. "We'll load the gear into the raft, tie the kayak to it, and have it ready to launch. Then we'll build the campfire up and throw some food on it to create a scent. Jerry and I'll stay on the river side of it. You two take up positions on the other side, fire some warning shots over his head and tell him he's under arrest. If he tries to bolt, wing him. If he comes after you, defend yourself with lethal force the way we were trained."

We readied the raft and then Loq and Liz disappeared into the bushes to take up positions. I fetched a can of beef stew and punctured two holes in the top with my pocketknife. The blade made me remember the antler-handled obsidian dagger November had given me. I retrieved it from my gear bag and strapped the deerskin scabbard to my calf. I set the can of Dinty Moore next to the flames and waited.

Twin fumaroles of smoke rose from the blackening can. I looked left, right, and straight ahead. I thought about Dr. Cannon and Sgt. Hardass again and how humans were animals. Wolves had eyes in the front of their skulls to look for prey while rabbits' were on the side to look for wolves. No animal, humans included, had eyes at the back of their head. And that was our downfall.

I smelled it before I saw it. The corpse of a deer came flying in from behind me. It landed on the fire and sent sparks flying. The dead buck was followed by a roar and splashes as Jasper emerged from the river directly behind me.

By the time I wheeled around, a caveman club was sweeping

toward me. I managed to duck and threw myself to the ground. The club continued its powerful arc and caught Jerry square in the face. Blood the color of the streaks that had earlier painted the sky shot everywhere. Jasper cocked the club back to take another swing at me. His hands were bear paws.

They're gloves, I told myself, as I raised the 12 gauge while still sprawled on the ground and pulled the trigger. But Jasper moved faster. He snatched Jerry's lifeless body and shielded himself from the blast. As I pumped in another shell, he flung the fisherman's corpse at me and knocked the barrel sideways.

Liz rushed out of the bushes holding her .38 in a two-handed grip. "You're under arrest! Drop your weapon!"

Jasper swung his club at her. She twisted to get out of its way, but took a glancing blow on her shoulder that sent her flying. As he went after her, Loq jumped between them and emptied his six-shot revolver. A magnum slug struck the club and knocked it loose, but the rest of the rounds found only the flapping bearskin coat as Jasper twisted and turned with amazing speed.

Then the killer abruptly stopped. Four red eyes trained on Loq. His and those of his badger-skin cap.

"Ya no brave warrior, *Maklak*," he snarled. "I'm gonna eat you the same as I ate *Newe*."

Loq dropped the empty .357 as he switched the skinning knife from his left hand to his right and launched himself, trying to get inside Jasper's massive reach. I aimed the shotgun again, but Loq was too close to risk a shot.

The two clung to each other like love-drunk dancers as they grappled, each trying to kick the other one's legs out from under him. Loq couldn't pull his arm back far enough to get leverage to drive his blade past Jasper's thick coat while the killer pounded on his back and tried to sink his teeth into the top of his head.

I charged in to push the shotgun right up against Jasper, but he sensed me coming and spun so Loq's back was toward me, forcing me to pull up short. He bared his teeth. So did the badger. Then Jasper pushed Loq away while swinging his bearpaw gloves. First left, then right. Sharp claws shredded shirt and skin as they raked across Loq's chest.

The Klamath was still between me and a clean shot at Jasper. A bolt of adrenaline surged through me and I dropped the 12 gauge and unsheathed the obsidian dagger. "Chief Washakie's knife!" I shouted. "The power of all Shoshone living and dead is in it."

Jasper's and the badger's eyes locked onto the knife. "Where'd'ja get that?"

"From a Paiute medicine woman more powerful than *Tsa-ahu-bitts*. Her husband descended from the great warrior chief. They are with us now and hungry for revenge."

Jasper growled and raked the air with his bear claws. I bent my knees and shifted my weight to the balls of my feet, ready to spring and plunge the stone dagger into him, but he abruptly turned away and lumbered into the darkness.

Loq fell to his knees, clutching his chest, blood seeping between his fingers. "How . . . how did you come up with that?"

"Must've been November talking through me. Doesn't matter. We got to go."

I sheathed the dagger and helped him to the raft. By the time we reached it, he collapsed. I laid the unconscious warrior in the bow and clasped his palms over his chest to keep pressure on his wounds.

Then I ran back to collect Liz and our weapons. She was on her hands and knees shaking the stars from her head.

"Let's go," I said. "Jasper ran off, but not for long. Come on. Hup two. Double-time."

I locked arms with her and half-dragged, half shoved her toward the river.

"Where's Loq?" she said.

"In the raft. He's wounded. You'll need to ride up front with him and make sure he doesn't bleed out."

"And Jerry?"

"He didn't make it."

"But we can't leave him."

"If we don't, we'll join him."

Jasper's roar rent the night air. I swiveled to look where it was coming from. Another bolt of adrenaline surged through me and I saw silvery animals streaking through the bushes like comets. I threw our guns into the raft and gave a running push as Liz scrambled into the front. By the time I jumped in and swung us around, rocks began raining down. The front tube thumped like a kettle drum when one struck. A sharp crack sounded as another hit the kayak trailing behind us. Finally, the current caught the raft, sweeping us into darkness.

I thought of Dr. Cannon again as I steered blindly, relying on feel and sound to try to keep away from boulders. Running from a fight wasn't something I was used to, but with Jerry dead and my two partners wounded, retreat seemed best no matter how bitter it tasted. Not knowing what we were fleeing to didn't make swallowing defeat any easier. It could be safety or it could be an even greater threat, like a river that raged as dangerously as a killer who'd never tire of hunting us.

Loq never would've gone along with my decision to run if he hadn't passed out. I was also sure Pudge Warbler would've stayed and fought too. I wasn't looking forward to telling the old sheriff that I'd turned tail. The best I could hope for was he might understand when I explained that his daughter and grandkids had been top-of-mind. That is, if I was able to get down the river alive to tell him.

The roars from Jasper and the rapids told me it was a mighty big if.

19

THE MEAT LOCKER

Sheriff Pudge Warbler's eyes blinked open and stayed blinking. It was dark. Pitch dark. And cold. Ice cold. A thought that he was dead flittered, then fled. So did the idea that he'd been buried alive in the family plot on the ranch. After his wife died and he was left with a five-year-old, Pudge asked November to promise that if he ever got shot on the job and pronounced dead, she'd make sure by stabbing him in the hand with the long beading needle she used for making bracelets and decorating deerskin pouches.

The ranch. Henrietta. November. Gemma. Nick. Hattie. Johnny. He saw their faces. Knew who they were. That had to be a good sign.

His head ached. So did his back and shoulders. He moved his arms. Moved his hands. That was another good sign. Felt around. Black air above. Black air to the sides. Black something hard beneath his back. He touched it with his fingers. Cement. Cold cement. A cement floor. He wasn't outside, he was inside. But inside where?

And then it came flooding back.

Driving Dill McCaw to Salem. The pass closed. The lodge at

Turtle Lake. The confused old man in the red-and-black plaid hat. William? Wilbur? Something like that. Wilmot. That was it, Wilmot. The girl with the silver moon with a winking eye and frilly apron. Catherine? Christina? Short for it. Tina. The bearded man with the toolbelt. Carl? Calvin? No, Caleb. Hot coffee. A hammer.

Guess Wilmot wasn't so doddering after all.

The sheriff slapped at his hip and felt for his gun. It wasn't there. He reached for the buckle to his holster. It wasn't there either. Not only did they take it, but they also got the leather pouch on it that held the keys to the handcuffs and shackles as well as to his pickup. His hat was also missing, but at least they'd left his jacket on him. He would've frozen without it.

Pudge tried moving his legs. It was as if they were stuck to the cement. Maybe they'd gotten wet and then froze to it. He tried wiggling his toes. There. He felt them move. First the left ones, then the right. Another good sign.

He remembered another time he'd been knocked flat, knocked out. His company of Marines were storming the beach at Iwo Jima. The air was whistling not from wind but machine-gun fire. The ground was shaking, not from crashing waves but exploding shells. The sky was black with smoke. Too black. Something was ringing in his ears. Someone was screaming. Pudge was lying on his back, his legs folded beneath him. A helmet clanked against his. A face was inches from his. "Get up, Private!" the face belonging to his sergeant screamed. "Get up!" And so he did. Kept running forward, kept shooting as he tried to shake the ringing from his ears. Never could shake the ringing the whole time he was on Iwo.

Get up! Pudge yelled to himself. Get up!

He pressed his forearms against the floor and tried to raise himself to a sitting position. His biceps burned. His shoulders ached. He raised his head off the cement. His shoulders. But then his head exploded with flashing lights, screaming sirens, and burning flames. He fell back. His head thunked on the cold cement. Pudge blacked out again.

Get up, Percival! Get up! His father was yelling at him to get up after he'd been thrown from his pony. Get up, Percival! Get up! He hated the name. Told his father he didn't care that it went back to England where his ancestors once lived, back to King Arthur's time, Sir Percival being a knight of the Round Table. Sir Percival being the real hero in the Quest for the Holy Grail before being replaced by Sir Galahad in literature, before being replaced by Pudge who took his own nickname as his given one.

Get up, Pudge! he yelled to himself. Get up!

His eyes blinked open again. Kept blinking. This time he knew what had happened. Knew where he was. He was still in the two-story lodge by the lake that was the shape of a turtle. For how long, he wasn't sure. Pudge rubbed his chin, his cheeks. He'd shaved before he left No Mountain that morning. But it was no longer that morning. His whiskers told him that. There was at least a day's worth. Maybe two.

Instead of trying to raise himself on his forearms, he decided to roll on his side, get on his stomach, and do a push-up. He'd always been good at push-ups. Much better at push-ups than sit-ups. In boot camp before shipping off to the Pacific. In the physical when he applied to be a deputy at Harney County Sheriff's. In the calisthenics he did on the ranch to keep in shape. Nearly twenty years after Iwo when JFK ballyhooed a new President's Council on Physical Fitness, Pudge took the test at home and passed it with flying colors despite being on the first hole of his belt.

He started moving his hips, tried raising his feet, his knees, his legs. His pants became unstuck from the cold cement floor. He finally got enough momentum and rolled onto his side. Took a breather. A long breather. Ignored the pounding in his head.

The shooting pain. The shooting stars. He rolled again, this time onto his stomach. Again he took a breather.

Pudge worked his palms under his shoulders and pushed. Nothing. He tried again. Still nothing. Then he pictured Dill McCaw's face. Heard him caterwauling. That godawful noise he called singing. He pictured Caleb's face. The black beard. The half-lidded eyes. He pictured Tina. The face of sweet innocence. The silver moon with a winking eye. The murder in her eyes when she pitched the coffee in his face.

It was that look that made Pudge angry. Real angry. He pushed harder. His chest came off the ground. He raised his hips and drew his knees up and then rocked onto them. On his hands and knees, he pushed off the ground and stood. Wavering at first and then getting his balance to stand tall as the faces of Dill, Caleb, and Tina flashed. He struggled to catch his breath, struggled to shake the sound of Dill's singing and guitar picking ringing in his head.

Only it wasn't in his head. It was coming from somewhere above him. Dill was still in the lodge. Someone had retrieved his guitar from the pickup for him. That surely meant Tina and Caleb were still there and believed his BS about record royalties. Nobody had skedaddled. Nobody thought he was alive. They'd dragged him down to wherever he was and threw his body inside. But he wasn't dead. Not yet. And that meant he still had a chance to stop them, still had a chance to deliver justice.

The idea of him doing the delivering eased the pain in the old lawman's head, eased the fact he couldn't see.

Standing put him eye level to a murmur of cold air. Pudge wetted his finger and held it out. The wet finger turned even colder. He wetted it again, held it out, and took a tentative step forward. The cold murmur grew to a whisper. He took another and then another and still another. He bumped into something, reached down and shoved it to the side. Took more steps and bumped into something again. Only this time it was his outstretched finger that bumped first.

It was a wall. A wall with cold air leaking through it. Leaking from a seam. He ran his fingertip along it, reading it like it was braille, felt a hump, hooked his finger under it, and pulled. Pulled hard. Got another finger under it. Pulled even harder. Metal screeched and light flashed and he shut his eyes to keep from being blinded.

A blink at a time. That's how Pudge let his eyes grow used to the thin line of light shining from behind the pulled metal. He could see it was a square of tin that had been hammered around a thick pipe as a flange or gasket of some kind. He peeled the tin square back on all four sides to let more light in. The pipe extruded through a hole in the wall. He could see light. He could see snow. His head was even to the ground.

Pudge turned around. With the light shining over his shoulder, he saw shelves lining the walls of a rectangular room. Some held empty Mason jars. Others, cardboard boxes. He looked inside the closest one. Several withered apples blackened the bottom. Another had a bedding of wilted lettuce dotted with shriveled carrots. Pudge looked up at the ceiling. Hooks dangled from chains, but anything that once hung from them, be it deer, ducks, or sides of beef, had all been consumed.

He'd been tossed into the lodge's cold-storage room, a meat locker.

The sheriff wondered how long Tina and Caleb had been living there, holding Wilmot hostage, eating his food, plundering his wares, stripping the lodge like a gang of thieves stripping a car and leaving behind only a chassis resting on its axles.

It didn't take any guesswork to know what they'd do to Wilmot when they finally took off to sell their stolen loot and look for a new victim. They'd lock him inside and burn the old lodge to the ground, burn any fingerprints and evidence left behind.

Pudge gritted his teeth. He'd be damned if he was going to wind up as ash at the bottom of a cold gray pile.

He searched for a door. Shuffling around, he kicked something. Something soft. It skittered on the floor. The sheriff looked down, expecting to see a rat. It wasn't. It was his hat. He picked up the short-brim Stetson, reached inside the crown, and used his thumb to push out the dent made by the hammer swung by Caleb, thankful that the brute had hit him with the face and not the claw.

Pudge clamped the Stetson back on his head and started feeling almost whole again. He resumed his search for a door and found it. A thick metal one. The handle wouldn't budge. Must be locked on the other side. No light leaked around its jambs. Must have rubber seals all the way around.

Pudge took a step back and thought. If he was in a meat locker, then it had to rely on some kind of refrigeration. He studied the walls again. Saw no vents. Saw no refrigerator coils. Saw Wilmot in his mind. Heard the old codger tell him he'd owned the place free and clear. An old codger who did things the old way to save money. He wouldn't need refrigeration during the winter when the meat locker was below the frozen ground, not when nature would do the job for free. But in summer when the lake was warm enough to swim in and the lodge open and full of hungry guests, how to keep the food cold? A variation of the same way in winter. Bring in big blocks of ice. But how to get them there?

Pudge pictured a sled sliding down the hill behind the ranch house. A sled he used to ride as a kid. A sled he watched Hattie ride. A sled he wished he could talk Johnny into riding. Maybe he would one day. Maybe the boy would get over his fear and anger and allow himself to be a kid.

If he was ever going to see that happen, then he had to get a move on. The sheriff started by moving shelves, patting walls. Finally, he found a hatch cover. Pried it open. Looked inside. A dark tunnel. A tunnel with a slippery wooden slide angling upward into the dark. The ice chute. It was as wide as his shoulders. He'd crawled through tunnels in Iwo Jima to go after General Tojo's boys who were holed up in caves. If he could crawl through them, then he could crawl up it.

The trick was doing it on his back. That way he could apply pressure against the sides with his palms while using his feet to push off on the rough top of the wooden chute that hadn't been slickened by decades of ice sliding down it. Scoot up it inch by inch. Like a caterpillar crawling upside down on the bottom of a leaf.

The trick worked and Pudge's head was soon pushing against another hatch door. His thick skull had withstood a hammer and he figured it would withstand hammering against the door too. He set his feet against the rough ceiling, pressed the sides with his palms, and scooted forward again. Old nails, pounded into old wood to hold the latch, juddered and squealed and then gave way. The hatch door swung open and Pudge slid out as slick as one of the newborn calves his daughter was probably delivering on a ranch back in Harney County right then.

He landed on a soft blanket of snow, but didn't stay put to enjoy being free. He knew he'd never be completely free until Caleb, Tina, and Dill no longer were.

Rolling onto his side, he did another push-up, and got to his feet. He stayed in a crouch as he made for the snowy woods that surrounded the ice-covered lake, all framed by the snow-mantled mountains. They weren't the only cold things. So was the ice in Sheriff Pudge Warbler's veins.

20

Shrieking wind shot sleet as pounding whitewater scoured the river canyon's walls that were the same color as the moonless night. Liz Bloom rode the raft's bouncing bow like a bronc buster, one hand pressing a folded shirt doubling as a compress to Loq's bloody chest, the other held high as she trained a powerful flashlight on the rapids ahead. We were both wearing headlamps, but mine was doing little to help light the way. Its beam bobbed and weaved with every push and pull of the oars as I fought to keep us in the main channel and out of chutes narrower than the gray Avon was wide.

"We're losing air," Liz yelled, her words quickly snatched away by the wind.

"Where?" I yelled back

"Front left tube."

"How can you be sure with all the water we're taking on?"

"Because it's sagging. Must've gotten punctured from a rock Jasper chucked."

I looked port, then starboard. My headlamp revealed what I

already knew. With nowhere to pull ashore and patch a leak, a deflated tube would sink us.

"Let's get some weight off it. You and Loq need to move to the stern."

"I'll need help lifting him."

I let go of the oars and got my hands under Loq's armpits. I heaved and Liz shoved his hips. We wrestled him over the thwart and onto the floor at my feet.

"He's good right here," I said as I grabbed the oars and straightened us out. "Now you."

Liz scrambled over the first and second thwarts and sat on the right rear tube beside all our gear. I kept one foot on the compress plastered to Loq's chest while I rowed.

We hit another long stretch of rapids. Liz was shining the flashlight over my shoulder. The bow was plowing into whitewater rather than surfing over it because of the sagging tube. Sink and we'd have to ride it out in our life jackets. That is, if we could manage to keep our heads above the sucking, churning cauldron.

"We need to lighten the load," I said. "Start tossing stuff overboard. Pots, pans, and the stove first. If that doesn't do it, then tents and clothes next. Weapons last. First landing spot we see, we beach it. Patch Loq and the raft."

"I weigh as much as all those things put together. I'll ride in the kayak."

"Too dangerous to try to board it in this whitewater. It'll capsize for sure."

"Watch me."

I cranked a look back. My headlamp illuminated Liz hauling in the towline. The red kayak nosed against our stern.

"Lift the right oar," she said.

I pulled it out of the water and pushed the blade toward the bow. She maneuvered the kayak until it rode alongside like a pontoon.

"You only have one shot," I said.

"I got this."

Liz held the kayak paddle in front of her like a tightrope walker's balance pole and swung her legs out and aimed her feet at the cockpit. She bounced up and down on the tube for lift and then launched herself, hovering in midair for what seemed way too long before knifing feet first into the cockpit. The force of her landing shot the kayak away from the raft, but the towline yo-yoed it back.

"I need to put the oar in the water," I said. "Fall back and I'll tow you."

Her headlamp jerked back and forth. "No, I'll lead and light the way."

Before I could say a word, she untied the towline and the kayak shot forward again.

I dipped my blade and began rowing after the much speedier craft as the raft's slumping bow continued to drag.

The blades on Liz's paddle were whirling as she dug and stroked to keep the narrow-hulled kayak straight. I was falling farther behind when the canyon entered a sharp bend to starboard. The weight of the water pouring over the punctured tube pulled the raft to port. I fought to stay with the main current, but steering was akin to turning a rudderless barge.

The canyon wall loomed ahead. I glanced over my shoulder and saw Liz's headlamp grow fainter. Her fate was in her own hands now. That and the Bruneau's.

"Brace," I yelled to Loq even though he lay unconscious beneath my foot.

The half-flat tube made a thwapping sound when it slapped the wall. I gave the oars all I had to fight the resulting suction and pulled the raft free. My headlamp lit flat water ahead.

Hoping it was a shallow along a bank, I stroked for it. At the last second, I let go of the oars, grabbed a throw line tied to the chicken line, and used the middle thwart as a trampoline for my own acrobatic leap.

Luck was with me when I hit the water—I only sank up to my knees. There was no time to enjoy good fortune. I quickly sloshed across to terra firma, hauled the foundering raft to shore, and tied it off. A quick survey revealed we'd landed on a rockfall at the base of the canyon wall. I spotted an opening beneath overlapping slabs. It was deeper than I was tall and had room to stand. Best of all it was dry inside. I fireman-carried Loq to it and placed him on the ground. Then I returned to the raft, unloaded some gear, and strung a tent fly across the mouth of the shelter to dull the wind's teeth.

Sticks had washed inside during a previous flood stage. They were dry and lit with little effort, not by smacking rocks against each other as the castaway fisherman claimed he'd done or with a Zippo that Chief Warrant Officer Jim Craig had given to Johnny Da Den, but by striking a waterproof match from the aluminum tube I carried in my pocket.

While the fire produced light and heat, I kept my headlamp switched on as I opened the first-aid kit and laid out fishing tackle. I was stripping olive feathers and gold thread from a fishhook tied to mimic a stonefly when Loq wheezed, gasped, and coughed.

"Where am I?" he rasped.

"A rock shelter downriver."

"You mean we ran?"

"To live and fight another day. Remember what happened?"

"Jasper needs a nail clipper."

"You've lost blood but not your sense of humor. That's going to help."

Loq wheezed and coughed again. "Where's Liz? Is she—"

"Alive, but the raft sprung a leak and she changed horses in the middle of the stream to help keep us afloat. She and the kayak are somewhere below us."

"Meaning on her own and you don't know where."

"Save your breath. You're going to need it."

"Why?"

I held up the featherless fly clamped by a pair of needle-nosed forceps I used for removing hooks from trout. "You need patching."

"Thought you were combat, not a corpsman."

"I helped medics more times than I care to remember."

"Hope they taught you how to sew."

"Marines don't do hope, right?"

"Seeing you with that needle, this one does now."

I pulled a length of monofilament through the eye and crimped the hook's barb. "You better bite down on a stick."

"Don't want to break off any teeth. Need all my weapons when Jasper tries to finish us off."

"We may be on the same side of the river as his cave, but we're miles downstream from it."

"You know he can go anywhere he wants."

I crouched over him. "Go ahead and pass out again so I don't have to kneel on you while I stitch."

"Can't. Got to stay awake."

"And I say, take five. If Jasper shows up, he won't get past me."

"No! It was my heart he tried to rip out. It's my fight. I earned that right."

"He could kill you next time."

"Then I'll greet my ancestors with honor."

"Have it your way."

I pulled the blood-soaked folded shirt from Loq's torn chest. Jasper's bear claws had sliced through his *Semper Fi* tattoo. I splashed the wounds with alcohol from the first-aid kit and dabbed them with clean gauze. Then I poked the homemade suture into flesh at the top of the first slash and pulled the fishing line tight.

Loq didn't wince. "When you're through, leave me the Shoshone knife and get out of here."

"I'll go, all right, at first light to search for Liz. Maybe there's enough room to hike along this section of the canyon. She could've found a place to take out like I did. Maybe she's sheltering nearby."

"That's one too many maybes. If she didn't drown, then Jasper found her and did to her what he did to the fishermen."

I concentrated on closing his wounds so I wouldn't have to think of her that way. "You know the rule. It's the same here as it was when we were in country. Nobody gets left behind. Not the living or the dead."

"We left Liver-Eating Johnson."

"Like you said, he could've been a *sko'gs*."

"Could be you and me are already *sko'gs* and don't know it yet."

"And could be this is all a nightmare, but it isn't since we're both awake. Now close your eyes and let me concentrate."

A howl piercing the veil of night silenced the river's thunder and rode an icy gust past the tent fly.

"Stitch faster, brother," Loq said. "*Tsa-ahu-bitts* is hungry."

"Roger that," I said and jabbed him with the fishhook needle again.

21

Loq lost his battle to stay conscious and I lost count of how many surgeon knots I tied closing his wounds. The ones that weren't too deep got taped shut after I packed them with gauze slathered with some tinctures in the first-aid kit that November had made from plants and who knows what else. Clean T-shirts torn into strips served as dressings to wrap his chest.

I added a couple of sticks to the fire when I finished and slumped against the slab wall with the shotgun across my lap. The howls had stopped along with the shrieks of wind. Even the sleet pelting the tent fly quieted. I knew I should catch twenty winks myself, but didn't want to miss a chance at blowing Jasper's head off if he poked his badger-skin cap into the rock shelter.

It wasn't rage, revenge, or bloodlust that drove me to that thinking. It was a cold, hard calculation of what gave me the best odds of surviving. Reason was the missing ingredient in Dr. Cannon's theory. While adrenaline pumped into the bloodstream certainly triggered a fight-or-flight reaction, my observations in the field led me to conclude that wild animals could choose between the two.

I'd seen crows at the Malheur refuge display intellect by learning how to clutch sticks between their beaks to pry seeds from crevices when food grew scarce. The same with herds of wild horses when they looked for plowed roads after a blizzard to speed their search for life-saving graze. A wildlife biologist I worked with theorized that bears exhibited intelligence comparable to higher primates after she documented them choosing certain models of cars over others to break into while prowling for groceries. The burly predators knew which ones had the easiest door handles to open.

Jasper was still a no-show when dawn broke and the color of the tent fly grew lighter. Loq's breathing was steady and blood hadn't seeped through his dressings. After putting more wood on the fire, I placed the obsidian dagger in his hand, shoved gear and a fleece pullover into a backpack, and started hiking downriver.

The rockfall had created a bank at the base of the canyon wall. It showed no sign of a trail made by animals, either the four-legged or two-legged kind. Little vegetation had gotten a roothold, so picking my way up, over, and around the slippery slabs took as much concentration as exertion. Thirty minutes later I reached the end of the bend where I'd last seen Liz Bloom and the red kayak. I pulled out my binoculars and started scanning.

The rapids were daunting with the nearest stretch roller-coastering over submerged boulders. The trenches between the frothy crests were half as deep as the fourteen-foot Avon was long. I brushed away the image of the much smaller kayak nose-diving into them and Liz leaning as far back as she could to try and keep from being catapulted out of the cockpit.

The big rocks on the river bottom didn't stay submerged for

long. Dark basalt haystacks broke the surface and acted like bumpers on a gigantic pinball machine. Running the gauntlet without getting bashed to pieces would take an expert kayaker. The odds against a novice being able to do it at night were unfathomable.

Gorge rose in my throat as I thought of Liz capsizing and then struggling to keep her head above water as the angry current hurled her against rocks and whirlpools dragged her battered body down.

Though she hadn't revealed much about her personal life, something in her past had given her plenty of courage. She showed that when she fended off the Backwoods Rapist, tried to arrest Jasper, and again when she boarded the kayak midriver. I liked the way she'd turned it right back on Loq when he asked if she was a senator's daughter. Maybe things had been easy for her because of who her father was, like going to the best schools or spending vacations at a family compound in Maine where he helped her land a summer job at the state wildlife agency that turned into a full-time position and a stepping stone to the district supervisor's job with the US Fish and Wildlife Service. But guts weren't handed down. You had to grow them on your own.

I wondered what her favorite music was, if she liked to dance, if she had brothers and sisters, a best friend, a boyfriend. No matter how easy Liz may have had it, I vowed to do for her what I'd done for every one of the KIAs in my squad. After I took the Freedom Bird home, I visited their loved ones, told them how courageous their son, husband, father, brother was, how he'd spent his last days, and how he fought like hell up until the moment he died. I'd do the same for Liz if she'd drowned, no matter if her father was a senator, governor, carpenter, or boilermaker. They deserved that. And most of all, she did.

The Bruneau appeared to exhaust itself past the lethal chain of black haystacks. The water returned to its usual color of tea. I caught a snatch of bright red and zeroed in on it. The kayak was wedged between two rocks near shore. I slowly moved the binoculars up and down and from side to side. No paddle filled the field of view. No Liz either. Alive or dead.

I focused further downriver and repeated the search pattern. Still nothing. I scanned back upriver, stopping at each haystack to see if maybe Liz had been able to crawl on one after capsizing. Nothing.

Swallowing gorge again, I started to lower the binoculars when rays from the rising sun reached the canyon and reflected off something. I twisted the focus knob. The shiny aluminum shaft of the kayak paddle stood upright between two slabs on the same rockfall shelf where I stood not thirty yards upriver. Liz was curled beside it.

She didn't respond when I yelled for her as I scrambled down. She still didn't respond when I rolled her on her back. Blue lips stained a lifeless face with skin the color of campfire ash. She was icy to the touch, her headlamp and wool cap were missing, and her tousled hair was streaked white with frost.

I tilted her head, pinched her nose, sealed her cold mouth with my lips, and blew for a full second. Once. Twice. Three times.

"Breathe, dammit!" I shouted. "Breathe."

I pulled her into a sitting position, slapped her back, and laid her down again. I unbuckled her life jacket, threw it aside, and was about to begin chest compressions when I realized I needn't have bothered.

Without the thick vest on, I could see her chest rising and falling. She'd been breathing on her own all along, but so slowly and shallowly that I didn't sense it when my lips were pressed against hers. It was no wonder she seemed dead at first touch.

Hypothermic after having been tossed from the kayak and spending the night soaking wet in the freezing wind, her core body temperature must've dropped ten degrees.

"Got to get you warm," I told her. "Got to light a fire."

I reached for the aluminum tube of waterproof matches in my jeans pocket, but stopped; they were useless with no wood on the rocky shelf. Not even a dried sagebrush in sight.

My mind raced. Sitting in Mrs. Wilsey's stuffy office at the Medford orphanage flashed and then another sweltering room came into view. High school. Science class. A teacher trying to keep the attention of his drowsy students as he explained the laws of thermodynamics. Heat exchange, he droned, occurred when two bodies brought in contact would change their temperatures until they reached the same degree. Friction was another law. Finally, he got attention. Winks and laughs erupted as girls giggled and boys made jokes. The teacher threw up his hands. "Class dismissed!"

The down in Liz's wet jacket was clumped. I unzipped it and pulled it off. As I unbuttoned her shirt, I began talking to her.

"It's Nick. You're drenched. Freezing. I need to undress you. It's the only way to save you. Trust me, okay?"

I stripped off her shirt and T-shirt. Her skin was ashy and had no goosebumps. Her boots, socks, and jeans came off next. The heavy wet denim had stuck to her legs and was hard to pull down. Still no goosebumps. The only items left were her bra, panties, and the choker of polished turquoise beads. I kept my eyes fixed on it, telling myself it must be a good-luck charm since the rapids hadn't torn it off when she went in the drink. No way I was going to mess with magic right then, and so it stayed put.

Although her underwear was soaked too, the instinctive sense that I was walking right into danger like I used to get on patrol warned me to halt. But another look at her blue lips and ghostly pale face swept away any reservations. Leaving them on would reduce heat transfer and could make the difference between saving or losing her. It was all or nothing.

"You got to trust me, Liz. Just trust me," I said and slipped her bra and panties off.

Using the fleece pullover as a towel, I rubbed her from head to toe, but blood didn't rise to color her skin nor did she wake up. I removed my jacket and put it on her, leaving it unzipped. Then I ripped open my shirt, sat down, and pulled Liz onto my lap. I wrapped her legs around my waist, encircled my arms around her beneath the jacket, and hugged her, pressing my bare chest against hers, tucking her head beneath my chin to keep it from lolling.

I started rocking to create friction, humming to help keep time. I heard the music I listened to in high school, listened to how The Beatles had changed everything. Heard the songs and bands we blasted on tinny transistors in country to get amped up before heading out on patrol. "Born to Be Wild." "Gimme Shelter." Janis Joplin. Cream. Heard the coming-down songs we played when we got back from a fire fight. Crosby, Stills, and Nash. Marvin Gaye. Otis Redding.

I kept humming, kept rocking, kept remembering, kept rubbing Liz, and lost track of time until goosebumps started rising beneath my palms and nipples grew hard against my chest. Eyelashes fluttered on my throat, followed by a moan and then a sigh. I stopped humming.

"Fire," Liz mumbled. "Fire and..."

"Can't light one," I said. "Got matches, but nothing to burn."

"Rain," she mumbled.

"It stopped. The wind too."

"Song. Guessing game as kids."

I stopped rocking to and fro, loosened my hug, and gently pulled away so I could see her face. The lips were still tinged with blue, but her skin wasn't nearly as ashy. Her pupils were dilated, but life was returning to the brown irises.

"Welcome back," I said.

"James," she mumbled.

"No, it's Nick."

"James Taylor. His song. 'Fire and Rain.'"

"Oh, what I was humming. Score one for you. I've seen fire and I've seen rain, sunny days and lonely times." I kept track of her breathing, kept track of her eyes, urging the pupils to constrict.

"Mmm, good. But 'Light... Light My Fire' be better."

I hummed the opening notes. "That one's easy. The Doors."

"Who's... who's talking about Jim Morrison?"

That got a laugh and Liz managed one too, though it was weaker than the way she'd laughed before. Still, it was a good laugh, and even better because it meant she was alive.

"Tell me what happened," I said.

"Don't want to. Don't want you to stop holding me." She slipped her arms around my neck and nestled her cheek against mine, burrowing even closer against my skin as if she could extract more heat from every pore.

I started rocking her again, starting humming again. Some Neil Young. Loggins and Messina. Linda Ronstadt too. My mind drifted to what I'd seen on wildlife refuges, things I'd learned about animals and their behavior. From crows with sticks and bears opening car doors to what different species did to ensure their kind's survival. I saw bighorn rams butting heads over ewes at the Sheldon refuge, doe pronghorns at Hart Mountain who selected the bucks for mating, and a western grebe pair dancing a pas-de-deux at Deer Flat as part of their mutually-agreed-upon courtship ritual.

I felt the slow burn of Gemma and me dancing around each other for months on end before finally letting down our guards and admitting what we'd both known the moment we met, saw her sleeping next to me beside the woodburning stove in the old lineman's shack, our wedding on a rise behind the ranch with a view of Steens Mountain, the birth of our daughter, the day we brought Johnny home. I felt the strain of all the responsibilities we'd taken on and how it was starting to wear us down as relentlessly as time and sun and wind loosened a slab of rock on a canyon wall and sent it tumbling into the river below.

But mostly what I felt was Liz's bare skin beneath my palms and her breasts pressing against my chest and the laws of thermodynamics reaching a boiling point.

I stopped rocking, stopped humming. "Tell me what happened on the river."

"Why?"

"For the record. The one the sheriff will want."

This time her laugh was a little stronger. "My turn." She started humming. "Need a hint?"

"Nope. Rolling Stones. 'Play With Fire.'"

"Story of my life."

I sang the lyrics in my head. A girl with diamonds, pretty clothes, a chauffeur to drive her car, and the refrain. Don't play with me 'cause you're playing with fire. Maybe she was a senator's daughter, after all.

"Tell me what happened on the river, how you saved yourself, because that's who you really are."

"Think so?"

"I know so. Come on, tell me what happened. I learned talking about something harrowing . . . well, like combat, and that's what you went through, talking can help."

"They tell you that at Walter Reed?"

"Among other things. Face your demons."

"Like facing Jasper?"

"And eventually I will again, but right here and now, tell me what happened on the river. How you did it. Why you did it."

Liz took a deep breath and shuddered. I could feel it all the way down her body, right down to where her naked rear was weighing on my groin.

"Thought I was drowning. Dying. Didn't want to. It was the river or me and it wasn't going to be me."

"And so you fought to stay alive."

"Damn right."

"Did the kayak hit a rock, a wave capsize it?"

"I turned around to look for you. Couldn't see you. Wanted to. And then rolling upside down. Happened so fast." Liz took a deep breath and when she exhaled, it moaned against my cheek. "Held the paddle. Never let it go. Here somewhere."

"It is. You stuck it upright to signal. Smart move. It's how I spotted you."

"Mmm."

I rubbed her sides, her back. "You're strong in body, mind, and spirit. As my old friend Tuhudda Will would say, 'Life's fire burns bright inside you. This is so.'"

"He related to Nagah Will?"

"His grandfather. He raised him."

"But he doesn't live on your ranch."

"Tuhudda journeyed to the spirit world last year."

"Do you miss him?"

"Every day, but we still speak. He honored me by choosing to become my spirit guide."

"What's that?"

"I'm still learning, but basically a way to open your eyes to all the worlds around you."

"Mmm. I could use some of that myself. I wish I could meet him."

"Maybe you still can."

"How's that?"

"Tuhudda has a way of showing up."

"Like you." Liz shifted again and wrapped her legs tighter around my waist. "Thank you."

"What for?"

"Not giving up on me. Coming to look for me. Warming me this way."

"Heat exchange," I said. "The laws of thermodynamics."

"I meant in here." Liz leaned back, causing the jacket to fall open even more. She took my hand and held it against her breast. Her polished turquoise choker gleamed, and so did her brown eyes. "I don't trust easily, Nick, but I trust you."

As I felt her heart beat beneath her breast, felt the fire flaming within it, she closed her eyes and lifted her chin. Her lips parted and they were no longer blue, but beckoning. The sun rose higher. The rays grew stronger. The rapids' roars loudened in my ears. The river's call became a siren song and I saw fire and I saw rain because I knew if I kissed her, it would be like putting in on the Bruneau at flood stage. There'd be no turning back. We'd be swept away with no stopping until the take-out, pushing and pulling with and against the current the whole way. It'd be reckless and thrilling and dangerous and remind us over and over that we'd both survived Jasper's attack and drowning and were alive. Very much alive.

22

Loq was sitting beside the raft studying a topographical map when we got back. I didn't raise an eyebrow that he was up and around, but he raised one at me when he saw Liz holding onto my arm and wearing only my jacket and the fleece pullover tied around her waist like a slit skirt.

"You didn't drown," he said to her.

"And you didn't bleed out," she said.

"I underestimated you. It won't happen again."

"Nor I you, even if you decide to wrestle a giant with bear claws again."

I asked how he was feeling and if the stitches were holding. He looked down his high cheekbones as if to say, "What stitches?"

After putting the kayak paddle down, I retrieved Liz's gear bag from the back of the raft. She carried it inside the rock shelter to get changed, closing the tent fly behind her.

Loq nodded at the paddle. "Where's the kayak?"

"Further downriver. I couldn't get to it."

"But you got to the paddle."

"Liz had it. She never let it go after capsizing in a wicked stretch of whitewater. When she made it to shore, she stuck it upright as a signal and then blacked out from hypothermia. I might've missed seeing it if I hadn't gotten there right when the sun rose and shined on it."

Loq looked up at the sky. It was past daybreak. Long past. He looked back at me. "How far away was she?"

"About a thirty minute hike. The rock shelf here ends where she was."

"She doesn't look frozen now."

"Not anymore."

He looked downriver. "Don't see smoke from a fire."

"Couldn't make one. Nothing to burn."

He looked at the sun's position again and then at the rock shelter where Liz was changing and then back at me. "So I see."

"What's that supposed to mean?"

"You tell me."

"If you got something to say, then say it."

Loq grunted. "She's lucky you found her."

I let it go. "What's with the map?"

"I discovered a way off the river."

"You mean, hike out instead of running it all the way to the take-out?"

"We'd still have to run it."

"Then why get off it?"

"So I can go back to the box canyon. Three weeks from now when the Bruneau drops, other people will be coming down it. Jasper can't be left free to do to them what he did to the two fishermen and tried to do to us."

"That's why we're going to get to the take-out as fast as we can and call for backup. Our plan, remember? And then there's the little matter of that fishing line holding your chest together. You really think you're in any shape to go up against Jasper again? I treated the wounds with medicine November concocted, but you need real antibiotics, not to mention a real surgeon and real sutures."

"November's medicine is stronger than anything a hospital has. And there's nothing wrong with my memory either. Especially the part where Jasper nearly sent me to the spirit world. You could've bought it yourself. Still could. The raft could spring a leak again or flip and none of us get lucky next time. No one left alive to warn anybody about Jasper."

He mimicked a hawk's warning cry. "Gemma would alert the sheriff's department when you're overdue getting home. They'd launch a search party. You know she'd demand to be part of it. Pudge too. You want them to run into Jasper?"

There was only one answer and I could hear Sgt. Hardass yelling it loud and clear.

"Show me on the map," I said.

"Show you what?" Liz said as she joined us and handed back my jacket and fleece.

"Loq found a possible route back upriver."

Her head cocked at me. It wasn't that long ago I was looking at her face thinking she was dead, only to see her come alive in my arms.

"You mean, back to the box canyon. The cave. To prevent Jasper from killing again." They weren't questions.

"It's what I aim to do," Loq said.

"No, it's what *we* aim to do. District supervisors take the same oath as rangers to uphold the law. We go together or no one goes at all."

"Works for me," Loq said.

"One for all and all for one," I muttered.

Liz mimed a rapier's parry and thrust. "A regular d'Artagnan, aren't you?"

I didn't laugh because it would take more than gallantry and fancy swordplay to defeat Jasper. The fact he hadn't hunted us down during the night told me he was one step ahead and waiting for us to return to hunt him on his turf and on his terms.

We huddled around the topo map and Loq pointed out a spot where the contour lines showed a drop in elevation on the near side of a thin blue line that ran perpendicular to the river.

"It's a feeder spring to the Bruneau and comes down a draw from these hot springs. From there we can climb up and then cut across this plateau." He drew his finger northwest across contour lines. "It'll put us right on top of the box canyon."

I checked the map's scale and did the math. "Looks to be about a seven-mile hike as the crow flies. Of course, crows don't have to worry about contour lines. We'll have to scramble up and down gullies and then climb down the cliff to get to a spot where we can rappel to the canyon floor."

"And that's our way back up and out," Liz said. "Like Jerry said, we leave a rope hanging."

Mentioning the dead fisherman cast a pall, but it also served to remind me what I'd said over Only Owen's cairn about finding justice for his family. I'd do the same for Jerry Johnson whether he was a *sko'gs* or not.

Despite having nearly sunk us, the puncture on the raft's tube was only the size of a thumbnail. I fetched the repair kit, dried the surface around the hole, and made short work of applying a patch. We broke camp while the glue dried, and when it had, we reinflated the patched tube with a foot pump and shoved off.

Liz and Loq rode on the front thwart and I took up my rowing position on the ice chest. Having scouted the rapids when I was searching for Liz helped when I lined us up for the nasty stretch of whitewater at the bend. The raft shot up the face of the first wave and plunged into the trench behind. At that point, momentum took over and I concentrated on working the oars to keep us straight as we rode the roller-coaster.

I'd already made the decision to favor the left side when it came time to run the gauntlet of haystacks. It was a good plan as whitewater rafting plans went, but the river had other ideas. We shot between the first two stacks and slid past the third, but colliding currents on the backside hurled us straight at the fourth. If I cranked it and cut too close, the oar would strike rock and snap. Cut too wide and there wouldn't be enough time to steer past the next one.

"Grab the chicken line," I yelled. "Going to play bumper pool."

Praying the patch would hold, I aimed directly at the haystack. We rode a boiling cushion of water up it. The bow bumped rather than struck bare rock and I used the recoil for a boost as I heaved back on the oars to slide us off while spinning us right. The current grabbed the stern and pulled us backward around the stack. Once clear, I jammed the oars down and spun the Avon around so we faced downriver again. I raised the left oar out of the water, shoving the blade behind me. We squeaked safely past the last stack.

"Nice move," Loq called over his shoulder.

"Kayak's up ahead," I said as we entered the calm stretch of tea-colored water.

The red hull bore scratches, but no holes or fractures. Liz tied a line to the bow and it trailed behind us as we drifted down to where the feeder creek from the hot springs joined the Bruneau. The bank was flat and made for an easy take-out. Enough water was coming down the creek to let us drag the boats up a short distance.

"That should keep them safe in case a downpour raises the river any higher," I said.

"We got another hour of daylight," Loq said. "Want to camp here or at the hot springs? It's not far."

"Hot springs," Liz said. "I'd love a bath as long as it doesn't smell like rotten eggs."

I unfastened the perimeter line from the D-rings and shoved it into a pack along with the throw lines and a bag of carabiners and pulleys. We carried that and other gear up the feeder creek to two pools ringed by sagebrush and flat rocks.

"The ancient ones used these hot springs," Loq said, pointing to petroglyphs on a rock face.

"One's a directional," I said. "Not sure what the other is."

"It's a warning about an evil spirit in the area."

"*Tsa-ahu-bitts*," Liz said. "Are you still convinced the demon is real?"

"The ancients did. Who am I not to honor their beliefs?"

"What about you?" she said to me.

"Jasper's clearly a monster, but I'm of the opinion he's the human kind."

"What makes you say that?"

"The ladder in his cave. If he's an evil spirit or a giant that can leap across rivers, why's he need one to climb up and down? I'm sticking with him being an extra-large-sized poacher dealing in exotic animal parts. Making people think he's *Tsa-ahu-bitts* by hanging dead elk from trees and dressing like Sasquatch is a pretty effective 'Keep Out' sign."

"And if they ignore it, he murders them?"

"My hunch is Jasper doesn't see the difference between four-leggeds and two-leggeds anymore after having killed so many animals. He's developed a taste for hunting humans because we're more of a challenge than a deer is."

"It's all the more reason we have to prevent him from doing it again," Liz said.

"You know he's not going to let himself be captured and taken to jail. Not by us. Not by anyone."

She nodded. "But we have to try. That's our job. We have to

protect the public and wildlife too, especially the endangered species. He can't be allowed to kill anything again."

Loq and I set up camp and lit a fire while Liz undressed and slipped into one of the pools. "Ah, it's hot," we heard her say as she settled into the water as darkness settled over the high lonesome. "Wonderfully hot."

"You going to take a bath too?" Loq asked me.

"No, I'm going to go over the map some more and figure out how we can find an element of surprise to spring on Jasper. Knock yourself out."

Loq shook his head and waved a hand in front of his chest. "I don't want to dilute the power of November's medicine. We can figure out a plan together."

"Let me make some tea first. You need to keep drinking so you'll keep producing blood to replenish what you lost. You can't afford to lose another drop."

"I don't plan on spilling any more. At least none of my own."

I put a pot of water on to boil and saw Jasper's red eyes glaring in the flames beneath it. I blinked his image away. After the tea steeped, Loq and I drank it while laying out scenarios and poking holes in them until we agreed on one that seemed good enough to start putting X's and O's on the map to show who'd go where and who'd do what.

Liz finished her bath, got dressed, and brought fixings for supper over to the fire. "How does lobster ravioli for dinner sound?"

"Blackpowder packed a lobster in the ice chest?" I said.

"I wish. It was a favorite dish when I lived in Maine and thought we could pretend that's what this can of Chef Boyardee is."

It broke the tension we'd all been feeling, and we grinned like fools as we ate the spaghetti and meatballs.

23

After supper, Loq said he was going to turn in so he'd be ready to stand watch in four hours. I washed dishes in the creek and then brought them back to the fire to dry. Liz was still sitting there, her knees drawn under her chin.

"You must be beat too," I said. "There's no need to have two people standing guard tonight."

"I know I should be exhausted, but I'm still keyed up. It's like having a hangover in reverse. Has that ever happened to you?"

"All the time until I discovered November's tea. That and stargazing." I looked skyward. "After last night's weather, it's good to see them again. They tell stories like my old friend Tuhudda Will does."

"Can you see him up there?"

"Sometimes. He travels among them."

"What makes the stars so different here?"

I brought her a mug of white sage and peppermint tea and sat beside her. "You can see them better because there's nothing around to drown out their stories. They sparkle brighter here than any place I've ever been."

"Does that include Vietnam?"

"Especially Saigon."

"I still want to hear the rest of the story of how Johnny got from there to here. What happened when his mother was murdered by the owner of the boom-boom club?"

"He fled and had to fight to survive on the streets. It was either them or him and he decided it wasn't going to be him. Sound familiar?"

"I knew there was a reason I liked him." Liz leaned her head on my shoulder. "Tell me more."

∼

JOHNNY THREW himself on his mother's body and began to wail after the GI with the tiger tattoo shot Duong Pham. Only his name wasn't Johnny then. He didn't know what it was. His mother had always called him *cho con*, my puppy.

The girl who'd been entertaining the GI came running from her curtained cubicle. She pulled Johnny off Thien and told him to run. "As fast as you can and never come back. Duong Pham's wife will beat all us girls, but you, she'll kill." She grabbed Johnny's tobacco tin that the boom-boom club owner had found under the bed, scooped some of the scattered *xu* coins into it, and clasped his hands around it. "Take it and run. Never look back. Never return." When Johnny didn't budge, she slapped him. Finally, he scampered away, and she buried her face in her hands and cried.

Johnny ran out the back and was quickly swallowed by the hustle and bustle of Tu Do Street. Crying and clutching the tobacco tin and occasionally checking his pocket to make sure he still had the silver lighter with the fire-breathing red dragon's head on the front, he careened between honking, sputtering motorbikes and three-wheeled bicycle taxis whose drivers cursed at him to get out of their way. A water buffalo pulling a cart blocked his path. He tripped while going around it and fell to the pavement. It was strewn with garbage and broken glass.

Crying and bleeding, he crawled into the nearest doorway and huddled inside it. The river of people flowing past never slowed. No one stopped to check if the frightened little boy who was hurt and alone needed help. To them, he'd already become invisible.

His stomach eventually drove him from the doorway. "I'm hungry," he told a hunched old woman who was carrying crates of live chickens roped to her back. She never broke stride. "I'm hungry," he told a man who was leaning against a motorbike and smoking a cigarette. The man looked up at the gloomy sky and blew smoke rings. "I'm hungry," he told a girl who wore lots of make-up and was dressed like his mother. "We all are," she said and kept walking.

Johnny saw the cart where just hours before Thien had bought *banh pia* for them. He asked the vendor for a mooncake. The man ignored him. "I want mooncake," he said again. The man finally said, "Twenty *xu*." Johnny opened the tobacco tin and started to fish for a coin.

The man grabbed the tobacco tin and shoved it into his pocket. Johnny asked him to give it back. "Beat it," the man said. When the boy started crying, the man hailed a passing policeman. "This little thief is trying to steal my mooncakes." The policeman seized Johnny's ear and dragged him down the street, beating him on the back of his shoulders and legs with a bamboo baton. When he finally let him go, he said, "Come around here again and I'll take you to the field of dead dogs."

Johnny huddled in another doorway, hugging his shins, and burying his face in his knees. The policeman scared him. A field full of dead dogs scared him. He rocked back and forth and sobbed for his mother.

"Why are you crying?"

He looked up. A little girl was standing before him. It was hard to tell from all the grimy tangles, but her hair seemed almost as yellow as his mother's special friend from the boom-boom club, Jim Craig. Patches of pale skin showed through the streaks of dirt on her bare arms and legs.

"Why are you crying?" she said again.

"Because my mother is dead and I'm hungry and a man took all my money."

"You had money?"

He nodded.

"How did you get it?"

"From American GIs."

Her head cocked. "You mean, you stole it."

He shook his head. "They pay me."

"What for?"

"Bring cigarettes and beer."

"What man took your money?

Johnny pointed up the street at the *banh pia* cart.

She took Johnny's hand and pulled him up. "Come with me."

As she led him, she whistled. Two scrawny boys dressed in filthy T-shirts and ragged shorts stepped out of an alleyway. They were a little bigger than Johnny. The girl said something to them and they quickly ran ahead and whistled.

The yellow-haired girl didn't let go of Johnny's hand. She walked right up to the mooncake cart.

"Give him back his money," she said.

The vendor ignored her.

She said it again.

He backhanded her. "Scram you filthy little *bui doi* or I'll turn you into a mooncake and eat you."

The yellow-haired girl whistled.

A bunch of kids led by the two boys dressed in filthy T-shirts swarmed the cart. While they grabbed mooncakes, the girl pickpocketed the man. She whistled and then took off running, dragging Johnny with her. The other kids scattered as the man screamed for the policeman.

The girl and Johnny raced down Tu Do Street with the policeman and *banh pia* man in pursuit. They cut through alleys and entered a rabbit warren of tin-roofed shacks and thatched hooches that lined both sides of an open ditch filled with raw sewage. She halted at one shack, moved a loose board, and pulled him inside. It was a goat shed.

They pushed their way through the bleating animals and crouched in the far corner among piles of dung. "Shh," she said, and held a finger to his lips.

Footsteps echoed outside. The policeman was striking the walls with his bamboo baton while the man who sold *banh pia* described what'd he do to the yellow-haired girl when he caught her. He'd tie her up in his shack and have his way, and then after he tired of her, sell her to other men like he sold them mooncakes. The policeman made a grunting noise and said he'd be his first customer, but, per usual, wouldn't pay. Of course not, the *banh pia* seller said quickly.

When the sounds of the men's laughter and the bamboo baton striking the walls grew fainter, the loose board swung to the side and the two boys with filthy T-shirts slipped inside.

The bigger of the pair looked at Johnny. "Who's he?"

The yellow-haired girl shrugged. "What's your name?"

"*Cho con,*" Johnny said.

"That's a pet name for a baby."

"So?"

"You need a real name. American GIs give you money. All GIs are Johnny. We'll call you Johnny. Johnny *Da den* because you have black skin."

"My skin is black?"

"Blacker than mine. Blacker than theirs." She pointed to the two boys with Amerasian features.

"What about my *xu* coins?"

"Not yours, ours. We are like Uncle *Ho*. Like Viet Cong. We share everything. But you can have this back." She handed him the empty tobacco tin.

The smaller of the two boys held out a mooncake. "Here Johnny *Da den*. You're one of us now."

From that day on, Johnny *Da den* was no longer a *cho con*, but a *bui doi*, a child of the dusty streets. He shared everything with the girl and two boys, everything except the silver lighter with the fire-breathing red dragon's head on it. That was his and his alone. Every time he looked at it, he pictured his mother. She'd become a powerful, magical dragon and would always protect him.

Weeks passed. Months. A year. The days were a blur for Johnny. He and his three young companions continued to live in the goat shed and spent their waking hours always hungry, always scrounging for scraps of food on the streets, always avoiding the policeman with the bamboo baton.

Whenever Johnny spotted American soldiers, he'd go up to them and speak the words he'd learned at the boom-boom club. "You number one GI. You want boo coo boom-boom? I take you. You hungry? I take you to boo coo chop chop. You want dew? I get for you. Number one dew. No swamp grass."

Sometimes they'd laugh and flip him a coin or two. Other times they'd have him guide them, tipping him on their way in, tipping him for bringing them packs of L&Ms and Kools, bottles of beer, and joints.

He shared his earnings with the yellow-haired girl and two boys. She took the money and bought food from street vendors and the *mama-sans* who raised chickens in their tin-roofed shacks and hooches, had little gardens out back. The four would huddle in the goat shed and eat what she brought back, washing it down with milk they squeezed from their stablemates.

One night, Johnny went up to a group of four GIs drinking beer outside a club on Tu Do Street. He was about to tell them he could take them to eat boo coo chop chop when he noticed one soldier had a patch with a fire-breathing red dragon's head sewn on his uniform.

"Orient Express number one," he said, pointing to it.

"Right on, my man. We kick ass," the soldier said. "Say, how you know about the Seventh Transportation Battalion. You some kinda pint-sized spy?"

"Jim Craig. Number one friend of my mother. Give me this." Johnny flashed the silver lighter with the dragon head and motto crest.

One of the soldiers cracked, "Looks like whoever this Jim brother be gave the mama more than a Zippo."

The four clinked their beer bottles. "Hooah!" they cheered.

When the laughter died down, Johnny said to the one with the dragon insignia, "You know Jim Craig? You take me to him?"

The GI shook his head. "Sorry, my man. Can't say I heard of him. Battalion's got lots of units, hundreds of personnel. Why?"

"He number one. Can help me."

"Help you how?"

"Give me job. I work hard."

"You work as hard as you're hustling now, I don't doubt it. When's the last time you saw him?"

Johnny shrugged. A year? Maybe longer."

"That's a tour or two ago. He's long gone and wearing civvies by now." Seeing Johnny frown, he quickly added, "Tell you what, my man, I run into this Jim Craig, I'll let him know you're asking for him. Okay?"

"Okay," Johnny said. "You want chop chop now? Boom-boom? I take you. All number one."

"That's okay. We good here, but take this. Buy yourself sumpin' to eat. You skinnier than my grandma's cat got locked in the basement with last year's Christmas lights." He handed him a 500 *dong* bill.

Johnny said thanks and raced back to the goat shed. The yellow-haired girl was there. He handed her the money. "We eat plenty tonight."

She clapped her hands. "We'll have a feast. I know a *mama-san* cook up *ga nuong* for us."

"And get something sweet too," the bigger of the two boys said.

"*Banh pia*," Johnny said, remembering the sweet mooncakes he'd eaten with his mother.

"Yes, mooncakes for everyone," she said.

The three boys' mouths were watering as she slipped out of the goat shed. They were still watering an hour later when she hadn't returned. "It doesn't take this long to cook chicken and rice," the bigger boy said. "Maybe she's still looking for mooncakes?" said the smaller boy.

Mooncakes, Johnny thought. He shouldn't have mentioned them. All this time, they'd gone out of their way to avoid the man with the *banh pia* cart.

"I'll go look for her," he said.

"We'll go too," the bigger boy said.

They squeezed through the opening by moving the board and split up. The two boys with the filthy shirts ran down the alley to the first *mama-san* who raised chickens. Johnny headed back to Tu Do Street and the mooncake cart.

People were lined up in front of it. He didn't see the girl with the yellow hair. He also didn't see the man who sold mooncakes. Someone in line said he'd be back in a few minutes.

Johnny started to turn away when something stung his arm.

He turned toward whatever it was and saw the bamboo baton swinging at his head. Crack! He didn't duck fast enough.

"Got you," the policeman said.

He grabbed Johnny's ear and yanked him into the alley, striking him a few more times with his baton.

"Let me go," Johnny cried. "I didn't do nothing."

"You're *bui doi*. No different than a dog run over on the street. And that's where I'm taking you."

Johnny grabbed onto his wrist to try and get him to let go, but the policeman only tightened his grip on his ear as he dragged him down the alley. The little boy cried for help, but nobody did anything to help him. Nobody said a word to the policeman or tried to stop him. Most looked down at their rubber sandals.

The alley grew darker the farther they went. The policeman gave Johnny another swat with the bamboo baton when he stumbled.

"I knew you'd come looking for your little *bui doi* friend with the yellow hair," the policeman said and smacked his lips. "She's a mooncake now."

Johnny's tears turned from ones of rage to fright. The strength was giving out in his legs and when he stumbled again, the policeman dragged him like a sack of rice through puddles and mud and over rocks and refuse.

Finally, they stopped. Glowing embers hovered like fireflies in the smoke that rose from piles of burning garbage and filled the night air. Johnny's eyes stung from the fumes and stink.

"The field of dead dogs," the policeman said. "Listen! The *con ken ken* are feasting. Can you hear the crack of the dogs' bones and ripping of their flesh? The vultures here eat day and night. Soon they'll be eating you."

"Please," Johnny cried. "Please don't kill me. I'm only a little boy."

"No, you're not. You're *bui doi*. Worse than filth. Worse than dead dogs."

Johnny threw up his hands as the policeman raised his bamboo baton, readying to bring it down on his skull.

But then one of the dead-dog bones being eaten by the vultures cracked louder than all the rest and an ember firefly bigger and brighter than all the others landed on the policeman's forehead. The bamboo baton fell from his hand and then he fell too.

A figure cast in red by the flames of the burning garbage walked toward Johnny. The red dragon had come to save him.

"Mama," he cried.

The red dragon kicked the policeman with the bullet hole in his forehead and then holstered a pistol. He reached out a hand, not a claw, to the boy.

"Come, little comrade," the man dressed in the all-black uniform of the Viet Cong said. "Policemen are the people's enemy. Saigon is falling. Victory will be ours."

Johnny *Da den* took the guerrilla's hand and his journey from Tu Do Street to No Mountain continued.

24

Loq kicked the foot of my sleeping bag, bringing me wide awake with my gun drawn. He didn't flinch seeing it aimed at his chest. "Coffee's on."

A few stars still twinkled overhead. Most had melted away. It'd been four hours since I finished telling Liz about Johnny, and Loq took over watch.

"All quiet on the western front?" I said as I threw off the sleeping bag and pulled on my boots.

"Too quiet."

"That one of your lines from when you were making the movie?"

"The big-money star playing the gunslinger said it. Took a few takes because every time he did, someone would sneeze 'cliché.'"

"You," I said.

He shrugged.

I hooked my thumb at Liz's mummy bag. "Aren't you going to wake her?"

"Let her sleep while we talk by the fire."

"About the plan."

"That too."

"What's the *too*?"

Loq waited until I poured myself coffee and we were standing beside the campfire. "You and Liz."

"We may not be *Maklak* warriors, but you know what I bring to a fight. As for Liz? She's proven she's brave."

"That's not what I'm talking about. There's a hundred different ways today can go sideways. Now's the time I need to know how many of them could be on account you're thinking more about her than what needs doing."

"You mean, thinking if I'm doing everything I can to keep her from getting killed? The same as it's been all along. Liz may have forced this trip on us, but it doesn't mean you and I are any less responsible for her. Or to each other, for that matter."

"If your eyes refuse to see what's going on, let mine tell you. I saw the way you two were when you came back from finding her and again last night sitting by the fire."

"You're seeing it wrong."

"Then tell me how?"

"It's none of your business."

"Today makes it mine."

I drank some coffee. Breathed in, breathed out. Calm was there somewhere and I needed to find it right away.

"This one time. There won't be a second," I said. "Liz was half-frozen and at the edge of death. We exchanged trust and body heat. It created a bond between us, like a sacred obligation to honor the trade because it gave her back her life and made me responsible for it. I can't find any better way to explain it than that."

Loq didn't let go of me with his gaze. "Word of advice? Find one before you get home or you'll lose something you'd already found."

As I watched him cross the campsite to wake Liz, I recalled

November's warning that I risked losing myself on the Bruneau. First the old healer and now Loq. What did they know that I didn't? I looked at the coffee swirling in my mug, but it held no answers.

Liz got up and helped herself to coffee while Loq busied himself breaking camp. I made everyone hot oatmeal because I'd learned in 'Nam that Napoleon was right: an army marches on its stomach. After breakfast, we double-checked our gear and moved out.

Loq led the way up the side of the draw to the plateau above. There was a trail of sorts and I wondered if it had been made by animals that Jasper drove over the edge of the cliff to the bone pile at the bottom of the box canyon or by *Newe* ancient ones who'd camped by the hot springs and carved a warning about *Tsa-ahu-bitts*.

The sun rose and at every turn of a switchback I looked down on the Bruneau. From a distance, it appeared benign, but it was anything but. If we succeeded in stopping Jasper, we'd still have to climb out of the canyon, hike back to the boats, and run the rest of the river through the deepest part of the canyon where the largest rapids raged.

We reached the plateau and halted for a water break. Liz brushed away my asking how she was feeling and Loq did the same when I said I should check on his stitches. I chalked it up to what I'd seen in combat when soldiers became so focused on the mission they tuned out pain and discomfort. Ignoring fear was different. Everyone held onto a little bit to give them an edge —the good ol' Dr. Cannon kind of fighting-rather-than-fleeing edge.

I walked point after the break and Loq took sweep. I stayed alert for shadows, noise, and movement. Jasper surely had a way out of the box canyon and up to the plateau. The animals that had been driven to plunge lemming-like over the cliff was proof.

He might've set dead-elk "Keep Out" signs up on the plateau or trip wires that would trigger rock slides as early warning systems.

Liz hurried to close the gap between us. "What's that?"

I froze and scanned the field ahead. Nothing moved. Not even a shadow. "What did you see?"

"Those holes in the ground over there. They look like, I don't know, meteor strikes."

Loq caught up to us. "What is it?"

"There," I said. "Bomb craters."

"Flyboys missing their targets again."

"Would one of you care to explain?" Liz said.

"On the other side of the river is a hundred-thousand-acre patch of high lonesome used by Mountain Home Air Force Base for training. They conduct live-fire exercises there and sometimes the bombs they drop and the missiles they fire don't hit where they're supposed to. This looks to be one of those places."

"How far away is the base?"

"It's a little past where we were watching eagles and falcons above the Snake River, but only a blink of an eye for a trainee at the stick of a fighter jet or missile launcher."

"Are we in danger of them dropping a bomb on us?"

"We're more at risk of tripping over UXO."

"What's that?"

"Unexploded ordnance. Wherever there's military, there's UXO. In a theater of war, on a base, at a live-fire training range. Stuff gets ditched or forgotten or doesn't go boom."

Loq grunted. "UXO could be our element of surprise."

"Good idea. Let's see if the flyboys left us a present."

Craters got less of our attention than surface tunnels of heaped earth that looked like giant moles had dug them. They meant something had burrowed into the ground but didn't go off. We were about to call it quits when Liz started waving her arms as she stood atop a hillock.

"Hurry!" She pointed to a slender green metal tube with short tail fins sticking out of a very thick clump of sagebrush.

"Looks like the tail of an old Redeye," I said. "I saw them in country, but never fired one. You?"

Loq nodded. "Men were getting trained on them during my last deployment, but since the enemy rarely put birds in the sky, I stuck with my M16."

"The Redeye is an old surface-to-air missile," I explained to Liz. "A soldier fired it with a bazooka-like launcher. It got its name from the infrared signal in the nose cone that locks in on hot exhaust from aircraft."

I motioned at the finned green tube. "This has been here for a while. My last tour was in sixty-eight and I heard it was redesigned and renamed two, three years after that. Now it's called a Stinger."

"Shouldn't the whole thing have blown up when it landed?" Liz said.

"In theory. It has a direct impact fuse that explodes the warhead, which is between the nose and tail. That and the frag generated by the exploding rocket and motor is more than enough to bring down a plane."

"Does that mean it's a dud?"

"Either that or when they were doing live-fire it missed its intended target and kept flying until it ran out of gas and fell from the sky. Landing on sagebrush instead of striking a rock around here is, well, take a look around. A one in a million."

"Then it could still be a live round."

"And go off if it was struck," I said, finishing her thought.

"I'll have a look," Loq said. "I got on-the-job demo training in country. One army's bomb was another army's booby trap."

I didn't try to talk him out of it; he wouldn't have listened anyway. Liz and I withdrew and crouched behind a pile of dirt and dirt rock that had been thrown up by a bomb that had gone off. We watched through our binoculars as Loq approached the clump of sagebrush. He circled it a couple of times, dropped to his knees, and began gently spreading the branches so he could get a closer look inside the nest of foliage. His head and shoulders soon disappeared. After a couple of minutes, he backed out and pulled the finned green tube from the silvery shrub.

Holding the slender four-foot-long missile aloft like a lance, he whooped and shuffled his feet in a *Maklak* war dance. "*Wey heya. Wey heya.*"

25

The top of the plateau turned into thin air where it met the box canyon. A brisk breeze was threatening to become a cold wind as the temperature started to drop. We looked over the edge. Hundreds of feet down the Bruneau snaked past the bank where Jasper had attacked us. It disappeared from view beyond the butcher pile of animal hides and bones. Though we couldn't see its mouth from our position, the killer's cave was right below us.

Twenty yards in front of it was the hollow no deeper than a chrome moon hubcap. The bare trunks of five juniper trees had been staked around it. The lenses of my binoculars filled with horror. Jeremiah "Jerry" Johnson dangled from the closest, pinned to a sharpened limb that stuck out of his chest. What was left of Only Owen hung from another. Two gutted deer bucks festooned two more trunks while a doe was impaled on the fifth.

The genders of the animals weren't lost on us. Liz gasped. Loq's silence was deafening.

"Jasper's been expecting us," I said, "but that doesn't change a thing. Let's take another look at the topo. We won't be able to once it's go time."

We backed away from the edge, put down our packs, and huddled around the map. I traced the routes each of us would take and ticked off our objectives. Then I pointed out designated fallback positions.

"Visualize them up here," I said, tapping between my eyes. "See them so you can find them in the dark. If you can't reach the first, go to the second."

"There's no falling back," Loq said. "Not now. Not ever."

"But one of us has to," Liz said. "Other people's lives are at stake as long as Jasper is on the loose. Let's promise right now that if two should fall, the third leaves immediately. No ifs, ands, or buts. It's return to the boats and get downriver ASAP and radio the sheriff's department."

She raised her right hand. "I promise."

Loq did the same. So did I. We didn't blink or cross our fingers when we said it, but I knew he and I would never honor it. Loq didn't have flee in him and I couldn't live with myself if I ran again. It was time to face my demons, starting with Jasper.

Plenty of daylight remained. I showed Liz how to make a climber's harness out of rope with loops tied around her thighs and waist with a combination of bowline and square knots and a carabiner attached in front.

"We only have to rappel the bottom thirty feet of the cliff," I said. "Wear your gloves. Control the speed of your descent by using the line running through the carabiner as a brake. Bend your knees and feel the rock through the soles of your boots. Hum a song and walk backwards."

"'Up On the Roof,'" she said.

"The game," I said. "Okay, Carole King wrote it, but I like the way Laura Nyro sings it better."

"Me too." She smiled. "What about going back up?"

"We'll leave a rope hanging with loops knotted in it for hand and toe holds so we won't have to shinny up."

"I meant, how will we get Jasper back up?"

"You still believe he's going to let us arrest him? Not after what we just saw. He even dug up Only Owen."

"Arresting him has to be our intention when we report in. Understand? What he intends is up to him, and whatever that might be, well, then we'll be within our rights to react to it."

"He's never going to go willingly."

"He will if we shoot him in the legs."

"Fine. We'll start off trying to wing him. If it works and we can 'cuff him, then we'll haul him up that section of the cliff with the ropes and pulleys we brought. If they can handle winching a raft wrapped on a rock midriver, they should be able to lift a four-hundred-pound giant off the ground."

"Time to check gear," Loq said.

I ran down the list. "Weapons. Check. Binoculars. Check. Flashlights. Check. Gloves. Check. Ropes. Check. Climbing hardware. Check. Canteens. Check. Am I forgetting anything?"

Liz pointed at the green metal tube with the silver nosecone and short tail fins leaning against a boulder.

"Right. The Redeye. Check. I'll also take the Winchester."

Loq and I swapped long guns. He held out the fringed sheath. "Here. Shoots While Running's knife."

"You keep it. You'll be seeing Jasper before me."

He redid his belt so the obsidian dagger and his skinning knife were both strapped at the back of his waist. Then he cupped his palm, added pinches of ochre dirt, and spit in it. Stirring the mixture with a finger, he made a paste as he chanted a blessing in *Maklak* and painted slashes across his high cheekbones.

Liz said, "If those give you strength, I could use them too."

He obliged and the ochre slashes on her face brought out the brown in her eyes and made the blue in the turquoise beads in her choker shine like a robin's eggs.

When he finished painting, I held up my wrist and read off the sweep hands on my field watch. Liz checked hers. Loq did the same by looking at the sun.

"Go time," I said.

I watched as the pair shouldered their packs and followed the edge of the plateau to a ravine that dropped toward the canyon floor before ending at a sheer rock wall.

When they'd disappeared from view, I grabbed the Winchester and the years-old Redeye and returned to the edge of the plateau. I sat cross-legged and scanned the box canyon while humming some tunes we used to blast before going on patrol. "Who'll Stop the Rain" led into "Born Under a Bad Sign" and into "Voodoo Child." Jimi Hendrix's electric lyrics rang in my head: "Well, I stand up next to a mountain and I chop it down with the edge of my hand. I'm a voodoo child. Lord knows I'm a voodoo child."

The music stopped when movement on the canyon floor caught my eye. Loq stumbled up from the river to the copse of corpses surrounding the hubcap-deep hollow. His boots and the bottom of his jeans were wet. He'd ditched his pack, sidearm, and shotgun. He stopped, swayed as if barely able to stand, and then shouted. Its echo rose to my perch.

"*Tsa-ahu-bitts*! I know you. I smell you. I don't fear you. Come out so I can destroy you."

Loq waited and then yelled again. "My name is Loq, *Maklak* for 'Bear.' You killed and skinned my brother for your coat and gloves. Come out and I'll give you a taste of my claws."

He raised his hands, curled his fingers, and raked the air. "*Tsa-ahu-bitts*! Stop hiding and meet the demon more powerful than you."

Loq's echo faded away, but was soon filled with another. "Ya no demon, *Maklak*. Ya no brave warrior neither. I'll eat ya heart. I'll eat ya liver."

"Come and try," Loq yelled back.

"Where be the other two, missy and the white man with the *Newe* knife?"

"Dead. Dead like my brother bear. Dead like these men here. Like the two bucks and doe. You drowned them with your rocks. The raft sank."

"And your guns?"

"Went down with the raft, but I don't need them. Come down and meet the demon more powerful than *Tsa-ahu-bitts*."

"And who be this powerful demon?"

"Revenge!"

I took the binoculars off Loq and searched for Liz. According to the plan, she was supposed to be hiding close by. Could be she was well camouflaged. Could be she'd found a better hiding spot than the one we'd picked on the map. What she couldn't be was running away in fear. In her mind, it was Jasper or her, and it damn sure wasn't going to be her.

While I hated not being able to confirm Liz's position, there was no stopping a thunder-and-lightning storm. Jasper had climbed down the ladder and was lumbering into view. The badger cap still rode on his head, the long bearskin coat hung from his shoulders. He'd reclaimed the club he'd used to bash in Jerry's brains and carried it on his shoulder, caveman style. I zeroed in on his hands. No surprise there. He was wearing the bearpaw gloves.

When he neared the trees strung with Jerry, Owen, and the animals, I gripped the Redeye, and leaned over the edge. "Fire in the hole!" I shouted and hurled the missile straight down.

As the twenty-pound rocket plummeted, a vision of high-school science class flashed and the drone of the teacher lecturing in the overheated room filled my ears. A chalkboard full of equations spun. Words in a textbook ran together. Newton's laws of motion. Terminal velocity. Acceleration due to gravity. How to calculate when a falling object would reach the ground. An apple, a feather, a missile. Did weight even matter? Was it height multiplied by final velocity equaled time? Was it one second per sixty feet or was it one per one hundred?

I should've paid more attention. All I could do now was count until the Redeye hit.

One second. Two seconds. Three.

26

THE SECOND FLOOR

Sheriff Pudge Warbler stood among the trees and looked back at the two-story lodge made of peeled logs on the frozen shores of Turtle Lake. His footprints leading from the basement meat locker were clearly visible in the snow despite the wan light of late afternoon. There was nothing he could do about them. If Caleb, Tina, or Dill McCaw spotted the tracks, they'd know he was alive and on the loose. That'd be fine if he had a weapon, but he didn't, and so he kept moving.

He made his way to where he'd left his pickup. It was gone. When they'd taken his holster to retrieve the keys to Dill's handcuffs and shackles, they'd also gotten the keys to his rig. Pudge wasn't surprised they'd moved it. Leaving it in the open would've been a mistake. The Oregon State Police trooper who'd directed him to the lodge could've driven down for a cup of coffee himself. Another driver needing to wait it out until the two-lane was reopened could've done the same.

Pudge rubbed his chin and felt the whiskers again. What was he thinking? He'd been knocked out for at least a day or two. Surely the pass had been cleared and traffic given the green light. The prison in Salem would've sounded the alarm when he didn't show up. Orville Nelson would've gotten word and orchestrated a search party. Help could be minutes away.

But if so, why wasn't anyone driving down the toboggan run of a road to the lodge to look for him?

Thinking of why nots, what ifs, and wouldn't it be nices was a waste of time. His gut said he was on his own and his gut never lied. The old sheriff moved closer to where his rig had been parked and recognized the pattern of its knobby snow tires in the tracks coming in and again as they backed out. Both sets were dusted with fresh snow.

He pictured Wilmot in the red- and-black plaid hat, and wrenching Wilmot's double-barreled shotgun from his grasp and tossing it into a snowbank. Tina had left it there when she'd guided the old man back to the lodge. The sheriff eased out of the woods and starting kicking snow. His boot struck the buried side-by-side. It didn't matter it wasn't loaded. He picked it up and held it hip level as if it were.

Pudge followed the reversing tire tracks that were crisscrossed in places by the tank-like tread marks of the bright orange Sno-Cat. They led to a fork and backed up left toward the boathouse and disappeared behind its closed double doors. The right fork was the steep road that led to the highway. He didn't recognize the tire tracks on it and followed them.

Around a curve, the way was blocked by a utility trailer covered by a tarp and hitched to the rear of a green pickup with a camper on it. He snugged the empty shotgun to his shoulder as he crept closer until he could see the pickup's windshield. Hoarfrost clouded it. Pudge tried the doors. They were locked.

He went back around to the rear and tried the camper's door. It was locked too. He set the shotgun down, stepped up on the rear wheel and wiped a peek-a-boo into the dirty, frosted window. The inside was crammed with boxes of crockery and cutlery, bedside lamps, and paintings. He hopped off and peered under the tarp covering the utility trailer. Plumbing fixtures, throw rugs, and small furniture odds and ends had been loaded into it.

The camper and trailer rig was a roadblock, stolen loot transport, and getaway vehicle all rolled into one.

Pudge cocked his head and listened for the clatter of snow chains on the highway above, the deep growl of big rigs in low gear, the squeal of brakes coming downhill. All he could hear was the distant echo of heavy machinery way up on the pass. They were still working to clear the two-lane.

He slogged back to the boathouse. The double doors were latched but unlocked. The rusty hinges screeched when he opened them. He closed them behind him so no one could catch him by surprise.

Relying on a row of small windows beneath the eaves for light, the old lawman poked around. On one side of the boathouse was a pile of outboard motors. On the other were boxes of tools and hardware. They'd been stacked close to the door for easy loading and hauling away. In the low light, Pudge nearly tripped over a dinghy on a boat trailer that had been pushed into the middle of the room. He walked around it and made out a faded-green canvas tarp covering something big. He flipped up a corner. All but winking at him were the headlights of his own pickup, which had been backed in.

Pudge tried the driver's door. It was locked. He felt under the bumper and found the magnetic hide-a-key box. The rig was so new, he'd yet to have a reason to use it. He inserted the spare key into the door lock and twisted. Click.

Leaning into the cab, he saw that the 12-gauge pump and Winchester .30-30 had been taken from the gun rack. That confirmed what his gut had been telling him. Caleb, Tina, and Dill weren't about to go willingly if he knocked on the lodge's front door and told them they were under arrest.

The sheriff reached under the front seat and dragged out a steel box. It was fitted with a combination lock. Pudge lined up the four numbers of the year he'd married Henrietta. Another click. He lifted the top. A twin to his .45 wrapped in oil cloth was inside. He checked the magazine and made sure it was loaded before tucking it into his waistband. The steel box also contained a second loaded magazine, a box of .30-30 rounds, and another of 12-gauge buckshot. He left the rifle ammo, but pocketed the magazine and a handful of shotgun shells.

Pudge plucked two more shells from the box, opened the breech of the double-barreled, and slid one into each chamber. As he snapped it closed, he heard Tina's voice calling it a dinosaur that Wilmot lugged around like a teddy bear. He blinked away a warning about antique shotguns with Damascus barrels. The ancient method of twisting iron and steel together into ribbons for gunsmithing wasn't strong enough to handle modern ammunition. Pull both triggers of the side-by-side at the same time and it was all but guaranteed the twin barrels would blow up in his face.

The sheriff took a flashlight from the glovebox and backed out of the cab. He locked the door, put the key on top of the front wheel, and flipped the canvas tarp back down. Taking a final look to memorize the layout, he walked out of the boathouse, relatched the door, and returned to the woods, sweeping the loaded shotgun in front of him as he trudged through the snow.

Pudge's plan of what to do next was the same as his company of leathernecks had followed the day they stormed Iwo. Go in and make it up as you go.

He crossed the narrow road that continued around the lake. It was covered with snow and marred only by tread marks made by the Sno-Cat. The windows on the lake side of the two-story lodge were curtained like all the rest. Caleb and Tina weren't staying there to admire the postcard pretty view of the lake and snowcapped volcanoes beyond. They kept them drawn because they didn't want anyone to see it was being ransacked.

He spotted a door and tried the knob. It opened into a dark and cold hallway. Closed doors lined both sides. All had numbers except a pair, one signed "Gents," the other "Ladies." He opened the nearest door. It was crow-wing dark inside. He shined the flashlight. The guestroom had been stripped bare of everything except the heavy furniture. He knew where the room's missing bedside lamps had gone.

The next room was more of the same. Discolorations on the wallpaper outlined where paintings once hung. The next two doors wouldn't open. Pudge let them be. In the Gents bathroom the sink was missing. So was the toilet. The same with the showerhead and tub faucet.

A stairway rose at the end of the hall. Pudge stepped on the first tread. It creaked. So did the second. He widened his stance and stepped close to the walls to help muffle his footsteps as he climbed to the second floor.

A hallway led from the landing back toward the lake. It was lined with guestrooms too. He checked a few. They'd been stripped like the ones downstairs. He reached the end of the hall. The door to the last guestroom on the second floor was bumping in its jamb. In and out. Like breathing. Pudge twisted the knob and pushed the door open with the twin barrels of the shotgun.

Drawn curtains were dancing from the wind blowing through an open window. As they flapped, a shaft of light blinked from the gap in the middle. It cast a broken stripe on a bed pushed against the wall. Wilmot lay on the bed, a rope tying his ankles to the footboard, another cinching his hands to the headboard. His feet were bare, his eyes open, his mouth ajar, his face whitened not by whiskers but frost.

Pudge reached for the old man's wrist to check for a pulse

out of respect. Between the freezing wind blowing through the second-floor window and rigor mortis, Wilmot was as white and stiff as the dock's piers that poked like whale ribs out of the frozen lake.

The sheriff reached behind the curtains and closed the double-hung window. He nodded to Wilmot, told him to rest easy, that he could count on him to do the right thing. Then he walked out of the room and down from the second floor to a reckoning with the trio responsible for the poor old man's murder.

The first-floor hallway led to the lobby overseen by the two mounted deer heads and three rainbow trout. Pudge paused in the doorway before entering. He listened for any sounds that might give him a bead on the whereabouts of the three killers.

It didn't take long to pinpoint the guitar picker. Dill's caterwauling was coming from the other side of the swinging kitchen door. Tina's and Caleb's muffled voices echoed from somewhere further away. They were soon replaced by the loud clomps of steel-toed work boots crossing the lobby's wood-planked floor. The front door to the lodge opened and slammed shut. The bright orange Sno-Cat started and revved. When it drove off, lighter footsteps soon click-clacked across the kitchen linoleum, where Dill's singing now kicked it up a notch and Tina was giggling.

Pudge gave it another minute to make sure Caleb was gone, but not more than a minute. He knew it wouldn't take long for the hammer-wielding brute to spot the footprints leading from the ice chute into the woods. He'd follow them on the Sno-Cat and eventually wind up at the boathouse. Looking inside and seeing it was as he'd left it, he'd notice the sheriff's footprints returning to the woods. He'd follow them to the lake side of the lodge and the door to the hallway and the stairway to the second floor.

The old lawman entered the lobby and strode quickly across. He pushed open the swinging door to the kitchen and left it open so he could hear the Sno-Cat's return and Caleb's steel-toed boots on the wood-plank floor.

Tina was sitting crosswise on Dill's lap nibbling his ear. His arms were around her as he continued strumming his guitar and singing. Seeing Pudge and the shotgun made the tune fall from his rubbery lips. He swallowed his shock and gave a nervous chuckle.

"I gotta tell you, Sheriff, I'm a helluva lot gladder to see you than Caleb. He's got some temper on him."

Tina let go of Dill's ear and gasped at the sight of the old lawman pointing the double-barreled at the pair. When she tried to scramble off the singer's lap, Pudge motioned for her to stay put.

"There's two ways to play this, Dill," he said. "One is for you to get back to being on your way to Salem. The other is being on your way to where Wilmot's gone." The short brim of his Stetson nodded at the ceiling.

Tina gasped again. "I don't know what you're talking about."

"Sure you do. Caleb didn't have to use a hammer on old Wilmot, just tie him to a bed on the second floor while you opened the window." He sucked his teeth. "As to where you're going, it's the same two choices Dill's got. Frankly, I don't care which one you choose."

"Don't listen to him," she said to Dill. "He can't do nothing. The highway's still closed, his truck's hidden, and that old dinosaur he's holding isn't loaded. Move your guitar out of the way so we can take him."

"You willing to bet your life she's right?" Pudge said, jabbing the side-by-side at Dill's face.

The three-time killer's bedroom eyes turned wide awake.

"You're on top, doll," he said to Tina. "Why don't you take it from him?"

She hissed like a cat, but didn't move.

"Caleb know about your duets being more than singing?" Pudge said.

Dill gave a what-did-you-expect-of-me grin.

"Where did he go?"

Tina shrugged. Dill did too.

"Doesn't matter," Pudge said. "By the way, I know where my rig's at. The pass may still be closed, but the road down to the jail in Sisters isn't and my front winch will pull your camper and trailer out of the way. The three of us are walking out of here right now, with you two in front."

"That'd be suicide," Dill said. "Caleb's got your Winchester with him. He could shoot me by mistake trying to hit you."

That told the sheriff what he wanted to know all along, Caleb had been armed when he left the lodge.

"I like my odds," he said

"Well, I don't. Neither does Tina."

Tina touched the silver moon with a winking eye hanging from her neck. "Maybe I do, Dill. Caleb's an awfully good shot. He's likely to put one right between the sheriff's eyes. Worst you and me get out of the deal is a little blood splatter on our clothes. It'll wash out."

"You're crazy," he said.

"Like a fox," she said.

Dill's hair flopped on the top of his shoulders as he shook his head. "I'll take foxy any night of the week, doll, but not crazy. I don't need to die here."

Tina's frown was followed by an even meaner hiss. "And you call yourself a man in your songs. They're only made-up words, like you are."

Pudge glanced around the kitchen. His handcuffs were on

the counter, shining amidst a stack of dirty dishes. The bracelets were open, the key still in the lock. Keeping the shotgun trained on the couple, he shuffled sideways and reached over to retrieve them.

Removing the key and holding them out, he said to Dill, "Left or right?"

"What?"

"You're gonna snap one bracelet to your wrist and the other to Tina's. I'm giving you a choice seeing you fancy yourself a guitar picker. Left or right?"

"Neither," he said.

"Then hold up your guitar."

"What for?"

"So I can blast it with this shotgun to prove I'm not fooling around here. It's loaded with buckshot."

"I'm telling you he's lying," Tina screeched. "We never let that senile old fart carry around a loaded gun. We hid all the shells."

"But not the ones in my pickup under the canvas tarp in the boathouse," Pudge said.

Tina's shoulders sagged from the weight of the truth.

"Left," Dill said. "It's only good for working the frets. I'm known more for my string work."

"You chicken shit," Tina said.

"Sorry, doll, but I ain't gonna risk my guitar. That Gibson is one of my signatures."

Dill leaned the six-string against the table and Pudge tossed him the handcuffs. He quickly snapped one around Tina's right wrist and the other around his left.

"Make 'em click so I know they're good and tight," Pudge said.

But he heard a roar instead.

"What the hell you been up to?" Caleb shouted from the

open doorway, his gaze on Tina sitting on Dill's lap, but the Winchester pointed at the sheriff.

The mudroom, was Pudge's first thought. Caleb had taken off his steel-toed boots, why he hadn't heard him clomping across the wood-planked floor. His second thought was one trigger at a time and maybe, just maybe, the Damascus steel wouldn't blow up in his face.

With no time for a third thought, he pulled it.

27

No lightning flashed. No thunder boomed. Nor did the Redeye when it struck. The echo of metal clanging against rock rose to my perch on the edge of the plateau. It sounded like a pickup's muffler falling off on a gravel road.

The noise wasn't enough to spook Jasper into turning around as we'd planned, but that didn't stop Loq. Drawing the obsidian dagger and skinning knife from behind his back, he raked the air with them like his own set of claws. The sudden appearance of the blades stopped Jasper long enough for Loq to spring. He took a baserunner's slide and swiped at the giant's calf below the hem of his protective bearskin coat.

Jasper howled as the skinning knife sliced through britches and found flesh. He pivoted as he unshouldered his club and gave a mighty swing, but only swatted dirt. Loq slid out of reach, leapt back to his feet, and spun around, the knives readied again.

The Winchester was our Plan B. I tucked the .30-30 against my shoulder, put the post of the front sight in the notch of the rear, and fired, careful to aim at the ground short of the fighters. Given the distance, drop, and angle, the chances of hitting a target even as large as Jasper in the legs were low while an errant shot or ricochet striking Loq were high. I levered another round, sighted, and fired. Bam! And again. Bam! And again.

The gunfire and its echoes and the dirt the slugs kicked up got Jasper's attention. He glanced in my direction. Loq used the distraction to take another running slide past the killer's tree-trunk-sized legs. He slashed with the Shoshone knife this time and drew an even louder howl.

The cuts missed tendons and didn't fell the giant, but they did make him jump. So did my barrage of gunfire. Instead of going after Loq again, he bolted for a thicket of pinyons and junipers near the bone pile. Loq held back to give me time to pursue him with lead. The distance and drop only grew farther and steeper as I aimed and fired. When I failed to bring the monster down, Loq waved me to stop and then gave chase himself, slowing only to scoop up the shotgun and sidearm he'd cached.

I grabbed my pack and raced across the plateau for the ravine that led to the canyon floor. Without wasting time to rig a harness when I reached the sheer wall, I took hold of the rope Loq had left hanging and slid down. When my boots touched ground, I was off and running toward the ladder to the lava tube.

Liz came at it from the opposite direction. We were both sucking wind by the time we reached it.

"Why didn't the Redeye go off?" she said between gasps.

"Faulty impact fuse, I guess."

The nose cone that contained the infrared sensors was dented, but still attached. The tail fins were bent at awkward angles. A deep gouge in the middle of the metal tube revealed a glimpse of the explosive inside.

"What should we do now?"

Loq hailed us before I could answer.

"Did you get him?" I said.

"Came back to warn you. He's got a back door hidden among the pinyons and junipers."

"Another lava tube. The box canyon is Swiss cheese like Jerry said."

"If that's the case, then he's going to get away," Liz said.

"Jasper's not running from, he's running to."

"Where?"

I pointed at the cave's entrance. "He's coming home, and like any house, his has a front and back door."

Loq said, "I'll chase him up the back-door tunnel to make sure he doesn't turn around. We'll trap him between us." He held out the Shoshone knife. "Here. He's got a head start. You might see him first."

I strapped the sheath to my calf while Loq ran back to the pinyon-juniper thicket. Then I picked up the damaged Redeye and started climbing the ladder.

"What are you going to do with that?" Liz said.

"Hope it still works."

"I'm coming with you."

Liz's nose wrinkled when she reached the cave's mouth. "What a stink! It's easier if I think of him as *Tsa-ahu-bitts* rather than a human being living like this."

I went to the dark pile that I'd seen the first time I helloed the cave. It was a stack of animal skins. Deer and elk and bighorn and wild horse and burro. Bear, mountain lion, and coyote too. Badger, beaver, raccoon, opossum, skunk, squirrel. From biggest to smallest, every type of four-legged mammal that called the high lonesome home was there. I put the missile on top for safekeeping while we searched the rest of Jasper's lair.

"No, no, no!" Liz cried out.

She was shining her flashlight on crude baskets woven out of dried twigs and branches. They were stuffed with feathers, some still on the wing. The tails of bald eagles were hard to miss. The same with the black-barred back feathers of peregrine falcons. The bodies of downy falcon chicks that had been plucked from nests were arranged like a dozen large white eggs on a dark brown turkey vulture wing. I made out the long feathers of a great blue heron, snowy ones from egrets, emerald greens from mallard drakes, and the carcasses of a dozen different songbirds.

"He's more than a monster," Liz said. "He's evil incarnate."

The floor of the cave was thick with gore, not all of it dry. A smaller, but filthier pile of hides was heaped in a corner, his bed I presumed. Another was an assortment of flotsam and jetsam dragged up from the river. There were mismatched shoes, a variety of hats, a plastic ice chest, a broken kayak paddle, an oar, two fishing rods. A life jacket peeked out from the bottom. The bottom half of green rubber fishing waders did too. I knew Only Owen's legs were still in them.

"What do you think are in those?" Liz said. She aimed her light at four large wooden casks that looked old enough to date back to wagon train days. "Drinking water or gas for an outboard motor? Maybe that's how he gets up and down the river."

"Neither," I said. "Don't open them."

"Why?"

Because they're full of animal organs, probably pickled in brine. The exotic parts he's trafficking."

The wave of disgust cresting across her face made the ochre stripes Loq had painted on her cheekbones curve downward. Then just as fast they snapped back into straight lines of anger. "Forget what I said about arresting him. I intend to kill him right here and now."

Her words echoed inside the cave and I realized everyone had a demon inside, waiting to be unleashed.

"Let's see if we can find anything in here that ID's him and his buyers. They need to be stopped as well."

The Demon Skin

We searched the cave, but found only hides, gore, and junk. There wasn't any kind of paper at all, not even a dollar bill.

"It's like he's in it for the murder, not money," Liz said.

"And he's coming our way. We need to find the entrance to the connecting lava tube and be ready for him."

The cave narrowed as we walked deeper into it, shining our flashlights as we went. The floor was flat and the ceiling arched like a cathedral's. The walls were relatively smooth, bored not by the spiraling steel of a gimlet but a force more powerful than anything—liquid fire spewed from the bowels of Earth.

I stopped. "You feel that?"

"What?" Liz said.

"A breeze."

I bathed the wall with light.

"I see it," she said. "There."

Liz aimed her flashlight while taking my wrist to redirect my beam. She didn't let go as we stared at an opening large enough for Jasper to squeeze through.

I clicked mine off. "Kill your light and back away. We don't want to alert him."

"He may have already seen it and turned around."

"Jasper won't retreat, but even if he did, there's Loq. We'd hear gunfire."

We returned to the main part of the cave still lit by the late afternoon sun. The stench hadn't lessened any and I couldn't imagine ever getting used to it. Liz stood tightlipped with nostrils clenched.

"I have a bandana," I said. "It might help mask the stink. Want it?"

"I'm fine. If you need it, go right ahead."

The bandana stayed in my back pocket.

"You know what you should've said when I didn't take it?" she said.

"What?"

"A regular Faye Dunaway, aren't you?" Liz waited. "You know, *Bonnie and Clyde?*"

"Didn't see it."

"Too bad. Then you'd know beautiful women can play badasses too."

"I don't need a movie to know that."

A glow appeared at the back of the cave. I raised the Winchester. Liz brought her flashlight and .38 into a cross-handed grip.

"Let him get closer," I whispered.

I sighted down the barrel of the .30-30 and slowed my breathing, ignored my heartbeat. The light grew closer. My finger started to squeeze the trigger.

"Friendly. Don't shoot," Loq called out.

He followed his flashlight into the cavern. Liz and I lowered our weapons as he looked around. Something glistened on his eyelashes as he took in the skins and feathers and casks.

"No wonder why so many animal spirits wander at night," he said softly.

"Where did Jasper go, another tunnel?" I said.

"If there is one, I never saw it. He was ahead of me until I reached here."

"You saw his flashlight?"

"Jasper doesn't use one. Doesn't light a torch either. He can see in the dark like the *loq* who used to wear his coat."

"Tapetum lucidum," I said.

"What?" Liz said.

"It's the name of the lining at the back of a bear's eyeball. It reflects light back through the retina and gives him a second look. Night vision."

"Great. Then how are we going to catch him now?"

"We need to triangulate him," Loq said. "I'll go back the way

I came. There must be another tunnel or a spider hole he's hiding in. One of you should wait here and the other return to the juniper thicket in case he loops back."

"I'll go," Liz said.

Loq nodded and then stepped back into the darkness.

Liz headed for the ladder and started to climb down. Before her head dipped below the ledge, she said, "Do me a favor, Nick."

"Sure, what is it?"

"Don't get yourself killed, okay?"

"Don't worry about me."

"I'm not." She said it too quickly. "The thing of it is, I'm . . . well, I'm still in my six-month probationary period and if you died, they'd . . ." The words trailed off in a self-conscious laugh.

"Hey, Liz," I said.

"What?"

"See you on the ground."

28

Something occurred to me after Liz left. There were no signs of a fire ring in the cave, no charred ends of sticks, no blackened tongues of smoke licking the walls or staining the ceiling. Jasper must be afraid of fire, and fear could be a powerful weapon. It was time for Plan C.

Like Loq, I'd gotten on-the-job training in booby-traps during my three tours. The unexploded Redeye might've had a faulty impact fuse, but there was more than one way to detonate a bomb, and I was pretty sure the laws of thermodynamics would cover it.

Leaving the Winchester near the ladder, I moved the green missile with the dented nose cone and fractured fuselage to the wooden baskets filled with feathers. I propped it in the largest and stomped another into kindling and placed the dry sticks on top. Then I pulled a metal canteen out of my pack and twisted the top off, but didn't take a drink. I poured half of the contents into the basket, soaking the kindling, Redeye, and feathers beneath. The smell of camping-stove kerosene filled the air.

I poured a liquid fuse with the remaining fuel to the stack of animal skins, up its side, and stopped in the middle of the top one. Shaking the canteen and hearing a reassuring slosh, I placed the makeshift detonator upright so it would be in clear view of the five bare juniper trunks strung with Jerry, Owen, the two bucks, and the doe.

After taking a final look around the demon's lair, I slipped the Winchester's strap over my shoulder, and started climbing down the ladder. With each rung, I envisioned each step I'd take upon reaching the ground. Hustling to the hollow next to the five bodies, shouldering the rifle, aiming, and hitting the can't-miss metal canteen that was as bright and shiny as a chrome moon hubcap. The spark would light the fuse, ignite the wooden basket, and blow the Redeye.

Except, down was up.

Jasper's roar drowned out the cries of dead animals as he rushed from the dark recesses of the lava tube and yanked the ladder up and back into the cave. He raised it over his head before I could let go and smashed me into the ceiling. Then he shook me off and I landed in a heap atop the flotsam-and-jetsam pile. Before I could scramble out of the way, he slammed the ladder down on me.

Strobing white lights turned into deep purple as the blow sent me plunging into a vertical shaft of darkness. I reached out to try and touch the sides, to grab hold of something to stop my fall, but all I touched was air, all I heard was it rushing past me as I tumbled deeper and deeper into the black, a black without bottom, without mercy.

The rushing air turned into a familiar voice. "Nick Drake, I knew you were coming before you left."

"Tuhudda Will, my old friend, is that you?" I said.

"This is so."

"Help me. I'm falling."

"Only you can stop that."

"How?"

"Look behind you."

"I can't turn around. I'm falling down a hole drilled by lava millions of years ago."

"Measure time not in years but in what you have done and who you have done it with. Listen to them. They will tell you where you came from and who you are. Then you will know what to do."

And so I listened as I plummeted through darkness. I could hear my father and mother talking in the next room, their happiness when he came home from a mission, their sorrow when he left on another. I could hear him telling me when I considered enlisting not to do it for him or for myself, but for what I believed in—that it was bigger than the both of us. I could hear my mother's quiet resolve that spoke louder than any words she'd ever said when she received a medical death sentence.

I could hear boyhood friends laughing and teachers teaching and coaches coaching when I ran track in high school and the two years I put in at college. I could hear Sgt. Hardass yelling, DJ explaining the ways of the world, the men in my squad, both when they were alive and when they were dying alongside me.

I could hear Gemma telling me off the first time I met her, telling me not to stop the first time we made love. I could hear her fearless voice reading off spinning instrument dials on the lightning-stuck plane as we plunged from the sky and crash-landed on a mountainside. I could hear her joy saying "it's a girl" as she gave birth in the makeshift wickiup I'd built while snow piled up outside and help wasn't on the way.

I could hear Hattie's first cries in there and then her first words at home and the way she said "Daddy" when I read to her and rode horses with her and drove her to school. I could hear Johnny's frustrated curses and knew deep down in my heart they were cries for help, for protection, for love. I could hear Pudge's folksy manner of speaking that criminals often mistook for a lack of steel and resolve, Blackpowder Smith's cackle that belied his country wisdom, Loq calling me brother, and Liz Bloom saying she trusted me and not to die.

I could hear November tsking when I struggled as she taught me her language, tsking when I failed to look at the world through *Numu* eyes and *Nuwuddu* eyes, the animals Paiute considered to be the First People. I could hear her warning about the Bruneau River and *Tsa-ahu-bitts* and losing myself, and telling me I'd know what to do with her husband's knife when the time came.

The sound of rushing air came back. The sound of Tuhudda's voice did too.

"What did you hear?" he said.

"Everyone. I heard them all."

"And what did you learn?"

"That I wouldn't be who I am without them. That I'd lay down my life for each and every one of them."

"You do not fear death?"

"No, I only fear losing them when I'm gone."

"But you will not. You are part of them as they are part of you. As it is with the light of the sun and the moon and the stars that share the sky, so is it with the spirit shared by all peoples —*Numu, Newe, Maklak*, white, black, *Nuwuddu*. The spirit that shines within you shined in those who came before and will shine in those who come after."

"Then how do I stop falling? How do I stop Jasper?"

"Will it to be so and it will be. You will know what to do when the time comes."

"That's what November said about Shoots While Running's knife. She said it takes a demon to stop a demon."

"Girl Born in Snow is wise and you would be wise to listen to her. This is so."

Tuhudda's voice grew fainter and so did the rush of air. The shaft I was falling down turned from black to deep purple to light. Jasper's roar and stink rocked me back to my senses and I saw the ladder come swinging down again. I grabbed the broken kayak paddle lying next to me on the flotsam and jetsam pile and stood it on end, jamming the broad blade in front of a rung. It stopped the ladder's murderous arc long enough for me to roll away and jump to my feet.

Jasper flung the ladder aside and snarled. "I'm gonna tear off ya limbs and rip out ya guts. After I kill ya, I'll kill the *Maklak* and then missy too. I'll string the three of ya up with the others. I'm gonna kill everything in this canyon."

I sprinted around the stack of skins and skidded to the edge of the cave. The drop to the ground was a leg-breaker at best. Jasper would lower the ladder and be on top of me before I could crawl away.

A new round of voices began sounding in my ears. They were the cries of all the animals Jasper had butchered, the ones stored in the cave and those in the bone pile too. They were cries for justice and I swore to get it for them the same as I'd vowed to Only Owen and Jerry Johnson.

I took a last glance down and saw Liz and Loq standing near the pinyon-juniper thicket and turned back to face Jasper. The obsidian knife came out of the sheath with a swish.

"You want this? Come and get it," I shouted.

Yellow teeth as long as fingers bared. Jasper's red-rimmed eyes grew redder. So did the badger's riding on his head. He feinted left around the stack of skins and then lunged right, but I was a step ahead of him.

We circled the skins. I dug in the front pocket of my jeans and pulled out the silver tube of waterproof matches while continuing to show the knife. I flipped open the cap one-handed and shook out a match. It fell to the ground.

I shook out another, but couldn't hold on to it either.

Once more I tried, and this time got the match between my fingers. Without taking my eyes off Jasper, I struck its head with my thumbnail, felt heat, and smelled sulphur. I swung the knife at the canteen and tossed the lit match as it tipped over. The kerosene burst into flames.

At the sight of fire, Jasper threw his bearpaw gloves up in front of his face and howled. He backed onto the ledge and bared his yellow teeth at the liquid fuse as the flame ran down the side of the stack of skins in a red-and-yellow hurry. It sped even faster upon reaching the cave floor.

The flame blazed toward the basket holding the Redeye that was between me and the back-door tunnel. But as sure as I was that Jasper would never allow himself to be captured, so was I sure that I had to make certain he'd never harm a two-legged or four-legged again.

I roared. Louder than Sgt. Hardass. Louder than the biggest rapids on the Bruneau River. Louder than Jasper. I kept roaring as I ran straight at him, ducked under his claws, and plunged the obsidian blade into his chest. I held onto the deer-antler handle and drove him backward off the ledge. As I rode him down, I could see in his red-rimmed eyes the reflection of another demon's face staring back.

We hit the ground so hard it shook the five tree trunks with the skewered bodies. In the cave above, the flaming fuse ignited the kerosene-soaked basket, which detonated the explosive inside the fractured Redeye. The blast made the five trees quake again and sent the bodies dancing. A flame shot out of the cave's mouth but was quickly extinguished as the rock ceiling collapsed and sealed the entrance.

Loq and Liz came running. I gave the obsidian dagger a final twist to be certain Jasper was dead and then pulled it out, stood over him, and raised my chin and howled. I howled again and again and waved the knife at the sky as the demon's blood rained down on me. Liz's eyes went wide with shock and her lips formed a circle but no words came out.

Loq slow-walked toward me while singing about birds that never stopped flying and a boundless forest and a river that flowed back into itself. He placed a hand gently on my shoulder.

"*Wey heya*, brother. It's over. You can put down your knife. You can put back your demon. Jasper is dead. It was an honorable kill."

29

Daylight was fading as we took the bodies of the two fishermen down from their rood trees and placed them on the ground within the circle of bare trunks. We gathered rocks from the floor of the box canyon and built cairns over them for safekeeping. The two bucks and doe were lowered too and carried to the skin-and-bone pile so they could rest among their own kind. As for Jasper, we dragged him over the rocky ground and through the brambles in the pinyon-juniper thicket to the back-door tunnel. We shoved him inside and sealed the opening with rocks.

After marching back to the sheer wall, we climbed up the hanging rope and followed the ravine to the plateau. The sun sank behind the Jarbidge Mountains and crowned the jagged ridgeline in gold as we stood on the edge for a final look down. When the box canyon receded into darkness and we were about to turn away, wisps of light started to appear in the bone pile. The soft glows brightened and formed into shapes and began to spread out across the darkening canyon floor. I could make out deer and elk and bighorn. Squirrels and skunks too. Every kind of animal Jasper had butchered was there.

The spirit animals started circling. Around and around they sped, forming a whirlwind of silvery light that lifted from the ground and passed in front of us in one long thundering herd as they journeyed to join the stars above. The night sky became brighter, so bright, that when we finally hiked back down to our camp beside the hot springs, we did so without the need of flashlights.

When we reached it, I dropped what I was carrying, stripped off my clothes, and waded into the closest pool of hot water. I scrubbed Jasper's blood off my face and hands. Then I dunked my head and washed my hair. Finally, I held my breath and sank beneath the surface. The heat from the springs unwound my muscles and the tension of the past few days, indeed the past several months, began to melt away. I let the sound of bubbling water drown out the roars of demons and the cries of butchered animals, and in their place I heard the voices of the people I loved and knew who I was and what I wasn't.

Sitting back up, I watched the reflection of stars twinkling on the surface of the pool. They rippled as Liz slipped into the water and sat in front of me.

"How are you doing?" she said, her voice as soft as the water's caress.

"Better now," I said.

"Good, because I was worried there. Frightened too."

"You don't need to be. Jasper's dead and buried."

"About you. What you did and how you did it." She paused. "It doesn't frighten you that you have that capacity within you?"

I cupped water in both hands, splashed my face, and slicked back my hair. "What frightens me even more is if I didn't."

"I'm not sure I understand."

"I'll tell you about Dr. Cannon one day. Is Loq coming to wash off too?"

"No. He went to check on the raft and kayak. He took his

bedroll with him and said to tell you he wanted to be able to close his eyes and you'd understand."

"He said that, did he?"

"Mmm. What we saw, the ghosts of those animals, were they really there or was it some kind of, I don't know, hallucination brought on by mass hysteria?"

"Did seeing them make you afraid?"

"Quite the opposite. They gave me a feeling of comfort and peace. But were they really there?"

"I told you when we first met that things happen in the high lonesome that aren't easily explained. I've learned to accept them and let them teach me things I might otherwise not understand. Seeing spirit animals like that? Well, seeing is believing."

"I expected that of Loq, but you?"

"Spend enough time here and you may come to expect it of yourself."

"Would you like that, if I were to spend more time here?"

"I would."

"How come?"

I cupped water again. It was like truth. Some of it had a way of slipping between my fingers no matter how hard I tried to hold on to it.

"We can get a lot done together. A new refuge. More protection for wildlife, the endangered species. We make a good team."

"A team?"

"You, Loq, and me."

The laugh came out of the sides of her mouth. "I suppose we have worked well together. Run a dangerous river. Kill an even more dangerous demon. That hasn't always been the case down here?"

"Did you meet your predecessor, the previous district supervisor?"

Water sprayed off her shoulders as she shook her tousled hair.

"In all the years I've worked for the service," I said, "he never left his office in Portland to come down here. If he had, he would've been able to do a better job and wouldn't've gotten fired. I saw more of the regional supervisor who lived in Washington DC than him. He came to No Mountain right before he resigned."

"The one who said the Great White Father sent him?"

"Turns out he wasn't such a bad guy after all, just a politician."

"A politician?" Liz smiled. "You and Loq don't hold them in high regard."

"Politics is what sent us to Vietnam and kept the war going as long as it did. They cost a lot of good men and women their lives. The suffering of their loved ones too."

"I'm sorry, I didn't mean to make light of it." She skimmed her palm over the water. "By the way, my dad's not a senator like Loq suggested."

"He's not?"

"No, he's a lobsterman. Like his father before him."

"That explains the ravioli, but not the Rolling Stones song being the story of your life."

"'Play With Fire?' I'm the one singing the refrain that you'll get burned if you play with me, not the other way around."

"I think there's a much better song for you."

"What is it?"

"You sang it yourself. 'The Eagle and the Hawk.' You're flying with them now."

"Mmm." Liz sunk deeper into the water so it covered the tops of her breasts and lapped at her throat. The reflection of stardust framed her face. "Gemma's very lucky to have you."

"I'm the lucky one."

"She wasn't too happy with me when she learned we were going on this trip."

"And even less happy with me."

"What did she say about me?"

"That you're young, sexy, and impetuous. That I should watch out."

Liz splashed me with the wave she'd been making. "I'll take the first two, but the third? I'm not reckless."

"How about high-spirited?"

"Better," she said. "What are you going to tell her when you get home?"

"About the trip?"

"About you and me. The way you saved my life. Being naked in a hot springs and alone together under a night sky in the middle of nowhere."

"I've never lied to her. I'm not about to start."

"Will you also tell her how I tricked you and Loq into running the river?"

"Yeah."

"She'll hate me for it."

"She'll be pissed off at first, but in the end when I tell her about Jasper, she'll thank you. Gemma's the daughter of a sheriff. She doesn't countenance letting murderers run free."

The hot springs bubbled. The stars and moon kept shining. Liz said, "What happens next?"

"There's the rest of the river to run. The big water lies ahead, but if we get an early start and push it, we can get down in one day instead of two and radio the sheriff's department. That's one less night Jerry and Owen's families won't have to wonder what happened to them."

"I meant about us. I don't want to forget about that morning on the rock shelf. How it made us feel about being alive, about each other."

"You don't need to feel obligated to me. I spent enough time talking to shrinks after Vietnam to know that letting go of the responsibility for saving men's lives and keeping them alive was as hard as letting go of the guilt for having led them to their deaths."

"But something did happen and I don't want to forget it." She chewed the corner of her lip. "You felt it, you heard it. Didn't you?"

I was low in the water too and our eyes were level with each other's. "I felt your heart pounding against my palm, I felt the river pounding against the rocks. I heard both of them singing."

"All that, and you still wouldn't kiss me, make love to me. I wanted you to."

"I know, but I couldn't. Wouldn't."

"Because of Gemma?"

I nodded. "And Hattie. And Johnny. And Pudge, November, and everyone, including myself. But right then and there, mostly because of you."

"Me?"

"Because you put your trust in me. If I had, it would've swept us away and our lives wouldn't've been our own anymore."

Liz sighed. "My luck. A ranger who's a saint."

"I'm not."

"You mean, you haven't always been." She skimmed her hand on the water some more. "You know, in here, in the starlight, without a shirt on, I can see the tiger tattoo on your bicep. The tattoo like the one on the soldier who shot the man who killed Johnny's mother." Liz's eyes held mine. "Was that you?"

"I don't know. Could've been. I was in a bad way at the end of my last tour and don't remember a lot except Tu Do was the place to score smack, get stoned, find comfort." I swallowed hard. "I haven't told Gemma many details about how Thien died."

"But on the rock shelf, being with me, you do remember all of that."

"Of course."

"And the feeling between us. It was real, right? Is real."

"Yeah, we went through something together, all right. We put our fates in each other's hands and we came out the other side. We're both stronger for it. Our friendship's stronger."

"Friendship?"

"I hope so."

Liz met that with silence and then said, "What do you say, friend? Should we keep the part about pounding hearts and singing rivers between just us?"

"Like a secret handshake?"

She laughed and I did too. Then she said, "I'm torn between wanting to get to the take-out tomorrow and wanting the trip to go on longer. Jasper and nearly drowning aside, I've loved every minute of it. The how it makes you feel alive part. You know what I mean?"

"I do."

"Would you ever do it again, go on a river trip with me?"

"Preferably not at flood stage and when the weather's warmer, but sure."

"I could always order you to."

"You wouldn't need to."

"Right answer, Nick."

We let that sit a bit and then Liz said, "I'm getting out before I turn into a prune. Time for bed."

"Yeah, it's been a long day."

We dried off and zipped into our sleeping bags spread out on a tarp, and watched the stars twinkle and spin and shoot across the sky in bursts of hot white light. For the first time in a long time, I didn't need a mug of November's herb tea to quiet my mind and fall asleep.

If I had dreams, I couldn't remember them when dawn broke. A campfire had already been lit. Coffee warmed in a pot. Loq and Liz were huddled next to the fire. I pulled on my boots and joined them.

"How did you sleep?" Liz said.

"Without remorse. And you?"

"With the angels."

30

We carried our gear down to the boats, restrung the perimeter line around the gray Avon, put the throw lines back in their bags, and readied the static line and pulleys for easy access in case of emergency.

I showed Liz and Loq the map. "Looks like we have a stretch of about a mile or so of fairly easy water before we enter the deepest part of the canyon."

Liz asked if there were any breaks in the big water.

"Not many," I said. "The only chance we'll have for a pull-out is about midway down. If the raft flips anywhere but near there, we'll need to try and re-right it in whitewater. That's no easy trick. Same with the kayak."

"Meaning, we don't flip," Loq said.

"Not now, not ever," Liz said, mimicking his seriousness, but with a bit of tease in her voice.

"You haven't gotten a chance to row yet," I said. "Want to start us off in this first stretch? Be a good place to practice."

"You know I would."

"Then let's get to it."

We lined the boats down the spring to where it emptied into

the Bruneau. Loq slid into the red kayak while Liz sat on the metal ice chest and took the oars. I pushed us off and then hopped aboard and perched on the tube facing her.

She planted her feet and arched her back. I was about to tell her to pull on both oars to back us away from the bank and then pull with the left and push with the right once we were in deeper water to straighten us out when she did exactly that.

Rowing a fourteen-foot-long raft laden with gear was a lot different than paddling a nimble kayak, but Liz quickly showed she didn't lack for strength or the ability to read the river. We were soon gliding down without bashing into midriver boulders or getting sucked into wrong chutes.

I watched as Liz rowed and realized that she'd lost the got-to-prove-it attitude she'd had when we first met. It was as if she'd exorcised a demon of her own and had become more comfortable in her own skin.

The first mile of water went by without mishap, but then the gentle thrum of the river's current began to take on a bassier tone. Liz stood to get a better view downriver.

"Looks like we're knocking on the door to the deepest part of the canyon," she said. "It's weird. A layer of mist is hovering above the water like a cloud."

"It's spray from the rapids," I said.

"Wow, they are big." She took another look and then sat down. "Time to switch seats?"

"Only if you want to. I'm good right here."

Liz's brown eyes gleamed brighter than her turquoise choker. "Then better hold onto the chicken line, friend, because here we go."

Her laughter rose above the drone of the big rapids and then we were in them. The drops were huge and the waves crashed over us as powerful as storm-lashed surf breaking hard on a rocky headland. I caught occasional glimpses of the red kayak as

Loq alternated between leading us down a slalom course and then backpaddling in the lee of a wave to hold his position as we flew past so that he could shoot in and try to pick us up in case we flipped.

We came close, not from Liz mishandling the oars, but because the river was so strong and at times all we could do was submit to its power instead of trying to fight it. Bailing was a Sisyphean task to lower the water pouring over the tubes. Still, I didn't stop. The effort kept me busy as well as warm. I knew the same was true for Liz as she never quit working the oars to avoid slamming into midriver rocks and prevent us from broadsiding or wrapping.

The red kayak zoomed in front of us after a particularly nasty stretch of nonstop waves and swirling holes. Loq took one hand off his paddle long enough to point to starboard. Then he regripped and dipped the right blade and cut an angle. Liz followed suit and we were soon in a back eddy created by a bend in the soaring canyon wall.

Loq steered straight at a rock shelf lapped by water and surfed the kayak right on top of it. He was out of his boat in a flash, slid it further up so its nose was on dry ground, and then turned toward us. I heaved the throw-line bag like passing a football downfield. He caught the spiral as the line unraveled behind it and held it fast as Liz steered the raft's bow up onto the rock shelf.

With the boats secured, we stretched our legs and looked back at what we'd just run. The rapids appeared even bigger than when we were in the middle of them. Liz's cheeks glowed crimson with excitement of having navigated the kind of thrill ride only Mother Nature could create. Even Loq's usual stoicism appeared to have trouble holding back a grin.

"Well, how about that!" I said, not bothering to cover my own delight. Only I wasn't talking about the rapids. "Look."

They followed the direction of my finger. A pair of bald eagles were flying right below the opposite canyon rim.

"They're carrying sticks," I said. "They're building a nest."

"Those are the first raptors we've seen since the put-in," Liz said. "It's like they know Jasper is dead."

Loq grunted. "So they do."

We watched the white-headed, white-tailed couple work as they brought more twigs and sticks to a crevice.

"They may be the first to return, but they won't be the last," Liz said. "I'll do whatever it takes to get this place protected."

"Even if it means running the Bruneau again?" Loq said.

"Early and often."

"Then count me in."

"Time to go," I said. "We got a radio call to make."

Liz turned to me. "Would you take over rowing? I want to keep a lookout for more birds. Maybe I can spot a peregrine."

"How about you do it, Loq? I'd like a crack at the kayak."

We switched spots and set off. As soon as we were out of the eddy, we were back in the nonstop cauldron of raging whitewater. I hadn't been in the cockpit of a kayak for a while, and it took more mental than physical adjustment to get used to riding so low in the water. The first big wave came fast and I was up and over it and plunging down into a hole before I realized I was leaning too far back.

Forcing my mind to shift gears, I leaned forward instead as I remembered how to ride low like when I used to redline my Triumph 650 to outrun the demons of combat fatigue and addiction. The feeling of freedom that had come with beating them flowed through me as I paddled and surfed. I couldn't get to the next big wave fast enough.

After a while, I slowed and ducked into the lee of a midstream haystack and waited for the Avon to catch up. The raft pulled abreast and both Liz and Loq looked at me like I was crazy. I gave them a guilty-as-charged howl.

As I got in line behind them, I thought about Johnny. Maybe that's what he needed, the same as I had when I got back to the States. To get out and let it rip, to race across the high lonesome and leave the demons that were following him from Tu Do Street behind. I'd paint a fire-breathing red dragon's head on the gas tank, seat him in front of me, my forearms holding him tight, and we'd push the bike to the limit and do it again and again, flying across the salt flats as long as it took until he knew he'd finally outrun them, that he was safe and had a home and was loved.

The rapids went on and on, but as in all things in life, the river eventually changed. The canyon walls grew lower, the water grew calmer. I paddled ahead of the raft as the take-out came into view. I beached the red kayak and waded into the shallows to take hold of the Avon's chicken line and pull it ashore.

Liz stepped off first and waited beside me for Loq. When he joined us, she threw her arms around us and hugged tightly. "I love you guys. You're the best."

While they unloaded and deflated the raft, I unlocked Loq's rig and picked up the radio's mike.

"Owyhee County Sheriff's Department," a woman's voice answered.

I gave her my name and told her the situation and she put me straight through to the sheriff. He reminded me of Pudge Warbler the way he took in the information without comment or emotion and waited until I finished before responding with a plan of action. A helicopter bound for our location would be in the air within minutes. Sheriff's vehicles would also be dispatched. The chopper would pick one of us up to serve as a guide to the box canyon and location of the bodies.

Before the sheriff hung up, I asked him to transfer me back to his dispatcher so she could patch me through to home. November answered on the fourth ring.

"The Bruneau let you live," she said without preamble.

"It did," I said. "Is Gemma there?"

"Everyone is out. Even Jake the dog."

"When she gets back, tell her I'm safe and on my way home."

"Will you be here for supper?"

"No, I'm still in Idaho."

"We will not wait for you. Maybe I will leave some frybread for you if any is left."

She started to hang up without saying goodbye.

"Wait," I said. "I still have Shoots While Running's knife. I used it, but didn't lose it."

"I know."

"Did Tuhudda tell you in a dream?"

"Shoots While Running did."

"Your dreams are powerful."

"He also said to tell you that though the demon you battled is dead, *Tsa-ahu-bitts* lives. A legend can never die. Nor should it ever."

"I know. It's one of the many things I learned on this journey."

I backed the rig up to the river to load the boats and told them about the sheriff's plan. Loq said he wanted to be the one to ride in the chopper and then have them drop him back at the put-in and drive my rig home to No Mountain.

By the time we finished loading the raft, kayak, and gear, a helicopter circled and landed. The sheriff got out. He was younger than I'd pictured him. A deputy followed him. We all shook hands. The sheriff said another one of his deputies would be escorting the coroner's van to our spot where the chopper would ferry down the bodies, but they were going to be delayed a couple of hours because of a prior fatal traffic accident. He told Liz and me we didn't need to wait and could send him our reports. If he needed anything more than what Loq could tell him, we'd do it by phone. Then he and the deputy climbed back into the chopper.

"See you back at the ranch," I said to Loq.

He nodded and then turned to Liz. "You did pretty good up there."

She gave him a hard stare. "Only pretty good?"

He grinned. "Better than good, sister."

Liz and I watched as he ducked under the blades of the helicopter and boarded. The chopper lifted off and began following the Bruneau upriver. When it disappeared from view, we got in the pickup and drove away.

"It'll take several hours to reach No Mountain," I said.

"Change of plans," she said.

"How so?"

"Drop me off at the Boise airport. I can catch a flight there to Portland."

"Tonight?"

"Mmm."

"What about your rig parked at the ranch?"

"I have a plan for that. I'll tell you about it later."

The dirt road turned into blacktop and the two-lane got bigger and my speed grew faster as I steered toward Boise. Darkness fell and I kept my eyes on the road ahead while Liz stared out her window. She was quiet and I wondered if she'd fallen asleep. I was teetering on the edge of exhaustion myself.

The turnoff to the airport came and I followed the signs to the terminal and parked out front.

"Now, about the vehicle at your ranch," she said. "Hold on to it for the new ranger I'm assigning to your area."

"What new ranger?"

"Someone to help you and Loq out. You could use an extra hand so you can devote more time to the reports you never file."

"Does this new ranger have a name?"

"I'll let you know when I choose her."

"Her?"

"Creating new refuges for endangered species isn't the only thing I plan on changing in the district."

We both got out and I retrieved her gear bag from the back of the pickup. I didn't know if I should hand it to her or carry it inside. We stood staring at each other.

Liz said, "On the drive from the take-out, I was trying to think up a way to say this, but I couldn't find the words and so I'll go right ahead and say it." She took a deep breath. "Thank you for saving my life. Thank you for not kissing me and, well, going where that would've led. The Bruneau taught me it's not the rapids that define a river trip, it's the people you run it with."

She took her gear bag from me. "One other thing. Besides assigning a new staffer to the high lonesome, I'm going to need you to come up to Portland from time to time to work on the plan to make the Bruneau a national wildlife refuge."

"You got it."

"And when you're there, I want you to remember one thing."

"What you told me in the beginning. To call you Liz in the field but Supervisor Bloom in the office."

"Wrong answer. I want you to always remind me how the Bruneau made me feel alive. I never want to forget that when I'm swamped with paperwork and I never want to forget what you and I have."

Liz leaned forward and gave me a hug. "Also, next time I see you, you need to finish telling me how Johnny escaped from the Viet Cong and got to America. You left the story hanging and I want to know what happened." She paused. "There will be a next time, won't there?"

"Absolutely."

"Good. Tell Johnny from me he's the luckiest kid in the world to have you as a dad and if he's ever looking for a godmother, to give me a call. Now get on home to your beautiful family."

Liz walked toward the terminal. I wondered if she'd turn around and blow me a kiss or even run back and give me a real one, but she didn't.

And that was the right answer.

31

THE LAST DANCE

The old double-barreled shotgun boomed. Tina shrieked. Caleb clomped across the wood-planked floor for the last time as he was blown backward into the lobby through the open kitchen door. When Pudge Warbler rushed to kick the Winchester out of the fallen killer's hands, Dill McCaw whistled.

"Damn, Sheriff, you're a mean old bastard. But you're honest, I'll give you that. You weren't lying about that blunderbuss being loaded."

Caleb's bootless feet were twitching and the dirty wool socks covering them had holes, but they hadn't been made by buckshot and they weren't bleeding like the ones in his upper chest.

"You're a goner," Pudge said matter-of-factly as he looked down at the wheezing, sputtering brute. "Any last words?"

Caleb hawked blood. "I shoulda hit you with the hammer twice."

"Maybe, but I only needed to hit you once." The sheriff said it in a way that revealed neither triumph nor regret.

The light faded from Wilmot's killer's eyes and his feet twitched a final time. Pudge picked up the Winchester and turned around only to see Dill and Tina scurrying down a hall that led from the kitchen.

"Ah, for Pete's sake," he groaned and laid the side-by-side on the kitchen table and chased after the handcuffed pair.

The hall led into a dining room. The cutlery and crockery had already been pilfered, but the tables and chairs were strewn about as if blown by a strong wind coming down the mountains and across the frozen lake. Pudge shoved an overturned table out of the way and hurdled over an upended chair. He reached a door on the other side of the room and yanked it open. A metal trashcan that had been hastily propped against it fell toward him. He jumped back as it clattered at his boots.

Seeing Dill and Tina round the corner of the peeled-log building prompted him to reverse course and try to cut them off. He hustled back through the dining room and kitchen, around Caleb's body, and pulled the front door open to the whine of the Sno-Cat revving followed by the deep-throated rumble of its tank treads.

The sheriff moved fast for a man his size and reached the narrow road that followed the frozen shoreline of the turtle-shaped lake in time to see the bright orange vehicle rolling away. Pudge couldn't tell who was driving because the cab didn't have a back window, but it didn't matter. Dill and Tina were both killers, both fugitives. Both needed to be stopped.

He aimed the .30-30 and fired, hoping the sound of rounds striking steel would convince whoever was driving to give up. Gunpowder banged and metal clanged as the round hit, but the Sno-Cat didn't stop. He fired again. Another bang. Another clang. Still no stopping.

Pudge trotted back to the boathouse. He yanked the double doors so hard the latch broke loose. The doors were left swinging as he went to his pickup and tugged the corner of the green tarp. It billowed like a bedsheet and sailed to the ground. The sheriff grabbed the key off the top of the front wheel, got in, and turned the ignition. He threw it into gear and stomped on the gas before remembering he hadn't moved the trailered dinghy out of the way.

The sound of metal clanging this time was even louder than before as the front bumper bashed the trailer and sent it spinning. It wasn't the only thing Pudge hit. One of the double doors had swung shut. It splintered as he plowed through. He didn't flinch or duck as boards hurtled at the windshield. One struck and left a spiderweb. Another thunked on the roof right above his short-brim Stetson.

The sheriff fishtailed onto the narrow road and blew past the lodge, shooting up twin roostertails of snow. He steered onto the ruts carved by the Sno-Cat's tank treads and floored it. The chase quickly changed from a toboggan run to a bobsled race and he soon closed in on them.

Pudge decided it had to be Tina behind the wheel since her right hand was handcuffed to Dill's left. He hit the lights and siren in hopes they might scare her into stopping. They didn't. She cranked the wheel instead. The Sno-Cat veered off the road, plowed through a drift, and rumbled toward the frozen lake.

"You damn fool!" he shouted. "The ice won't hold you."

Pudge turned onto the freshly made tracks and aimed for the lake too. The bright orange vehicle slowed and shimmied when it reached the sheet of ice before the treads got traction. Soon it was rolling again. The sheriff pulled to a stop near the frozen edge and got out, leaving the engine running.

The Sno-Cat was heading across the ice in the direction of the two-lane and the closed mountain pass beyond. With enough diesel in the tank and treads able to climb over anything, it could reach it and carry the pair of fugitives to freedom. But then it suddenly shuddered to a stop.

The sharp crack of ice echoing across the lake was louder

than a .30-30. The bright orange front end dipped. The passenger door flung open and Dill spilled out, his handcuffed wrist pulling Tina with him. The pair tumbled onto the ice like dice and tried to scramble to their feet as more cracking echoed and the heavy Sno-Cat tipped further.

The old sheriff wasted no time. He flipped the release on the power winch mounted to the front of the pickup, grabbed the hook, and began walking out onto the frozen lake, pulling the cable behind him.

The ice was slippery and he was wearing cowboy boots. Any footing he was able to get was as solid as a lie. He gritted his teeth and flexed his legs and remembered the first time he danced with Henrietta. It was shortly after his discharge from the Marines and he'd returned to Harney County with an eye toward signing on with the Sheriff's Department. What caught his eye even more was the pretty girl in a chiffon dress at a VFW Saturday night social.

A band was playing and it took him a while, but he finally worked up the gumption to ask her to dance even though he didn't know two licks about tempo or tangoing. He was both smiling and sweating when she said yes and he led her onto the dance floor. His boots seemed to find her toes with every turn they made during the fox trot and when it came to the rhumba, he was all for throwing in the towel and skedaddling right out of there with his tail tucked firmly between his legs.

The bandleader seemed to sense his predicament and the group abruptly shifted to a waltz. Henrietta's hand was cool against his sweaty palm and she wouldn't let go. She leaned into him and put her cheek next to his. "Just imagine we're ice skating," she whispered as the music swelled. "Glide and circle. Glide and circle. The ice can't break beneath us because we're lighter than air."

That's what they did. Skated all around the dance floor, skated right out of the VFW and into each other's lives.

Pudge clamped his hat down, took a firmer grip of the winch-cable's hook, and started skating. He skated straight toward the bright orange Sno-Cat as thunderclaps of cracking ice rang out and the snow machine's front end tilted ever more crazily into the slushy water bubbling around its treads.

Eight-five feet went through the sheriff's mind. That's what the winch's manual said. The cable was eighty-five-feet long. He was nearing the end of it and he couldn't reach the pair by skating any longer. He skidded to a stop.

"Dill!" he yelled. "Grab hold of the hook when it lands and hang on. I'll winch you across."

"It won't work," the panicky singer yelled back. He and Tina were clutching at each other as they tried to remain upright on what had become a slippery, bobbing island.

"Trying to jump that crack in the ice definitely won't. You'll drown before you freeze. Grab hold or die."

The old lawman planted his boots as best he could, took hold of a coil of cable, and began twirling the hook over his head, using only his wrist. The wire cable started singing as it circled overhead and then he tossed it like throwing a lariat back at the ranch, feeding the coil as it flew. Silver flashed and then the hook bit ice. Bullseye.

"Don't let go, the both of you," he shouted. "It's gonna be a rough ride."

Pudge spun around without doing the splits and started skating back to the pickup. Glide and circle, he told himself. Glide and circle. After he and Henrietta had skated into each other's lives, he learned how to dance proper, learned how to be a husband, and a father to boot nine months after they were married. He was on top of the world and nothing could knock him off it. Like Henrietta always said, they were lighter than air.

Every time they made love, rode horses together, danced. Always when they danced. But when the cancer struck and they danced for the last time six years after the first time, Pudge fell back to Earth.

The ice turned crunchy beneath his boots when the old sheriff reached shore. He hit the winch motor and let it wind. The cable grew taut and Dill and Tina, holding onto the hook, suddenly lunged forward as it pulled them off their feet and slammed them down face-first.

An even louder boom of cracking echoed across the lake followed by a splash as the iceberg tilted and sent the bright orange Sno-Cat plunging into the lake. The cable kept winding and dragged Dill and Tina into the water. Pudge saw both of them let go as they submerged, but the hook caught the handcuff's chain and continued to pull them.

Seconds later the winch reeled them out of the slushy water and onto solid ice again. Pudge had planned to stop the motor once they were able to walk, but he couldn't be certain they hadn't drowned and so he let the winch bring them in the rest of the way.

Sixty feet. Forty. Twenty. Ten. Pudge switched off the motor when they neared the front bumper. The pair were drenched and their hair and clothes sparkled with ice. Dill McCaw lay on his back, Tina on her stomach. They looked like a stringer of freshly caught trout.

The guitar picker's left wrist was cocked at an unnatural angle and bleeding from where the bracelet had dug into his skin. Both his left elbow and shoulder appeared to have been pulled from their sockets. His signature rubbery lips had been torn by shards of ice.

Pudge toed him to see if he was alive. The three-time killer spit water and cried out in pain.

The lawman turned to Tina. The handcuff chain had

wrapped around her right wrist and cut off blood flow. Her fingers were purple with pooled blood. He unlocked the bracelet and rolled her onto her back. Snow filled her mouth and nostrils. The silver moon with the winking eye was gone.

Assuming she'd suffocated, Pudge studied her in the same matter-of-fact way he had Caleb. But then Tina's eyes fluttered open and she struggled to breathe. He quickly crouched, got an arm under her, and propped her up while smacking her between the shoulders. A snowball flew out of her mouth followed by a stream of bile. She started sucking air.

He gave her another pat on the back as her chest heaved and teeth chattered. Dill was still crying in pain. "My wrist. I can't move my fingers. You mean old bastard, you broke it."

Pudge sucked a tooth. "At least it's your left hand, Dill, so you don't have to fret."

"That's not funny."

Sheriff Warbler stood and yanked both killers to their feet. "You'll both live," he drawled. "In prison, that is. Let's go. Load up. I got a job to finish."

32

It was straight up midnight when I clattered across the cattle guard and pulled into the gravel drive in front of the ranch house. I parked next to Pudge's four-door pickup that didn't look so new anymore. The front bumper was bowed, the right fender buckled, the roof dented, and the windshield spiderwebbed. I put my hand on the hood. It was still warm.

The house was dark. I walked quietly up the steps and opened the unlocked front door, careful to keep the screen door from slamming. I went straight to the kitchen, hoping November had put out some leftovers. I hadn't eaten anything since breakfast on the Bruneau.

A handwoven basket with black designs was on the counter. It contained pieces of frybread dusted with powdered sugar and wrapped in a dishcloth. I fished one out and took a bite and then another. It tasted better than good. It tasted of home.

Pudge came in. The old sheriff was still dressed in his uniform, but he wasn't wearing his holstered sidearm.

"Thought I heard someone drive up. Gemma tells me you've been on the Bruneau."

"Got off this afternoon. Late night at the office or are you just getting home from Salem?"

"Right on the second count."

"I thought you were planning to be gone only three days."

"Son, the thing about making plans is, they don't always go according to plan. Especially in the sheriffing business."

The grizzled lawman reached in the cupboard above the fridge and took down a bottle of whisky and poured himself a generous nightcap.

"What happened, Dill McCaw try to escape?"

Pudge put the bottle back in the cupboard. "It's a long story and I'm beyond bushed. Suffice to say, I had to take the long way around to get him there, but get him there I did. Now, I'm gonna go to my room and drink this in the dark and then fall asleep and try not relive the whole damn business in my dreams. Come morning when I wake up, I want to be able to look Hattie and Johnny in the eye and not feel any different about them and don't want them to feel any different about me."

I was about to say I hoped I'd be able to do the same, when he said, "You and me can swap tales tomorrow because if you were fool enough to run the Bruneau River at flood stage and managed not to get yourself killed, then you probably got a taller tale than mine. Besides, I'm not the one you need to be talking with right now. Gemma's out in the stable waiting on you. It was the same way with me and her mother whenever we had to have the kind of talk that little ears don't need to hear. I expect you to make things right with her, son. G'night."

Pudge ambled across the living room to his bedroom. I folded the dishcloth over the remaining frybread. Hunger could wait til morning. Gemma couldn't.

The ground outside was starting to harden from the growing cold and crunched beneath my boots. As I walked toward the stable door outlined by a thin rectangle of light seeping between the jambs, I tried to put my thoughts in order—how best to tell Gemma what happened without getting into the details that would make her angry or jealous or drive an even bigger wedge between us.

I reached the door, hesitated before opening it, and then thought to myself, who was I kidding? It was Gemma in there. The only speech I'd ever rehearsed for her was the day we got married and that was only two words long.

Wovoka shook his mane and pawed the ground when I stepped inside and closed the door behind me. Sarah nickered. Gemma was wearing a thick sheepskin coat and sitting in Shelly's stall next to the sleeping foal. She had a palm on Shelly's withers, which rose and fell with every breath the little horse took. The scene was reminiscent of several years before when the horse doctor was tending to a poisoned mustang filly foal I'd found, a time when it was only the two of us and we didn't have a care in the world or let anything stand in our way.

"Pudge told me you were out here," I said.

"You didn't need him to tell you to know that," she said.

"You're right. I could see you sitting in here the whole time I was driving in from Boise."

"Why did you go through Boise?"

"To drop Liz off at the airport. She flew back to Portland."

"Good. Why are you driving Loq's pickup?"

"You looked out and saw that?"

"I didn't need to. I know the sound your rig makes. I've listened for it hundreds of nights waiting up in bed for you."

I almost said like I'd listened for her airplane coming home that many times, but knew it would go over as well as me telling her about setting off a Redeye with no intention of using an escape route.

"Loq went back upriver after we took out. He'll bring mine here from the put-in."

"Why did he go back?"

I sucked my teeth. It was the rapids all over again; there'd be no stopping. "To show the Owyhee County Sheriff where we left the bodies of the two missing fishermen we found and that of the man who killed them."

Gemma finally looked up to meet my gaze. "Am I going to want to hear about how he died?"

"Probably not, but if you ask, I'll tell you. I'll tell you everything that happened on the Bruneau."

"Then you'd better get started."

"Okay, but when I finish, I want to talk about you and me and the kids and what we can do to sort ourselves out so whatever this thing is that's grown between us will stop growing. We can either hope it'll wither on its own or pull it out by the roots. I'm in favor of pulling."

"Before that can happen, I need to know what went on between you and Liz on the river and if it's still going on and if you want it to."

"What makes you think anything went on?"

"Because I know you. I feel you. You inhabit me and I inhabit you. Our souls, our hearts, our spirits, whatever you want to call it. I know you want to tell me but don't know how to tell me but you have to tell me. We need to deal with that before we can deal with anything else."

I sat beside her and told her everything. How Liz's stunt and attitude pissed me off at first and then how she slowly won me over and how I saved her life and how we fought Jasper and ran the river and parted at the airport.

For a long while after I'd finished, the only sounds being made were coming from the horses. Gemma said, "When she was sitting on your lap after you brought her back to life, what stopped you from kissing her and having sex? And in the hot springs and sleeping under the stars every night too."

"Trust. Yours and mine. And Liz's trust in me."

Gemma bristled. "Are you saying our trust is the same as yours and hers?"

"No. Yours and mine is about me trusting you to put my life in your hands and you trusting me to put yours in mine every single second of every single day. It's about trusting each other with the lives of our kids. You fight for them and me no matter what, the same as I fight for you and them. We don't fight each other, we fight for each other. In the end, that's what it all comes down to."

"You believe our trust is that strong?"

"I know it is."

"Okay, then I trust you about Liz."

"That's it?"

"You say you faced down a demon on your trip? Seems to me, the real demon wasn't some hairy beast living in a cave that tried to kill you but your own doubt about us."

"And you never have a doubt that we can still make it together, raise kids, pay the bills, keep the ranch?"

"Of course I do, but I remember the passage Blackpowder read to us on our wedding day. About how two are stronger than one, for if they fall, one will lift the other up, and although one might overcome an enemy on their own, two always will. That's what got us through the plane crash on the mountainside, remember? And it'll get us through now and whatever comes next."

I let that percolate. "When I was on the Bruneau, I kept looking at the canyon walls and wondering if you and me were strong enough to endure the wind and rain and time and not split off from the rim and tumble into the river below. But then I realized, so what if that happens. We'll become part of the rock shelf and the water will run over us together. The canyon will still stand. The river will still flow."

We sat and listened to the horses nicker and watched the foal's withers rise and fall as she slumbered.

"You're a one-woman man, aren't you?" she said as she leaned into me.

"The same as I'm a one-horse man and a one-motorcycle man."

Gemma laughed. It was still the best laugh of all. "You know I love being compared to Wovoka, but to your Triumph?"

"Actually, I had a thought about that while kayaking." I told her about my plan for redlining it with Johnny.

"That's a great idea. See, whenever one of us has doubts, we need to trust the other to hold fast."

I stood and pulled her up by her hand. "How about we hold fast to each other in bed?"

We started to walk through the stables, but then Gemma stopped.

"What is it?" I said.

Her eyes went to the fresh hay in the empty stall next to Shelly's. "Remember our first time?"

"Like it was yesterday."

"Let's make it yesterday right now."

We grabbed at each other and fell onto the clean bed of straw thinking only about right then and there and not yesterday or tomorrow or the day after or demons or anyone else, and the fire we felt was good because it was of our own making and nothing and no one could ever put it out.

AFTERWORD

Cattle mutilations have been called the greatest unsolved crime spree in history as well as one of its biggest mysteries. Since the 1970s, more than ten thousand incidents have been logged across the United States. Experts believe the actual number could be ten times that since most mutilations go unreported.

While Rocky Mountain and Great Plains states have had the greatest number of cases, the epicenter of livestock mutilation appears to have moved to Oregon beginning in 2017. Since then, at least twenty-one cases have been reported, primarily on ranches in remote areas of central and eastern Oregon, including Harney County, the setting for the Nick Drake novels.

Similar to previous instances of cattle mutilation, the Oregon carcasses were cut up with surgical precision. They were inexplicably bloodless and were missing body parts such as anuses, ears, eyeballs, genitals, jaws, and tongues. No fingerprints, footprints, or horseshoe or tire tracks were found near the remains. Nor was there any evidence that the cows had been shot, stabbed, or strangled.

Speculation and conspiracy theories about the mysterious

killings abound, especially after an FBI investigation called "Operation Animal Mutilation" failed to establish solid conclusions about a motive or uncover any evidence leading to the arrest of perpetrators. Local law-enforcement agencies throughout the affected states have also been stumped in their investigations.

Explanations about the cause of the mutilations fall broadly into three categories. The first holds that they are normal cattle deaths and the bloodlessness and missing body parts are the result of evaporation, dehydration, and scavenger activity.

The second category comprises a variety of conspiracy theories. One blames the government for the mutilations. Theorists point to "black helicopter" sightings associated with the discovery of carcasses and allege that they were used to dispose of cattle that had been tested in secret laboratories for such things as mad cow disease and radiation exposure.

Another theory blames cults. This gained traction following an investigation of cattle mutilations conducted by the US Bureau of Alcohol, Tobacco, Firearms, and Explosives that surmised devil worshipers were responsible. A similar accusation was made by the Division of Criminal Investigation in Iowa. Both claims were later discounted when they failed to provide any concrete evidence.

The third category embraces paranormal activity. Theorists point to the sightings of UFOs over remote parts of the country and believe extraterrestrials are harvesting cattle for food as well as testing advanced weapons on them.

One of the more controversial theories professes that ranchers are mutilating their own cattle to express their economic anxiety and resentment of government regulation of agricultural activities, such as restrictions on water and grazing rights and price freezes on beef.

Given the sheer number of mutilations and locations, the span of decades, and the lack of hard evidence and eyewitness accounts, no single theory is a perfect fit to explain all these cases. Despite its gruesomeness, perhaps that's the most fascinating part of this nationwide mystery.

GET A FREE BOOK

Dwight Holing's genre-spanning work includes novels, short fiction, and nonfiction. His mystery and suspense thriller series include The Nick Drake Novels and The Jack McCoul Capers. The stories in his collections of literary short fiction have won awards, including the Arts & Letters Prize for Fiction. He has written and edited numerous nonfiction books on nature travel and conservation. He is married to a kick-ass environmental advocate; they have a daughter and son, and two dogs who'd rather swim than walk.

Sign up for his newsletter to get a free book and be the first to learn about the next Nick Drake Novel as well as receive news about crime fiction and special deals.

Visit dwightholing.com/free-book. You can unsubscribe at any time.

A NOTE FROM THE AUTHOR

Thank you so much for reading *The Demon Skin*. I'd truly appreciate it if you would please leave a review on the online retail platform where you purchased it (e.g., Amazon, Apple, Barnes and Noble etc.) or with your Independent Book Store. Your feedback not only helps me become a better storyteller, but you help other readers by blazing a trail and leaving markers for them to follow as they search for new stories.

If you belong to a book club, please consider encouraging your fellow members to choose *The Demon Skin* or any of the other Nick Drake Novels for discussion. Contact me directly if you would like me to join your club's meeting via Zoom to talk about the book, the series, and my writing process. My contact information is on my website where I also post a blog and information about upcoming book tours and events.

ACKNOWLEDGMENTS

I'm indebted to many people who helped in the creation of *The Demon Skin*. As always, my family provided support throughout the writing process.

I'm especially grateful to my reader team who read early drafts and gave me very helpful feedback. They include Gene Ammerman, George Becker, Terrill Carpenter, Jeffrey Miller, Kenneth Mitchell, John Onoda, and Haris Orkin. A special shout out to Terrill for his insights about strange things that go bump in the night.

Thank you Karl Yambert for proofreading and copyediting. My appreciation to the Bureau of Land Management for use of the photograph that graces this book's cover and kudos to designer-extraordinaire Rob Williams for creating it.

Thank you Sara Donart Gorham, Idaho native and outdoor adventurer, for joining me on an exploration of the Morley Nelson Snake River Birds of Prey National Conservation Area. Finally, much love and many thanks to my wife Annie Notthoff; her real life experience as one of the first women ever to raft the Bruneau River inspired me to write this novel.

I humbly offer my respect to the Burns Paiute Tribe of the Burns Paiute Indian Colony of Oregon for your inspiration and to the Klamath Tribes, whose mission is to protect, preserve and enhance the spiritual, cultural and physical values and resources of the Klamath, Modoc and Yahooskin Peoples by maintaining the customs and heritage of their ancestors.

Any errors, regrettably, are my own.

ALSO BY DWIGHT HOLING

The Nick Drake Novels

The Sorrow Hand (Book 1)

The Pity Heart (Book 2)

The Shaming Eyes (Book 3)

The Whisper Soul (Book 4)

The Nowhere Bones (Book 5)

The Forever Feet (Book 6)

The Demon Skin (Book 7)

The Jack McCoul Capers

A Boatload (Book 1)

Bad Karma (Book 2)

Baby Blue (Book 3)

Shake City (Book 4)

Short Story Collections

California Works

Over Our Heads Under Our Feet